(((((SUPERNATURALLY)))))

PRAISE FOR *PARANORMALCY*

"Strong characters, a clever premise, and a hilarious voice
all team up to make *Paranormalcy* the most refreshing
paranormal debut of the year."
(((((LISA MCMANN)))))
New York Times bestselling
author of the Wake trilogy

"A fast, flirty roller coaster of a ride. This story was everything
I hoped for—sassy, light-hearted and downright scary.
Oh, bleep! I'm in love!"
(((((BECCA FITZPATRICK)))))
New York Times bestselling
author of *Hush, Hush*

"*Paranormalcy* seduced me. The two sexy paranormals who
vie for Evie's affections each had their own victory; one won
Evie's heart and the other won mine."
(((((APRILYNNE PIKE)))))
#1 *New York Times* bestselling
author of *Wings*

"Kiersten White creates the perfect blend of light and dark.
Even as the stakes rose higher, *Paranormalcy*'s narrator, Evie,
kept a smile on my face with her cunning wit.
I can't wait for more!"
(((((CARRIE RYAN)))))
New York Times bestselling
author of *The Forest of Hands and Teeth*

"First-time author White shows the technique and polish
of a pro in this absorbing romance, which comes closer than
most to hitting the Buffy mark."
—*Publishers Weekly* (starred review)

"This witty novel hilariously challenges notions of
dreamy vampires, along with many other common assumptions
about paranormals. The romance is keenly realistic,
and Evie herself is a memorable character."
—*The Bulletin of the Center for Children's Books*

"A fast-paced, entertaining debut.
Alternately funny and tragic but never maudlin,
White's debut will have broad appeal."
—ALA *Booklist*

"Good, romantic entertainment."
—*Kirkus Reviews*

"Perky, insolent, fearless, and insecure,
teenage girls will recognize themselves in Evie.
Likely to be a popular read."
—*VOYA*

(((SUPERNATURALLY)))

KIERSTEN WHITE

HARPER TEEN
An Imprint of HarperCollinsPublishers

(((((HarperTeen is an imprint of HarperCollins Publishers.)))))

Supernaturally

Copyright © 2011 by Kiersten Brazier
www.epicreads.com

Library of Congress Cataloging-in-Publication Data
White, Kiersten.
Supernaturally / Kiersten White. — 1st ed.
    p. cm.
Summary: Sixteen-year-old Evie thinks she has left the International
Paranormal Containment Agency, and her own paranormal activities,
behind her when she is recruited to help at the Agency, where she
discovers more about the dark faerie prophecy that threatens her future.
    ISBN 978-0-06-198586-7 (trade bdg.)
    [1. Supernatural—Fiction. 2. Fairies—Fiction. 3. Prophecies—Fiction.
4. Identity—Fiction.] I. Title.
PZ7.W583764Su 2011   2010040426
[Fic]—dc22   CIP
                                                              AC

Typography by Michelle Taormina
11 12 13 14 15   LP/RRDB   10 9 8 7 6 5 4 3 2
❖
First Edition

TO NATALIE AND STEPH,
FOR HELPING ME MAKE THE STORIES
AND TO MICHELLE AND ERICA,
FOR HELPING ME MAKE THE BOOKS

OUT OF THE BLUE

Oh, bleep. I was going to die.

I was going to die a horrible, gruesome, painful death.

My hand twitched at my side, reaching for the pink Taser I knew wasn't there. Why had I ever wanted this? What was I thinking? Working at the International Paranormal Containment Agency might have been close to indentured servitude, and sure, I had some nasty run-ins with vampires and hags and creeptastic faeries, but that was nothing compared to the danger I faced now.

Girls' gym.

We were playing soccer—*without shin guards*. The girl

I was supposed to cover (a creature so hulking I swear she was a troll) charged toward me, steam practically flowing from her nostrils. I braced for impact.

And then I marveled at the clear blue autumn sky. Not a cloud in sight. But why was I looking at the sky? Maybe it was connected to my sudden inability to breathe. Come on, lungs. Come on. They had to start working at some point, right? Bright spots danced before my eyes and I could just see my obituary: *Tragedy Strikes During Soccer.* How mortifying.

At last, blessed air filtered through. A familiar face, framed by long, dark hair, leaned over me. My one normal friend, Carlee. "Are you okay?" she asked.

"Green!" a tenor barked out. I was pretty sure that Miss Lynn had a deeper voice than my boyfriend. "Get off your butt and get back in the game!"

Ah, Green. It seemed like such a cute last name when Lend made it up to fake my legal documents. However, the more Miss Lynn shouted it, the less I liked it. "GREEN!" Carlee held out a hand and helped me up.

"That's okay. I suck at soccer, too." She smiled and ran off. She totally did not suck at soccer.

It wasn't fair. Here I was, standing like an idiot on a muddy field, while Lend was away at college. What a waste of time. And who knew how much longer I had left, anyway? What if I was expending the precious remnants of my soul on soccer?

Maybe I could get a doctor's note. I could see it now: "To whom it may concern: Evie has a rare condition in which she doesn't have enough of her own soul to live a normal life. Therefore, she should be immediately and permanently excused from all physical exertion involving sweating and getting knocked down in the dirt."

Ridiculous. But then again, it might be worth a shot. Lend's dad had some connections at the hospital. . . .

I ducked as the ball whizzed past my head. One of my teammates, a vicious redhead, swore as she ran by. "Header, Green! Header!"

Carlee stopped. "Just fake cramps." She winked a mascara-heavy eyelid.

I put my hands on my lower stomach and shuffled over to Miss Lynn, who stood at the painted white line on the crunchy grass, surveying the game like a general at war.

She rolled her eyes. "What is it now?"

Hoping my pale face would come in handy for once, I whimpered. "Cramps. Bad."

She didn't buy it and we both knew it, but instead of calling my crap she rolled her eyes and jerked her thumb toward the sidelines. "Next time you play goalie though."

Thanks a lot, Carlee. Brilliant idea. I put some distance between us and slumped to the ground, picking at the sparse, browning grass.

This wasn't how high school was supposed to be.

Don't get me wrong, I'm super grateful to be here. I

always wanted to be normal, go to a normal school, do normal things. But it's all so, so . . .

Normal.

Since school started a month ago, there hasn't been a single catfight. No wild parties where the cops got called, either. And as far as masquerade balls and moonlit rendezvous and passionate kisses in the hallways, well, all I can say is *Easton Heights*, my former favorite TV show, has taken a serious hit in my estimation.

I still think lockers are awesome, though.

I kept a hand on my stomach for appearances. Lying on the ground was a much nicer position when voluntarily assumed. I watched a tiny wisp of a cloud stream across the sky.

I frowned. It was a weird cloud. All by its lonesome in the otherwise blank sky, and there was something else about it . . . something different. Was that a flash of lightning?

"I said, are you going to attend your next class?"

Startled, I sat up and grimaced at Miss Lynn. "Yes, absolutely, thanks." I hurried inside. Things really were boring if I was looking for excitement in clouds.

I spent my next class calculating the exact number of minutes left until the weekend, when I could see Lend. The answer was far too many, but figuring it out was more interesting than, say, paying attention to my English teacher's lecture on gender roles in *Dracula*—and don't even get me started on that book. An accurate researcher Bram Stoker was not.

My head was drifting toward an inevitable collision course with the desk when the door banged open and an office aide came in with a note. "Evelyn Green?" I waved a hand and she nodded. "Checkout slip."

I perked up. I'd never been pulled from school before. Maybe Arianna wanted to hang out. She was weird and moody enough to pull something like this.

Then again, not so much. She wouldn't come out during a day this bright, what with the whole being-a-vampire thing. My stomach dropped. What if something was wrong? What if Lend had an accident on campus, got knocked unconscious, and turned invisible? What if the government took him and he was being entombed in some IPCA facility?

Trying my hardest not to run, I followed the aide, a short woman with shockingly unnatural blond hair. "Do you know who's here to get me?"

"Your aunt, I think."

Well, that cleared things right up. Or at least it would, if I had an aunt. I ran through the list of women, all paranormals, who could pass for a relative. It wasn't a long list, and I couldn't think why a single one of them would be here. I burst into the office. A woman with sensible (read: ugly) shoes and black hair pulled into a severe bun was standing with her back toward me. It couldn't be.

Raquel turned around and smiled.

My heart jumped into my throat. On the one hand, it was Raquel, and she was the closest thing I'd ever had to a mom. On the other hand, it was Raquel, and she was one of the head honchos of IPCA, the organization that thought I was dead. The organization I really, really didn't want to find me. And the organization I *thought* Raquel was protecting me from.

"There you are." She shouldered her purse and gestured toward the double doors leading outside. "Let's go."

I followed her, thoroughly confused. Outside in the brilliant daylight at my normal high school, it felt wrong to be with the woman who represented everything I had left behind. I kept wanting to lean in and hug her—which was weird, since we'd never really had a hugging relationship. Of course, I also wanted to book it in the opposite direction. She was *IPCA*.

"What are you doing here?" I asked.

"Judging by your surprise, I'm going to assume that David has not been passing on my messages."

"Lend's dad? What messages?"

She sighed. My interpretation skills were rusty, but it sounded like an *I'm tired and this is going to take too long to explain* sigh.

A shadow passed over the sun and I looked up to see my wisp of cloud. There was definitely something underneath it, but not lightning. Something shimmering. Something paranormal. Something with a glamour that only I could see through.

"What is—" I was interrupted by my own scream as the cloud dove out of the sky, wrapped itself around me, and flew back into the blue.

FLYING LESSONS

I was still screaming when I ran out of air. Gulping a breath, I stared down at the ground. Tendrils of cloud shifted around me, not doing nearly enough to obscure the fact that the tree-filled landscape was *much* too far beneath us.

I forced back another scream and stared at my waist. Wrapped around me were two arms that both looked and felt terrifyingly insubstantial. I had no idea how something that seemed as light as the breeze was holding me up here, but I couldn't think about that right now. I had more pressing problems. Like where the cloud was taking me and why.

Even worse, tiny sparks were flying around us, and I didn't like my odds for avoiding electrocution. The hairs on my arms stuck straight out, tingling with the energy crackling around me.

So, so bad.

I was ready to bid the Earth good-bye when I saw my small town beneath us and something snapped. That was *my* town. I was done being manipulated by paranormals. If this thing could touch me, then I sure as Hades could touch it. And if I could touch it . . .

I closed my eyes and took a deep breath. It had to be done. It wasn't because I wanted to—this was a matter of life and death. Odds were it wouldn't work anyway. I might be an Empty One, able to suck the souls straight out of paranormals, but I'd only done it once before. And that was different; the souls had been trapped and they *wanted* to come to me. This thing probably didn't want to give me its life energy.

Still worth a shot. I threw my shoulder back, reached around, and put my hand flat against the first solid thing I felt, praying that whatever this cloud creature was, it had a chest.

I gave myself up, willing the channel between my hand and Cloud Freak's soul to open. *I want this*, I thought, my mind screaming desperation. *I need this.*

My eyes flew open in shock, the soul crackling with dry, charged heat as it flowed down my arm and into my core, filtering outward until every part of my body tingled.

The creature let out a shrill cry of surprise and pain. It jerked back, breaking the connection; my head spun, drunk with the rush of new, strange energy.

And then we fell.

What a brilliant idea, Evie, go ahead and *suck the energy out of the thing keeping you aloft thousands of feet in the air.* But it was still holding it together somehow. We were spinning out of control, but we weren't falling as swiftly as we should have been. If we could make it to the ground, we'd be okay.

It dropped me. I screamed, scrambling and grabbing onto its foot. It shrieked in frustration, kicking out, but I wasn't about to let go. We were in this together. The earth rushed up toward us, a green and orange carpet of trees.

Before I could brace myself, I slammed through the canopy, leaves flying around me as I bounced off a branch and let go of my cloud's foot. Another branch whacked my hip, slowing me enough that when the ground and I finally caught up with each other, it only felt like I'd been hit by a truck.

Every bone in my body had to be broken. There was no way I could be in this much pain and have any surviving appendages. I'd be in a body cast for the rest of my life. This was going to complicate cuddling with Lend. At least I'd get out of school for a while. And I'd definitely be off the hook for gym.

Electric tingling sensations rushed up and down my

body, replacing the pain and making me feel buoyant, like my limbs were fuzzy and disconnected.

Oh, bleep. I was paralyzed.

Panicked, I leaped to my feet, running my hands over myself in horror. Well, duh. If I could do this, probably not paralyzed. Why did I feel so weird then? And where was Cloud Freak?

"Horrible thing!" a voice like the wind through dead trees rasped. "What has it done to me?"

Still covered in clinging tendrils of cloud, the small creature crawled across the dirt toward me. Although shaped like a person, it was delicate—almost childlike. Its eyes flashed brilliant white like lightning, but the rest of its features were blurred and indistinct; even its color matched the pale shade of cloud. To anyone else it would look like an animated section of solid fog, but my glamour-piercing eyes saw everything.

I took a step backward, trying not to stumble on the exposed roots of the massive tree kind enough to break my fall. "Hey, I didn't ask to be snatched and flown off!"

"It took me—it took part of me away. Give it back."

I backed up against the tree trunk. The creature levitated, turning upright and hovering in front of me. Thin traces of lightning surrounded it like a web. Its limbs blended in and out of the cloud—sometimes there, sometimes not— but there was an undeniable sense of power and force to it.

I was so out of my league here. I held up my hand and

tried to look braver than I felt. "Leave me alone or I'll take it all." My voice trembled, part fear but part longing. My fingers tingled, my body yearned. A taste wasn't enough. I wanted the rest.

No, I didn't. I couldn't have it. I didn't want it. I wasn't that person. I'd give it back if I could, but I didn't know how.

Cloud Freak narrowed its large, flashing eyes at me. The air between us was dry and hot, charged with crackling electricity. It was going to kill me. I took a deep breath, wondering how much it would hurt, when the thing shot back up into the sky with a shrill blast of air. I watched as it went higher, occasionally veering to the side or losing altitude before climbing again. And then it was gone.

Letting out a trembling breath of relief, I leaned back against the tree. When I daydreamed about something happening to make my life more exciting again, this wasn't what I had in mind. Clearly I forgot what being involved with paranormals—real, uncontrollable paranormals— entailed.

Fear.

Lots and lots of fear.

And now I didn't even have Tasey with me for comfort. I stepped forward resolutely, taking stock of my situation. I had dropped my bag when Cloud Freak snatched me, which meant no cell phone. And while I was pretty sure we had been close to home when we fell out of the sky, who knew how far off course our fall had taken us? Still, how big could a forest be in the middle of Virginia?

No doubt I was going to find out.

By the time I hit a road an hour later I was tired, sweaty, and depressed. What were the odds that Raquel showed up the exact same time a paranormal tried to snatch me? What was she playing at, pretending to let me off the hook with IPCA and then coming back for me? I found it hard to believe that her goal had been to lure me out of the school so Cloud Freak could grab me, but it seemed the likeliest explanation. The idea that Raquel—who had been like a mom to me during my years at the Center—would do something like that broke my heart.

Fine, though. If IPCA wanted to play it like that, so be it. I stretched my hand and smiled, a vicious, smug thing. I could take care of myself now.

I shuddered, shaking out my hand to get rid of the tingles. No. I was never doing that again. Ever. I liked it too much.

My inner compass was better than I gave it credit for, because I managed to pick the right direction on the road. Practically crying with relief, I saw the turnoff to Lend's house. *My* old house, before he moved out and I moved in with Arianna to avoid the awkwardness of living with my boyfriend's dad. I ran up the long, winding drive and burst through the door into the family room.

Raquel was sitting on the couch.

"What the crap?" I shouted.

She jumped up and grabbed me before I could think to block. I tensed. And then I realized she was hugging me.

"I haven't seen you in months and you go and get kidnapped first thing! I thought you were trying to be normal!" She pulled back, looking at me with tears in her eyes.

"You mean you didn't send that thing?"

"Goodness no!"

"What was it?"

David stumbled into the room, a phone in his hand and a relieved look on his face. "You're okay!"

"Besides being kidnapped by a living cloud and dropped thousands of feet to the ground? Yeah, I'm peachy."

"So it *was* a sylph!" David pointed triumphantly at Raquel. "I told you they existed!"

Raquel's lips tightened, and it was all she could do to hold back a sigh. "Yes, it would appear you were correct."

"Wow." David ran his hands through his thick, dark hair, eyes lit up with excitement. "Wow. A sylph. I think that's the first confirmed contact ever!"

I raised my hand. "Umm, hello? Girl who was kidnapped by said sylph? Anyone want to fill me in on what it is and why it decided to give me an aerial tour of our fine state?"

"Sylphs are air elementals." Raquel spoke quickly, shooting a perturbed look at David, like she wanted to prove that even if she hadn't believed in them, she still knew more than he did. "Thought to be distantly related to faeries. It was commonly believed that they either never existed or had simply ceased to be, but this is because a sylph would never willingly touch the ground, thus making finding one impossible and looking for them an enormous waste of time." She shot another one of those looks at David.

"Oh, come on, just because my specialty was elementals and you focused on common paranormals like unicorns and leprechauns." David winked at me as if I were somehow in on this joke. "She's always been jealous that I know all the really cool ones."

Now I was the one holding back an annoyed sigh. "Air elemental, got it. Great. Now does anyone know *why*? You said they were related to faeries maybe?" All my annoyance squished itself into a ball of fear. I didn't want the fey back in my life.

Neither one of them said anything. Then Raquel cleared her throat, her voice strained. "We could always ask *Cresseda* if she knows anything." She said "Cresseda"—Lend's mom and the resident water elemental—with a strange emphasis.

"No, we can't, actually." David shuffled his toes into the carpet. "I haven't been able to get her to surface for a couple of months now. Ever since Lend moved out." His voice was soft, but the pain underlying his words was obvious. I wanted to hug him. It was bad enough that he fell in love with an immortal water nymph, worse still that she only stayed human with him for a year. But now for her to abandon him entirely because Lend was gone? I couldn't imagine the pain.

Actually, I could imagine it. I frequently imagined it. Some days it was all I could do *not* to imagine it. Being the mortal in a mortal/immortal duo was something I understood all too well.

I still hadn't told Lend he was never going to die, though. The thought that he might give up this life—the one here, with me—to figure out how to be an immortal terrified me. I'd tell him, though. Soon. Soonish.

Eventually.

Raquel straightened, looking pleased. "Well then, this is something I can help with. I'll get all my researchers on air elementals. It's strange that it would show up now, especially given recent upheavals in elemental populations. We'll figure it out. But it's not why I'm here."

I frowned. "Exactly why *are* you here?"

"IPCA needs your help."

JOB INTERVIEWS

Raquel." David's voice was low and annoyed. "Evie is not going to get sucked back into IPCA. What was the point of telling them she was dead if you come here six months later and bring her back in?"

"I told you, the situation is different now."

I held up my hand again, tired of them talking around me. "I can take this one, thanks. I miss you, sure, but I don't want to come back to IPCA. You sterilize werewolves!" That was one of the many crimes I had discovered the International Paranormal Containment Agency committed in the name of keeping the world a safer place.

Raquel got a tight look around her eyes. "That practice is no longer in effect. As I've already explained to David, things have changed drastically in the time you've been gone. Our policies toward nonaggressive paranormals have undergone serious revision, including greater werewolf rights. Any and all eugenics have been done away with entirely. There was a lot wrong with IPCA—there still is—but you and I both know how much good it does. And I'm a Supervisor now, which means I have final say in most policies."

I folded my arms, frowning. "I won't work with faeries." I hadn't seen Reth since he had come to visit me in the hospital after I released the souls, and I never wanted to again. Him or any of the other creepy, manipulative, amoral, psychotic, insert-further-negative-adjectives-of-your-choice-here faeries. Especially after today, if the sylph was with them. I wasn't about to draw their attention to me by holding hands through the Faerie Paths.

She smiled. "I understand. In fact, one of my first initiatives was weaning IPCA from faerie magic dependency. I think you'll be pleased to find that we now use them a mere forty percent of the amount we used to."

"Forty percent, huh? That's still about one hundred percent more than I'm happy with."

"We've got a way for you to be effective without any faerie interaction whatsoever."

"Effective doing what?"

She glanced at David, who scowled. "I'm not having any part of this."

"With that in mind," Raquel said, a haughty lift to her eyebrows, "I'd appreciate it if you left the room. I can't give classified information to *two* dead people, after all."

I was confused until I remembered that David had worked for the now defunct American Paranormal Agency eighteen or so years ago, at which point he faked his own death to get out. That seemed to be a popular option around here. Of course, I didn't fake mine; Raquel fabricated it for me, so that they wouldn't come looking after I disappeared.

David huffed. "You seem to forget that I'm Evie's legal guardian."

"And you seem to forget that there's absolutely nothing legal about your guardianship, considering all the documents were forged."

"Don't start with me about legality! An international organization acting with absolute impunity on American shores, not to mention—"

The front door flew open and Lend ran in. My heart did a happy flip in my chest, like it did every time he surprised me. His usual look, a dark-haired dark-eyed hottie, shimmered over his actual appearance, which was like water in human form.

And absolutely gorgeous.

"Evie!" He threw his arms around me, picking me up off the floor in a grip so tight I was suddenly aware that I had, in fact, sustained some serious bruisage.

I laughed through the pain, happy that at least I got some extra Lend time out of this whole mess. He put me down, holding me at arm's length and examining me. "Are you okay?"

"Just some bruises. I'm fine, though, really."

"How did you get away?"

Oh, crap.

Raquel and David gave me matching puzzled looks. "How *did* you get away?" Raquel asked. In their eagerness to bicker they had neglected to ask me. I kind of preferred that.

I bit my lip. "I, well, we were high? Really, really high. And it was this weird cloud and lightning and faerie thing. I didn't know where it was taking me or why, and I was so scared I did the only thing I could think of."

"Which was?" Lend prodded, worry shadowing his face.

I shrugged, a small, guilty gesture. "I took some." Hating the concern in his eyes, I rushed on. "Only a little bit—not enough to hurt it, really, just enough to surprise it, and then we fell, and it tried to drop me, but I grabbed on and some trees broke my fall. And afterward the Cloud Freak was okay, really, it was. Just kind of pissed. And then it flew off." I didn't mention the erratic flight pattern. It was probably woozy.

My story was greeted with dead silence. And suddenly instead of feeling guilty, I was downright mad. Who were they to judge me? It's not like I was going all Vivian, sucking the life out of everything around me. "I didn't have any other options! You should be glad I had a way to defend myself."

Lend quickly shook his head, squeezing my hand. "I am. Really. I just remember what it did to you before, and I worry that—"

"You don't need to! It was barely anything. Promise." Vivian had gone crazy and sucked the souls out of every paranormal she could find, under the guise of "freeing" them from this world, but really because she liked how it made her feel. Having all those souls in me after I took them from her—for a few minutes I was an immortal. It was strange and wonderful and dizzying to be that powerful, that disconnected from my mortal life. For a terrible moment I was tempted to abandon mortality entirely . . . to take Lend's soul away from him. I didn't like to think about it too much.

"Is it still inside you?" Lend asked.

I hadn't even thought to look. A nervous pit formed in my stomach as I held out my arms, searching for anything under my skin. Nothing. But there—a tiny spark under my palm. And then it was gone. It was probably nothing. Definitely nothing.

"Nope," I said with certainty. "Must not have taken enough for it to have an effect. Can't see anything but plain old Evie."

Lend grinned, pulling me in closer. "You've never been plain."

David cleared his throat. "Well then, as long as you're okay, that's what's important. Why don't you two go get something to eat?"

Raquel's lips pursed in annoyance. Apparently driving her crazy was a father-son thing for the Pirellos. Lend had the same knack for it. "I haven't finished speaking with her," Raquel said.

David looked ready to argue otherwise, so I jumped in. "Relax, it's okay. She can tell me what she needs to; what's it going to hurt?"

Lend and David wore matching frowns. There was no way Raquel and I would be able to have an actual conversation. And, unlike Lend and his dad, I liked her. A lot. I wanted to know how she'd been, find out how things went after I left, stuff like that. Suddenly my old life was sitting in the room with me, and I realized I missed parts of it.

Lish, especially, but she was gone forever.

I turned to Lend. "Why don't you go see your mom? Ask her if she knows anything about the sylph."

"Sylph? Really?" He looked at his dad, understanding how excited David would be over this. Or maybe Lend's interest was based on the fact that he was half elemental. I wondered how much that world called to him, how much he wanted to know about it and therefore himself.

Best not to let him dwell on it. I wanted him to stay

firmly in this world. "Yup. So your mom?" I would have offered to go with him later, but the truth was Cresseda still kind of scared me. Elemental immortals function on such a different plane than us, there's very little that connects. Speaking to one is like trying to understand theoretical mathematics before you have your times tables down—you come away doubting you even understood what numbers were to begin with.

It was so weird to think that Lend came from Cresseda. He was so human, so connected. But that'd have to fade eventually. Would he slowly stop caring, slowly become like his mother, beautiful and strange and forever *other*? Or would he just snap one day—give up this life for an eternal one? How long would it be before he became like the other immortal elementals?

"She's more likely to show up for you," David said to Lend. I looked over at him. He was so good at hiding the pain from his son, but I could see it written in the down-ward turn of his shoulders.

Please, please don't let that be me someday.

Lend seemed torn about leaving me with Raquel, but nodded. "I'll be right back." He hurried out the door.

"Before there are any more distractions, let me lay out the terms." Raquel steered me to the couch and sat down. "You would be working for IPCA as a temporary, contract employee."

"What does that even mean?"

"It means that you work for us because you want to, and only on the projects that you choose. If you want to stop, you stop. You don't have to come back to the Center. We'll call when we need you. There's no obligation, no oversight other than mine. You won't be back at IPCA, not really—you'll simply be helping me on some things that your abilities are particularly suited to."

I frowned. She was willing to admit that I wasn't really dead, and she had figured out a way for me to work *with* them without working *for* them. IPCA was all about control. If they were going to relinquish it to have my special glamour-piercing vision back, they must really be changing.

"How? What did you tell them? Didn't you get in trouble?" I asked.

"Stranger things have happened than paranormals coming back from the dead. Since we never had 'proof' that you were dead, my fellow Supervisors didn't question it when I said I'd found you alive. I made it clear that you wouldn't communicate with anyone other than me, and refused to contact you until it was unanimously agreed that you would be completely autonomous, no longer classified or regulated by IPCA."

"You didn't get in trouble?"

"After the severe mismanagement last April that resulted in so many deaths and disappearances, no one is left in a position to get me 'in trouble.'"

"But they agreed to all that? Really?"

Raquel sighed, an *I need a vacation* one. "Honestly, we're struggling. After Viv— After those unfortunate events, we're severely understaffed. We haven't been able to respond as quickly or efficiently to vampire or werewolf reports, our tracking measures seem to be failing us entirely for paranormals that usually stay in one specific area, and there are unconfirmed rumors that a troll colony has taken over a neighborhood in Sweden. Also"—she grimaced—"a poltergeist has targeted the Center and no one has been able to pinpoint its location for an extermination."

"Basically you guys suck without me." I couldn't keep the smug grin from my face. It was kind of gratifying to know that, without my eyes, IPCA was falling apart.

Raquel looked at the ceiling and heaved another long-suffering sigh. "That's one way of putting it."

"This isn't Evie's problem," David interjected. "If IPCA is tanking, I say good riddance." My eyes narrowed involuntarily, defensiveness for my old employers flaring up. Sure, the vamps here were self-regulating, but I had nearly been killed by one as an eight-year-old. The rest of the world wasn't a paranormal haven like this town. Things were scary. Things were deadly. And most people had absolutely no idea, which meant they had no way to protect themselves.

Raquel ignored him. "Your assignments would be simple and safe. And, as I said, entirely voluntary."

"How is that going to work? I'm in school." As boring as it was, I needed to do well. I had to get into Georgetown like Lend.

"We'll work around your schedule."

"That's sounding suspiciously Faerie Paths dependent."

Lend slammed the front door, his face clouded with worry. "She wouldn't come."

David shook his head. "She doesn't always. Don't take it personally." That was interesting—did Lend not know that Cresseda wouldn't show up for David anymore? Raquel looked sharply at Lend and then David; it was clear the wheels in her head were turning, but I had no idea why.

Lend rubbed a hand over his face, then looked at Raquel. "What are you doing here, anyway?"

"I'm here to ask for Evie's help with some projects. Yours, too, if you're willing."

David stood up straight and Lend's jaw clenched; even his glamour rippled with barely contained anger. "We're not."

Was he answering for me? As much as I loved him, that wasn't his call. "Lend, can I talk to you?"

He raised his eyebrows and followed me into the kitchen. The cheerful yellow walls didn't do much for me today. He grabbed my hand, pulling me in close, his frown deepening. "You're not seriously considering this, are you? I might have been the one they locked up, but you were just as much a prisoner there. After everything you've seen, how can you even think about it? And don't you find it a little suspicious that we haven't had any problems until Raquel showed up?"

Anger flared sharply in my chest. Sure, I had briefly thought the same thing, but she was *Raquel*. My Raquel. "She wouldn't do that. She was as worried as you. Besides, what am I even doing here? Going to class, working in the diner, counting down the days until the weekend? At least with IPCA I was helping people!"

"Yes, helping *people*! But how many paranormals were you hurting?"

Tears stung my eyes. He didn't understand. He never could see anything but evil in IPCA. But they'd taken me in, had taken care of me. I didn't even want to think where I would have been without them.

"How many paranormals am I helping right now, huh? Things have changed at IPCA. I can help paranormals, too, like werewolves who don't know what's going on, or this troll colony—I can find them and convince them to relocate before they get in trouble!"

Lend shook his head. "We can do that with my dad."

"We can't! We don't have the resources!"

"Like faeries?"

I hated that he was using my past against me. I hadn't been sure I wanted to work for Raquel before, but for some reason his insistence that I shouldn't was pushing me right toward it. It was all well and good for him, off at college, doing big important things for his future. A future that would last forever, even if he didn't know it. But I was stuck here, bored and lonely, slowly burning out with nothing to show for it.

I was struggling for a comeback when the brilliant outline of a faerie door wrote itself onto the wall.

OPEN SESAME

I blinked against the light, frozen with disbelief. I hadn't seen a faerie door since that night with Vivian and Reth. I had hoped I never would again.

Lend, however, wasn't frozen. Darting to the other side of the kitchen, he grabbed one of the cast-iron pans his dad always left out. A figure stepped out of the darkness, turning his head just in time to see Lend swing with all his might.

The faerie dove, executing a roll and jumping up several feet away. Lend turned around to close in again.

"Hey-oh, what's this?" the faerie said with a laugh.

There was something wrong, something off about the

whole thing. I narrowed my eyes at the faerie. My height, with sandy blond hair, brilliant blue eyes, dimples, and—

"Lend, *stop*!" Reacting to my shout, he pulled his arm up short from the swing, lost his balance, and stumbled into the granite counter. He looked at me, confused. I shook my head, feeling the same way. I had no idea how it was possible, but there was no denying what I saw underneath the boy's skin.

Nothing.

"He's not a faerie," I said. I looked back at the door, but it was already gone. I had watched the whole time; he was the only thing to come out. No faerie at all.

This was impossible.

"Are you sure?" Lend still held the pan at the ready, not taking his eyes off the boy. Or guy, really. He looked about our age, maybe a year or two younger.

The non-faerie smiled at me and winked, jumping up to sit on the counter. "Not quite the reception I was expecting, but I'll give your boy this—he's exciting."

Raquel rushed into the room, then fixed a scowl on Blondie. "You're late."

He shrugged and helped himself to an apple from the fruit bowl next to him. "I got lost." He took a big bite, crunching loudly before he blanched and spit into the sink. With a regretful sigh, he tossed the apple to Lend, who dropped the pan in his instinctive reaction to catch it.

The metal was still clanging when David came in

behind Raquel. "Who is that?"

"Not a faerie, that's for sure," I answered. Blondie stood up on top of the counter, his head nearly brushing the ceiling. Then, with a jaunty salute, he flipped off, landing on his feet.

I kept staring, looking for something, anything under his skin. There was no glamour. His clothes were normal, too, a light blue printed T-shirt and nice jeans. "How did you do that?" I asked.

"Lots of practice. You should see me walk on my hands."

"The door! How did you come through a faerie door by yourself?"

"Oh, that?" He ran a hand through his curls and looked back at where the door had been. "Easy. You walk up to a wall, and"—he leaned in close, all of us leaning with him, watching breathlessly—"open sesame!" He raised both arms dramatically in the air.

Nothing happened. "Huh." He turned around and shrugged. "Well, guess I'm stuck."

Raquel heaved a sigh I used to know well—it was her *Evie, Evie, Evie* sigh. But this time she followed it up with a tired, "Jack. Please stop playing around. We're here for business."

"Yes, ma'am," he said, eyes wide and earnest. Raquel turned around to go back into the living room and Jack tugged lightly on the end of my ponytail, then sauntered out after her.

Who on earth was this person?

Lend took my hand. "Do you have any idea what's going on?"

I shook my head. I had never seen anyone who could go through a faerie door or navigate the Paths unless they were accompanied by a faerie. You couldn't even let go of your faerie's hand on the Paths or you'd be lost forever in the infinite darkness. I still had nightmares about being there alone.

David, Lend, and I walked cautiously into the other room, tensed for an attack. But Jack was sitting, casual as can be, on the back of the couch.

"Jack is who I was trying to tell you about, Evie." Raquel smiled smugly at us. "Thanks to him, we can transport you to and from sites with the same speed as a faerie. You'll never have to work with the fey."

"How?" I had seen it with my own eyes, but I still didn't believe it. Then something struck me. "Take off your shirt!"

"I'm not that kind of guy!" He frowned thoughtfully. "On second thought, why not?" He pulled the shirt over his head, revealing a lean torso that under other circumstances might have elicited admiration, but today was only more confusing. Once again there was absolutely nothing shimmering underneath it. So much for my theory that he was hiding something paranormal under his clothes.

I blushed angrily and looked at Raquel. "What is he? I don't see anything!"

"He's not 'anything.' Just a talented boy."

"Then how did he make a door? How did he get through the Paths?"

"Wait, so am I allowed to put my shirt back on? Or did you want me to remove my pants, too?"

Lend and I joined forces in a dark glare. "Only if you want me to vomit," I snapped.

Raquel's communicator let off a small beep and she pulled it out, scanning the message. "Jack, we've got to go. Evie, think about my offer and we'll talk again in a few days." She looked up at me and smiled, this one touching her stern eyes and making her surprisingly lovely. "And it was nice to see you again."

I threw my arms around her in a hug. "You, too."

"David," she said, her voice tighter as she turned to him and nodded. He nodded back, his eyes lingering on her a little longer than they needed to. "Lend."

Lend shook his head, looking to the side in frustration.

Jack jumped off the couch, pulling his shirt back on. "Next time, if you'd like, I'll just come without one," he said, grinning at me. Taking Raquel's hand, he walked up to the living room wall and put a hand on it. For the first time his face lost its cocky, playful cast, and he seemed to be straining in concentration. Far slower than it would take a faerie, the bright outline of a door formed on the wall, opening into black. Raquel and Jack walked through, and it closed behind them, leaving no evidence that it had ever existed in the first place.

Lend turned to me. "Well, that was interesting. And a waste of time. However, since I'm already here, what do you say we make up for your sucky afternoon?"

I wished I could make him understand that Raquel wasn't just my former employer—or worse, my captor, as he seemed to view anyone who worked for IPCA. And Jack puzzled me to no end. But extra time with Lend quickly took my mind off those particular problems. "What are you thinking?"

"How about the Mall?"

"Wait—you mean the Mall, as in a bunch of museums in DC that we would wander around and I'd pretend like I understood modern art while really thinking, holy crap, a gremlin could have painted that and for all we know did, or the mall, as in picking out a new pair of shoes, eating food that's terrible for us, and making up life stories for all the people that pass us?"

"I can see now that I must have meant the second."

"What a smart boy." I smiled and he pulled me close.

"I still say that guy was CIA. Spy all the way."

I laughed, turning to face him as he parked in front of the diner. "Lend, he was like five foot nothing."

"Exactly! You'd never suspect him. He's the quiet, nondescript-looking guy, doesn't seem like a threat at all until—BAM. Say good-bye to all your country's secrets!"

"Okay, fine. He was a spy."

"We should have gone to that movie, though. I think some explosions would have done you good, helped you relax after a hard day."

"It's not my fault I wasn't allowed in without an adult and you forgot your license."

Lend rolled his eyes. Silver shot through his nearly black hair and I laughed, shoving him.

"Knock it off. That's creepy. Besides, if you pretend to be old to sneak me in, it'd be super gross if we started making out or something. No more gray."

"Fine." His hair rolled into corkscrew curls, turning a coppery red.

I laughed. "Quit it! Someone will see you."

His eyes got serious and his hair shifted back to its normal appearance. "Are you sure you don't want me to stay? I can blow off classes tomorrow if you aren't feeling well."

"You really don't have to." Lend never missed class; I loved that he was willing to skip for me, and part of me was tempted by the offer . . . but I'd feel too guilty.

He sighed. "I do have a bio lab. You're really okay? Nothing hurting from your fall? No weird side effects from the sylph?"

"I'm okay."

"Alright. I'll see you on Saturday."

"Not Friday night?" I hated the whine that crept into my voice. I wouldn't be that girlfriend, the whiny, clingy one who couldn't have a life outside her boyfriend. Even though she totally justifiably wanted nothing more than to spend every minute of her life with him. Nope. Not that girl.

"I've got a group project in vertebrate anatomy, and the only time we could schedule it was then. I doubt we'll get done early enough for me to get here at a decent hour, and if I stay in my dorm where there are no beautiful, fun distractions, I can finish up my homework and be absolutely yours all weekend. So first thing Saturday morning."

He leaned in and kissed me. I wished he could melt away his glamour and kiss me as himself, talk to me as himself, but it wouldn't do for someone to walk by and see me making out with a nearly invisible silhouette. The downside of dating a half-human, half-water elemental, I suppose.

Pulling back far sooner than I wanted him to (which, let's face it, could have been several hours—I never got tired of kissing him), he got out and opened my door for me. The second I stepped out of the car, a strange chill breeze wrapped itself around me. All the hairs on my arms stood up in response. Shivering, I hugged Lend tightly, ignoring my bruises.

"Don't do it, okay?" he whispered.

"Do what?"

"Work for IPCA again. Just—just don't do it."

I looked up into his face. "What if I can do some good?"

"You're doing enough good being yourself. I worry

about what might happen to you."

I frowned, making a noncommittal noise, which he seemed to take as an agreement, judging by his smile. "I'll see you Saturday." He kissed me again and then waited for me to walk up the steps before getting back in his car and driving away.

Long-distance relationships? Suck. Majorly.

Sighing, I walked in and through the brightly lit diner. David bought On the Hoof a decade ago as a front for his paranormal-hiding operation. It provided jobs for paranormals in need and a good place for everyone to meet and keep track of one another. The decor was cheerful, a slightly tired fifties theme. Nona, the manager, waved at me, her gorgeous blond glamour hovering over oaky brown skin and greenish, mosslike hair. Allegedly she lived in the upstairs apartment with Arianna and me, but really she went back to the forest at night, setting down roots until the sun came up. Tree spirits—another species of paranormals I'd never met on bag-and-tag duty at IPCA. I was all about the violence and mayhem back then.

I nodded distractedly at several of the regulars, mostly vamps and werewolves, noting yet another new paranormal I'd never met, who made my heart hurt a little—she looked like a cross between Lish and a human, complete with gills on her neck and fins lining her bare legs beneath the glamour. Lately we'd been seeing more and more species neither David nor I had ever come across.

Come to think of it, a lot of new paranormals other than the werewolf or vamp variety had been visiting Nona, hanging around the diner or meeting her out back. And the sylph was certainly new. Maybe Nona would—

I shrieked, narrowly avoiding tripping over the kitchen gnome, a particularly grouchy specimen named Grnlllll. At least, I think that was her name. Or his name. Hard to tell with gnomes. Maybe that's why she—he?—hated me. The glare seemed pretty feminine, though.

The desire to get away from Grnlllll's baleful looks outweighed my desire to talk to Nona, and I slipped through the kitchen door. Upstairs at last, I collapsed onto the faded, floral couch.

"Evie?"

"Yup."

Arianna skipped into the room, a glass in her hand. I deliberately did not look at what was in it. I never avoided looking at Arianna, though, even if her shriveled corpse body beneath her normal glamour (if you considered freakishly white skin and spiked red and black hair normal) creeped me out like all vamps did. It hurt her feelings, and despite our rough start last spring, I really did think of her as a friend. It wasn't like she asked to be what she was, and she never drank human blood. Plus, she could be pretty fun when she wasn't pissed off at me.

"Big afternoon?" Arianna settled onto the love seat and grabbed the remote, turning the television to our show.

"You could say that." I rubbed my tender hip, wondering how black and blue I'd be in the morning.

"Okay. Loser does dishes for a week. I bet Landon and Cheyenne hook up but have a fight and break it off by the end of the episode."

Trying to sound more enthusiastic than I felt, I countered. "No, Cheyenne rejects him because of some misunderstanding, and he starts shooting up again."

"You're on." Arianna leaned forward, devouring the drama playing out on the screen in front of us.

I looked forlornly at the ceiling, trying to ignore the faint tingling sensation in my fingertips. I knew I should listen to Lend, stay away from IPCA, be grateful for my normal, boring life. I should live for the weekends, when I got to see him, and ignore the nagging pain always pulling at the back of my mind that it didn't matter how much time I spent with him, how much I loved him, he could never really be mine because I was temporary and he was forever.

I was fine. This was enough. Besides, Lend didn't want me to help IPCA.

But Lend wasn't here, was he?

SPARKLES MAKE
EVERYTHING BETTER

*W*ake up," a voice like water rippling over rocks whispered in my ear. I smiled and reached out my arms until I found Lend's neck. I knew what I would see when I opened my eyes—almost nothing. My Lend in his true form. Squinting against the midmorning light, I looked into his water eyes.

"Good morning," he said, and I melted.

"Morning." I tried to pull him down next to me, but he laughed and ducked out from under my arms.

"Get up, lazy. Unless you want to sleep instead of hanging out with me?"

"I don't know." I closed my eyes again. "I *am* pretty tired."

He answered by tossing a pillow onto my face. I laughed and rolled out of bed, brushing my teeth and changing while he chatted with Arianna out in the living room. My room was tiny—a glorified walk-in closet, really—but I'd painted the walls "obnoxiously pink," to quote Arianna. I missed my posters from the Center, but I was slowly making the place mine. Sketches from Lend took up most of the free space, which made me feel like he was around even when he wasn't.

"Of course I'm a necromancer," Arianna explained to Lend. She was sitting in front of the sleek desktop, her favorite game running. "It's ironic. In real life I'm one of the hordes of the living dead, and in my online life I control them."

She spent nearly every daylight hour there, running quests with violet-skinned, scantily clad digital cohorts. A few weeks ago I was annoyed at never being able to check email and snarked that she should find something productive to do with her time. She made a point of showing me just how long a vampire can go without moving from a single spot.

It's a long time.

But even worse, a couple of days into her sit-in, I overheard her sobbing. I haven't mentioned anything since about how she uses her time. Having eternal life seems like a cool enough idea, but having it forced on you in that form? Not so much. Immortals like Nona try out being humanish every now and again for fun, but they were built to be forever. People weren't, and Arianna's corpse body under her glamour was a constant reminder to me of that.

"And that's why I had to kill him—the Knife of O'orlenthaal should have been mine all along, the little skunk. Now we have to fight his guild, which is where my ability to raise armies of the dead comes in handy."

"So what you're saying is, you've been busy." Lend grinned at her, and Arianna laughed. She treated him like a little brother. Lend, in turn, treated her like she was totally normal. I loved that about him; he took every paranormal at face value, and I could tell that it meant the world to ones like Arianna and most of the werewolves, who struggled with what they were. Lend had an amazing knack for balancing paranormal and normal and making everyone feel like they belonged.

"Totally busy. I also designed a few dresses—those reality show morons have nothing on me."

"I'm telling you, start a website! You could make everything here and then sell online. You show me your dress sketches, I'll make the site, and you and Evie can model."

Arianna shrugged, squirming in her seat. She had been in fashion design school when she was changed. Lend was always trying to get her to pick it up again, but for some reason she never went through with it.

He looked up and smiled when he saw me in the hallway. "Ready?"

"Always. Sure you don't want to hang out, Ari?" I asked.

Please don't want to hang out, I thought. We had plans for a movie with her this afternoon, but I wanted some time with just Lend for a few hours.

She waved a hand in the air, focused back on the computer. "Gotta finish this raid."

A burst of affection for that stupid game welled up inside my chest. Hooray for role-playing and its effectiveness in de-chaperoning me!

Lend took my hand in his as we walked outside into the brisk October morning, a breeze rising to greet us as soon as we stepped onto the sidewalk. Summer had lingered this year, reluctant to give up her hold. Only in the last week or so had a chill crept into the nights. The leaves were hinting at change, gold and red weaving their way in. After living in the climate-controlled Center for so long, I was definitely a fan of this whole seasons thing.

I was also a fan of my boyfriend. The sunlight gave an extra sparkle to his water eyes, and his nearly black glamour hair was shiny and oh so adorable. The day couldn't have been more perfect.

"I have a present for you," Lend said. Did I say the day couldn't have been more perfect? Because it totally just got better.

"What for?" I squealed, not trying to hide my excitement. Presents in the Center had been few and far between, and, with Raquel as the main giver, painfully practical. There was the travel-size first aid kit for my twelfth birthday, the infamous encyclopedia Christmas (honestly, who buys those anymore? It's called the internet), and of course, the pinnacle of craptacular gift giving: *socks*. Every. Single. Year.

But the box Lend took out of his pocket definitely didn't have socks in it. "Is it sparkly?" I bounced impatiently on my heels as he opened it.

He laughed and pulled out a delicate silver chain, threaded through an open heart-shaped pendant. Three pink stones lining one edge stood out in contrast to the dark metal of the heart. I pulled my hair off my neck and he clasped it there, the trace of his fingers against my skin raising goose bumps.

I fingered the cool metal. "It's beautiful!"

"Oh good. I've never given jewelry before."

"Well, you've set a ridiculously high standard for yourself. Should have started out with something tacky." I put my arms around his neck and hugged him close, breathing in his cool scent.

"It's not just pretty, though."

"No?"

"Practical, too. The heart is made of iron."

Warmth flooded through me, a spurt of affection I should have been used to by now but that still always managed to surprise me. Leave it to Lend to find a way to protect me with faerie-repelling iron. Of course, this meant that he was almost as practical as Raquel, but his practical was sparkly and pretty. I ran my fingers through his hair. "Perfect."

"It is?"

"*You* are. But the necklace is, too."

We kissed until an old lady walking her dog coughed loudly in our direction, reminding us that we were, in fact, on the sidewalk and not in our own little world. I smiled sheepishly at her, only then noticing that she was a glamoured paranormal. Her froggish face, mottled green, didn't really go with her floral housedress and slippers. This town? Weird.

She wouldn't quit staring; I couldn't figure out what she was, and suddenly I was nervous. I glanced at the sky, to check for errant clouds, but didn't see anything. Tugging Lend's hand so we'd keep walking, I shook off my unease. "What else is on the agenda for this morning?" I asked.

"Doesn't the necklace get me off the hook for planning things?"

"Fine. But it only buys you today. You still have to figure out something for us to do tomorrow. And as for right now, I think food is in order. Lots. I forgot breakfast."

"Okay, we can—" Lend's phone rang and he pulled it out of his pocket, frowning at the number. "One sec." He answered it and I plotted what to do with the rest of the hours in the weekend. The movies this afternoon with Arianna, after which I had a secret plot to drag her out for karaoke. She denied it, but I totally caught her belting

Duran Duran in the shower. If that didn't work out, I was thinking bowling. I'd never gone and was guaranteed to be horrible, but it'd be fun with Lend. Maybe we could even double with Carlee and whatever boy she was currently dating.

My stomach sank as I tuned into the conversation.

"All of it?" Lend asked, his voice tight. "Can you— No, calm down, it's okay, it's not your fault. I'm glad you didn't get hurt. I can come back up. Are you sure everyone's stuff is gone?" He closed his eyes, holding back a sigh. "Okay, give me an hour or two to get there." He hung up and stared at the phone as though he could erase the conversation.

And, just like that, my weekend evaporated. "What?"

"Natalie, a girl in my group, was in charge of compiling everything. Some guy stole her bag at the Metro station— took her laptop, all the notes, everything. We're screwed. I've got to go and help them put it all back together. It's three weeks' worth of work." His jaw was clenched with stress.

For the briefest moment I was tempted to tell him that getting a double degree in biology and zoology didn't matter. At all. In the grand scheme of his immortal life, this one stupid college group project? Not even a drop in the bucket. But . . . if he knew he was more elemental than human, would he quit school? Quit normal life?

Quit me?

Yeah, so not telling him. Not right then, anyway. I mean, if he had eternity, what difference did it make if I told him tomorrow or ten years from now? He wasn't getting any less immortal. Of course, maybe if I told him, I could be around him without feeling guilty. But I'd waited this long, and I didn't want to make today even worse.

"Evie?"

"What?"

"I'm sorry. I know this sucks."

"Oh, yeah. I mean, it sucks, but you gotta do what you gotta do, right?" I gave him my best *aren't I a supportive girlfriend?* smile.

We hurried back to the diner, the happy spring in my step dead. So the trees were changing color. Big bleeping deal. Lend made a few calls, but in spite of his best efforts it was clear he needed to be there to help fix it. He left me with a lingering, regretful kiss and nothing to do for the next two days except homework.

"Back already?" Arianna asked when I walked in, headphones on and voice way too loud.

"He had to go back to school."

"Lame." She actually looked up now and frowned, seeing my face. "That kinda makes your weekend suck, doesn't it. Wanna go . . . I don't know, hang out in some dark alley with me until the sun goes down?"

I forced a laugh. "No worries. You keep exacting virtual revenge. We're still on for the movie this afternoon."

"Fine, but I'm not holding your hand."

"Thank heavens for that."

She put her headphones back on. I trudged to my room and flopped onto my bed.

And screamed as my door slammed shut. A figure stepped out from behind it. "Rather pink in here, isn't it?"

A TRASHY LIFE

My heart stopped. For one horrible moment I thought Reth was in my room. And then I picked up the nearest object—a shoe—and threw it straight at Jack's head.

"What are you doing in here, you little weasel?"

He picked up my shoe from where it had clattered to the floor after hitting the door behind him. "How *do* you walk in these heels?" He sat and removed his own shoe, trying to jam his foot into my purple sling-back.

I stalked over and yanked it away. "What are you, five? Answer my question."

He looked up at me, impossibly big blue eyes wide with

innocence. "I thought we were friends, after you made me strip and all."

"I'm calling Raquel."

"Fine, fine. I was just doing some reconnaissance."

"Reconnaissance?"

"Oh, sorry, that's a big word, isn't it? It means I was scoping the scene, getting the—"

"I know what it means! What, is IPCA investigating me now? Screw them, they can forget about any help from—"

"Do you ever let anyone else finish a sentence?" He smiled at my glare, flashing his dimples. "That's more like it. You're much prettier when you aren't talking. True of most people, I've found. Anyhow, I needed to see the address Raquel gave me so that I could find it again."

"Why?"

"As you so graciously pointed out the other day, I'm not a faerie. I need to see a place before I can open a door there. Or at least open a precise door there. Otherwise it's anyone's guess how close I'll get."

I sat down on the edge of my bed. As long as the weirdo was already here, I might as well get some answers. It had been nagging at me: how he could do what he did? It shouldn't be possible. "How did you learn? To use the Paths, I mean."

His mouth twisted into an impish grin. "Don't let my good looks fool you. I'm terribly clever."

I rolled my eyes. "Clearly. But you still shouldn't be

able to use the Paths."

He shrugged, standing. "Watch and wait long enough, want something bad enough, and you can figure out a way to make it happen. I make a lot of things happen." Smiling enigmatically, he reached out a hand to my wall. "I'll pick you up later?"

"I haven't agreed to anything." I narrowed my eyes.

"Of course," he said, distracted as he focused on the white lines snaking out to make a door. "So, I'll pick you up later, then."

"No! Don't you listen to anything? Tell Raquel I'm not going to—"

Before I could finish my sentence he walked through the faerie door, muttering something that sounded suspiciously like, "Girls are annoying."

The wall formed again behind him, becoming the innocent recipient of my withering glare. Jack might look my age, but he was like a little kid on a sugar high—in need of a good spanking.

Good heavens, *that* sounded creepy. I lay back on my bed and closed my eyes. What a mess. I focused on letting the stress melt out of my body, letting myself drift into a restful, weightless state. It felt like if I could find peace, think things through, everything would be okay with my life, with Lend and me. I could figure out how to tell him the truth just right so that he wouldn't even think of giving up on his mortal lifestyle. I'd come up with some way for us to work, some way for me to have all the important people in my life *in* my life, for as long as I wanted them to be.

A loud rapping on the door jarred me, shattering whatever epiphany I was undoubtedly about to reach.

"EVELYN, GET YOUR LAZY, SCRAWNY, PALE BUTT OUT OF BED RIGHT NOW."

I opened my eyes with a roll, then walked out to the hall, feeling justifiably surly. "You have volume control on that mouth?"

Arianna shrugged. "You sleep like the dead. Nona needs help downstairs."

"Great. Exactly how I wanted to spend my weekend. Lend free and grease filled."

"Funny, I'd choose sleeping in and going shopping, but to each her own. Get down there."

"What about our movie?" I whined, hoping that Arianna would help get me out of work.

"Creature of the night and all that jazz. I'm good with a late show."

"Fine." I stomped down the stairs, sulkily pulling my apron down off its hook on the wall and fastening it. It was great having an income now that I didn't have an IPCA spending account (and, trust me, I missed that account something fierce), but working in a diner was a little less interesting than going on bag-and-tag missions.

And by a little I mean a lot. Keeping with the charming diner cow theme, we had to wear skirts—poodle-style skirts—in cow print. *Cow print.* There are many animal prints that are fabulous in any style. Cow is not one of them. It's insulting, really. Which was why I stubbornly kept my own skinny jeans on. I wasn't scheduled, I wasn't going to dress bovine.

Just my luck, Grnlllll (or was it four *l*'s? Or a double *r*, triple *l*? If you think Welsh is weird, try reading Gnomish) was in the kitchen. Gnomes are earth elementals and usually live under the ground, mining and digging. They even look kinda like moles, with furry heads of hair; small, squinty eyes; and noses more snoutish than anything else. They're happiest burrowing around in the dark and damp. What on earth Grnlllll was doing in this bright kitchen I had yet to figure out, but whatever it was, it certainly wasn't making her happy.

And her French fries? Not good.

Grnlllll growled something at me that I didn't bother trying to interpret, and I went out to take orders. Afternoon business was pretty typical—mostly the local paranormals, which meant an abundance of steaks so rare I could hardly stomach looking at them and shakes, the ingredients of which I didn't even want to think about.

Things picked up as evening began curling against the windows with its cold insistence. My feet and back ached, and if I had to smile one more time and pretend like I didn't notice the vamp in the corner licking his lips whenever I walked by, I was pretty sure I would scream. It was bad enough that half of the local vamps tried to use their mind-control powers to convince me I didn't want a tip.

I *always* want a tip, you undead creeps.

Still, it was kind of funny watching vampires get more and more frustrated when they couldn't persuade me. David and Arianna had kept my glamour-piercing abilities secret, which I appreciated. It made things less complicated.

I ripped off the bill and slapped it down on Lip-licker's table. "Fifteen percent, like always."

He scowled, then his face smoothed into a stunning smile. Stunning if you couldn't see through his glamour to notice that every single tooth was grinning out at me through his rotting cheeks. He reached out to try and take my hand, but I whipped it away.

"Seriously. Fifteen percent or I'm slipping garlic powder into your next Bloody Mary."

He fixed me with a scowl that could launch a thousand horror novels. I smiled. Muttering murderous things under his breath, he pulled out his wallet and handed over the money.

"Come back soon," I chirped, beaming as I went back to the cash register. I might not have Tasey on me regularly, but I could still best vamps.

Nona swished by. Even the way she walked looked like a tree swaying in the wind. Local guys, non-paranormals, came by the diner sometimes to watch her. If they could see her hollowed-out tree trunk of a back, complete with tail, they'd probably feel different.

Then again, you never know with guys. And she was a pretty hot tree.

She stopped in front of me, smiling. "Thank you for working tonight."

"Sure. Oh, hey," I said, remembering my earlier question. "I've been seeing more and more paranormals that I don't recognize. Does David know about them?" I met with him and Arianna pretty regularly to go over paperwork and details for their little operation, but I didn't know everything.

Nona waved a hand gracefully through the air. "There is no danger. Would you mind helping Grnlllll in the kitchen? She cannot get the trash out on her own."

My stomach sank. Trash duty. Great. The gnome was shorter than the trash bags, but of course we couldn't get smaller bags, oh no, so I got to be on call any time the filth was full. And taking out the trash meant the Dumpster, and I had to actually *touch* it to get it open, and it was sticky.

STICKY.

I'm really not a lazy person, but for the last eight years of my life all I had to do was pick up my things. I couldn't exactly take the Center's trash out to the curb, considering it was a sealed underground complex. Diner trash was enough to make me nostalgic for those sterile white halls. Better sterile than sticky and smelly.

Back in the kitchen Grnlllll pointed in the direction of

the trash—which she had let overflow and spill onto the floor. Trying to ignore the gag building at the back of my throat, I heaved the bag out of the can. It flopped into my leg, leaving a vile, dark smear of disgusting on my jeans. Brilliant.

Grnlllll's voice graveled something at me as she pointed angrily to the streak I was creating as I dragged the bag along the floor, but at this point I didn't care. I *should* have had this whole weekend off. I *should* have been snuggled up next to Lend right now, making fun of a bad movie with him and Arianna. I didn't ask for this.

Besides, she may have been too short for the Dumpster, but she wasn't too short to mop.

I kicked open the metal door leading to the dark back alley, gulping at the night air as the stench of rotten food assailed my nostrils. I could feel it lodging in my sinuses, and I wondered if I would ever be able to smell anything else.

The single light above the door flickered. I'd probably have to replace the bulb, too. Stupid gnome. Taking a deep breath, I walked to the Dumpster between our brick wall and the next building, flipped open the lid, and threw in the bag—and a big glop of something fell straight out onto my shoe.

"Bleep!" I screamed to the wall in front of me. "Bleep, bleep, *bleep*!" I kicked the Dumpster, then grabbed at my foot. Now I was dirty, my toes hurt, *and* I felt like an idiot. I closed my eyes, pinching the bridge of my nose. It was okay. This was okay. I would go upstairs, take a shower, and go to bed. For the rest of the weekend.

The light flickered off, then came back on. Too bright. Way too bright. I opened my eyes to see the lines of another faerie door forming on the wall next to the Dumpster.

"Go away," I snapped. "I'm not in the mood." If Raquel thought sending idiot Jack repeatedly would help her cause, she was wrong.

A figure, taller than Jack and more beautiful by far than anyone else I knew, stepped out of the door.

"Now really," he said, his voice liquid gold, "that's hardly the welcome I expected, my love."

EX MARKS THE SPOT

Reth. In front of me. In the alley behind the diner. I couldn't sort out whether the fluttering in my stomach was fear or excitement. How had I forgotten what a beautiful, beautiful thing he was? Looking at him now, glowing faintly with warmth in the cold dark, all the feelings for him I'd ever been overwhelmed with flooded back in.

Including all the terror and pain he'd caused, so yeah, I wasn't going to jump him or anything. But still, he was pretty to look at. And the last thing I wanted to see right now. Or ever, really. I held up a hand, palm out. "I'm not going anywhere with you!"

Reth raised one eyebrow. "There's no need for crass threats. I don't wish to take you anywhere. Except perhaps out of this alley, in an effort to escape *some* of the stench." He looked pointedly at my stained apron.

"Oh." I lowered my hand, deflated and confused, and put my nose surreptitiously to my shoulder. Did I really smell? And since when did Reth not want me? He always wanted me. But I didn't want him to want me—so why was I disappointed? Leave it to him to take me from angry to confused in five seconds flat.

"Walk with me? I would offer my elbow like a gentleman, but your hand looks rather sticky."

I scowled. "Why on earth would I walk anywhere with you?"

He held out one perfect, slender hand toward the kitchen door of the diner. "My apologies; by all means, go back in. No doubt more filth awaits."

I looked at the door, at war with myself. On the one hand, I hated doing anything Reth wanted me to. On the other hand, there was a mop with my name on it inside. . . .

"Fine, but if you try anything—"

"Really, Evelyn, how I've missed your charming company."

Keeping a wary eye on the faerie, I followed him through the alley. We made our way down the lamp-lined street, his step so light it bordered on dancing. I felt like a graceless clod next to him. Then there was the aspect of his ethereal, near-angelic beauty compared to my . . . well, for the sake of my self-esteem, it was probably best not to compare.

I hugged myself, shrugging inward against the cold, tickling breeze as my breath fanned out in front of me. I had no doubt I'd regret going with him, but part of me was glad for these strange new happenings. They reminded me I wasn't just a girl who was bad at soccer. Even though I no longer knew his true name and thus couldn't control him, for once I felt almost equal to Reth. The knowledge that I could hurt him if I needed to—if I wanted to—gave me a heady feeling of power.

It probably wasn't healthy.

Still, if he did something stupid and forced me to drain him, well, I wouldn't cry about it. "So, is there any point to this walk? Because I'm kind of cold."

Reth laughed, that silver, ringing laugh, and unconsciously I leaned in closer to him. Shaking my head, I took a firm step toward the street. We were nearing the border of thick trees that pushed in along the small town's edges. I looked over at him, noticing for the first time that he had his glamour on. Not that it was much less gorgeous than his real face, but it surprised me. When he was IPCA and required to wear a glamour he almost never did; I couldn't figure out why he would care now that he was free. (Which was mostly my fault, but, really, a girl can't be expected to outsmart a faerie when running from her own death, now, can she?)

"Still cold, my love? I can take care of that."

"Yeah, I remember. I think I'll pass." I rubbed my wrist, where I could see the faint pink print of his hand, forever burned there. I'd had enough of his warmth to last a lifetime.

Reth stopped and I did, too, reluctantly facing him. Latent rage welled up. I wanted to scream at him, attack him. It was his fault that Lish was dead—he was the one who let Viv into the Center. But if he hadn't, I wouldn't ever have gotten out of IPCA. And I definitely wouldn't have been able to rescue Lend. For all I knew, he would still be in a cell in the Center and Vivian would still be slowly but surely killing every paranormal around. It made me sick to think about.

Nothing was ever, ever simple with Reth.

"Why are you here?" I asked, all my pent-up anger draining away to exhaustion.

He reached out a finger, nearly touching my face but instead stroking the air in front of it. "Would you believe I merely wanted to see you?"

"Nope."

He smiled. "No, I suppose not. Initially I thought to take you. I could, you know. I've always been so gentle with you."

"Gentle?" I glared incredulously at him.

"Yes, I can't fathom it, either. Other methods would have been so much simpler. But for whatever reason I find myself charmed by you and concerned with your best interests."

"You just can't help topping your own levels of crazy, can you? My best interests? You kidnapped me! You burned me! You tried to force me to become something I never wanted to be!"

"Evelyn, dear child, simply because you cannot understand what is in your best interests doesn't mean that I do not. And if what is best for you also hurts you, well, that doesn't change the necessity of becoming what you should be."

"You're—I—*AUGH*! You have no idea how insane you are. If you really cared about me, you wouldn't hurt me. But you don't care, because you can't! You can't care about anything except yourself."

His eyes flashed, the gold darkening. "I care for you more than anyone in this sad, spinning world does. I couldn't have poured my own soul into you if that weren't true."

I was glad I'd let out whatever soul Reth had given me along with all the others. Knowing that I'd had part of his soul in me made me feel, well, icky. I raised my chin defiantly. "Lend loves me. He'd never hurt me."

"And no doubt he'd do anything for you."

"Yes!"

"Do whatever it took to protect you."

"Yes!"

"And if the only way to protect you and save your life was to hurt you?"

I snapped my lips shut against the yes that was about to

come out. Could I hit Reth? Could I please, please just hit him?

He smiled, knowing he had me there. "Lend can't love you because he doesn't truly know you. No matter how much you want this life, it isn't yours. It never has been. This isn't your home, Evelyn."

Angry tears pricked my eyes. "Go away."

"Come with me."

"Never! And you can't make me. If you really could have taken me, you would have by now."

He clicked his tongue impatiently. "My previous methods met with . . . disapproval from my queen. Sometimes I wonder if I chose quite right when aligning myself with a court."

"What do you mean? You're either Seelie or Unseelie." I might not know as much about faeries as I should, but I did know they were in one of the two courts: Seelie, meaning good—or rather, goodish, since no faeries were really good—or Unseelie, meaning definitely, *definitely* bad.

His smile shifted, and I saw something feral and primal beneath his refined features. "No one is either good or bad, my love. We all have bits of both; we simply choose to align ourselves with whichever side has a stronger pull. My choice to get involved was motivated by a very sad, empty girl with eyes like streams of melting snow."

So now Reth was saying he only went with the good court because of me? Or was he saying something else entirely? Only he could do this to me—make me feel this awful and confused. When I was with Reth, everything lonely and heartbroken in me seemed to well to the surface, begging to let him take it away. "I hate you," I whispered, my voice cracking.

He locked his eyes on mine, drawing me closer, his voice slipping around me like a golden net. "Nonsense. My queen's forbidden me to force you to come with me again, but I can't understand why I should need to. It doesn't have to be this way. It can be easy, safe, warm. And when you come home, none of this will matter—it will slip away, all the dark and cold, less than a dream. You'll never have to worry or wonder again. Just *choose* it, Evelyn. Quit clinging to this world of loss and come with me. I can fill all the emptiness that you are. Become what you should be, and help us get back to where we belong. *Leave with me.*"

I sighed, breathing in deeply, my cheek against his chest. The heartbeat there was strange, too slow, but he was warm, and his arms around me were wonderful, and how did I get here again? I didn't want his arms around me. Did I? There was someone . . . something . . . some reason. Did it matter?

Reth jerked away, his perfect nose wrinkled. "Oh, that necklace is monstrous. Where did you get such an abominable thing?" I blinked, dazed, and my fingers drifted up to my pendant. When I touched the cold iron, reality snapped back into place.

"Are you kidding me? You come here and use your stupid faerie mojo and then *you* back away from *me*? Is there anything in your golden head that makes sense? What, you thought, hey, Evie's probably having a bad night, why don't I go mess with her? While you're at it, there are probably some puppies you could kick!"

I whipped around, stalking back to the diner. I should have known—had known—this was a bad idea. Idiot Evie.

Turning a corner, I stopped short at the sight of Reth, leaning casually against a lamppost, surrounded by a puddle of light and looking like an ad for an impossibly perfect reality.

"You need to come with me. Things have been set in motion, and I cannot control all the variables. I can't hide you forever. I can, however, keep you safe and make you happy. Give me your hand." He held his out; I could almost see waves of heat radiating from it.

I frowned, thinking of the sylph. Clearly *something* had found out where I was. Come to think of it, who was to say he didn't set the sylph on me himself to trick me into thinking I was in danger? It would be just like him. The whole thing reeked of faerie mischief.

"Screw you. Me and my magic hands will be fine, thank you very much. I'm staying right where I am."

He smiled, straightening to stand in front of me. "Very well. Clearly this life you so desperately craved is everything you hoped it would be. It warms me through to see you this fulfilled and"—he leaned in, whispering right in my ear—"*happy.*"

I closed my eyes, clenching my jaw. If he thought he

could swoop in here and start messing with my life again, he was wrong. "Look, just because—"

I opened my eyes to find myself utterly alone. The lamplight that seemed to glow before was now harsh, creating shadows and sharp lines but illuminating nothing. The darkness of the night pressed in on me from all directions, and my teeth started to chatter.

"What am I doing here?" I whispered. And then quickly corrected: "*Out* here. I meant *out* here."

I walked back to the diner. Ignoring Grnlllll, I went straight upstairs, stripping off my filthy clothes and standing in the shower until the hot water ran out. Miserable and unaccountably sad, I wanted to call Lend. I never felt empty around him. But then I'd have to tell him about tonight, and he'd be worried that Reth showed up again, and I didn't want him to stress out about it. Instead I told Arianna I felt sick, climbed into bed, and willed myself to sleep.

Things would feel better in the morning. They had to.

My brain and body finally disconnected and I drifted off to blessed sleep.

"Hey, stupid," Vivian said.

"Oh, Viv." I broke into tears. "I'm so glad you're here."

DREAM ON

"What's wrong?" Vivian asked. We sat on a hill overlooking the ocean, stars in the black night sky reflected on the water. She put her arm around me awkwardly and I leaned my head into her shoulder.

When she first started showing up in my dreams again after last April, it scared the crap out of me. She was so lonely, though, and I couldn't help but talk to her. I still hadn't forgiven her for killing Lish—I don't think I ever will—but it was a topic we both avoided so that we could get to know each other. I understood now a little better where she came from, and I'd always sympathized with how deeply alone she'd been. Plus, being raised by faeries, she was bound to make bad choices. We treaded lightly around the hard topics, and somewhere along the way it felt like we really had become the sisters she always wanted us to be.

Except she never took my stuff, which was nice.

I wiped away tears. "I don't know what I'm doing. I'm sad, and I don't know why, and I shouldn't be—and here I am, complaining to you when you aren't even—" I stopped, unable to finish. Vivian wasn't going to wake up, ever again. When I took the souls from her, she hadn't had enough of her own soul to live a normal life. It was my fault.

"Hey, shush, don't you worry about me. I'm fine."

"You haven't visited in a while."

"Haven't I?" She looked thoughtfully out over the water. "I'm here, or I'm nowhere, or I'm somewhere else entirely. It gives me a lot of time to think. But I never seem to get anywhere with it."

"I'm sorry."

"I know. Me, too. I try to make my life different in my mind, be the one who was strong enough to let go."

"You were, though." I nudged her with my elbow. "You didn't take my soul."

"That's something, but it doesn't really make up for the ones I did take, does it?"

No. No, it didn't.

"Sometimes . . . sometimes I wish you had sent me with

them." She took my hand in hers, tracing the outline of the gate in the stars I had sent the souls through. Neither of us really understood what happened that night. We might both be Empty Ones, capable of opening gates between worlds, but that didn't mean we had any idea how it worked. "I wonder what would have happened if the faeries hadn't sent me after you, if they'd realized I had enough energy to open a gate myself. Lucky for us that my faeries were idiots, but I can't help imagining it. I think I'd like to see what's out there."

I let out a heavy sigh. "Someday we both will."

She laughed again. "Hey, stupid, it's not a bad thing."

"It's another way of losing people," I whispered. "I feel like I'm doomed to lose everyone, always. I can't seem to keep the people I love."

She squeezed my hand. "I know. On the bright side, I'm not going anywhere." Her voice had that edge of irony I remembered so well; funny that what used to scare me about her was now comforting, familiar. Being together was like a little touch of home—a foreign concept for both of us. She looked down at my hand; I thought I saw a tiny flash of light, along with tingling. "What was that?"

I had forgotten about the stupid sylph. This was hardly the place to bring it up. Another thing to worry about. "I didn't see anything," I said.

"If you're going to lie you really ought to get better at it." She lay back on the grass to stare at the sky. "So, you're sad. What's the problem?"

Sighing heavily, I lay back, too. "I don't know. I've finally got the life I wanted for so long. And it's great, really, and Lend—"

"I like hearing about him."

"I like talking about him. And he's wonderful. But I haven't . . . I still haven't told him."

"Yeah, I figured. You're not really good with the honesty thing."

"You're one to talk!"

"Hey, I was always honest about what I was doing." She flashed a wicked grin, reminding me that she wasn't as innocent as I liked to pretend. "But that's not what this new crying fit is about, because you've known about Lend's immortal soul for a while now."

I shifted uncomfortably. "Reth visited tonight."

"Really? Wish he'd visit me. . . ."

"Vivian!"

"What? A girl gets lonely in a coma, and faerie or not, he's *pretty*." I wasn't sure if she wanted him to mess around with or to suck dry—and equally unsure which option creeped me out more. "Go on, though."

"I don't know. He implied that I'm not really happy with the life I chose." I hated how he always seemed to see straight through me. If he didn't have to deal with squirmy, unpredictable mortal emotions, why did he have to be so good at reading them?

"Well, *are* you happy?"

"Yes! I am! Of course I am. It's what I always wanted."

"But . . ."

"Nothing. It's stupid."

"Well, duh. You, my darling sister, are stupid about a lot of things."

I glared at her. "Gosh, tender much?"

She shrugged. "Like I said, I'm honest. Go on. It's what you always wanted, and?"

"And it's not, you know? Lend's gone so much, and even when he's here I can't help but worry that this isn't the life he'll choose when he finds out that he's like his mom. And then Raquel showed up this week, which reminded me of how things used to be. They weren't great, but I kind of miss . . ." I thought about what my life had been like at IPCA, how much I had dreamed of being normal, of this life I had now. What was it that I missed? It wasn't the missions, the restrictions, the lifestyle.

It was mattering.

"I miss being special. With IPCA, I was special. They needed me. And in the real world, I'm . . . not." Tears started streaming again and I wiped them away, embarrassed. "I'm sorry. How lame am I, whining my whole life about being different, and then hating being the same as everyone else."

Viv pushed up onto her elbows, frowning at me. "But you're *not*. You've never been the same. So I don't get it—you haven't changed. What's the problem here?"

"I don't know."

"Get over it then. Do something."

"What?"

She waved a hand dismissively. "Whatever you freaking want to. That's the glory of being you, Evie. You've got a choice. I wouldn't recommend going on a massive paranormal killing spree, though. It didn't turn out so hot for me."

I let out a strangled laugh. "You're terrible."

"Tell me about it."

We were quiet then, both lost in our problems. Finally, Vivian took my hand in her even colder one again, pulling me up to sit next to her. "Well, enough with this pity party. If I've been gone for a while, there are important things we need to talk about."

"What's that?"

"Umm, hello? You need to catch me up on *Easton Heights*. I didn't listen to a rundown of the first three seasons for you to leave me hanging now."

I laughed. "Important, huh? Fine." And I shared what little I could of the outside world, here in my dark dream-world where Vivian and I met.

Sometimes it felt more real than anything else.

When I woke up in the morning my hand was still curled like I was holding Vivian's. I sighed. Viv nights always left me with the weirdest combination of well-being and regret. And then, of course, guilt over being friends with the girl who murdered my Lish, but Lish would understand. I hoped.

The faeries who raised Vivian never let her think she had any choices. She always felt like her life had been determined for her. I think she realized it wasn't, now that it was too late. It made me wonder if I had connected with her sooner, if I could have stopped it all.

It was enough to make a person crazy, thinking about it.

In the end Vivian had made her choices and paid for them. Thanks to the faeries, she was out of options. But I wasn't. I would make this life what I wanted it to be. Screw Reth—I'd be happy. I was going to have my cake and eat it, too.

Or rather, be normal and have my paranormal, too. I was special; why pretend otherwise? I needed to email Raquel. I was about to make her day.

LIKE APHRODITE
ON STEROIDS

Shut up." I laughed, closing my locker.

"No, really," Lend continued. "Dead serious. Dude's a leprechaun."

"Your technical writing professor is *not* a leprechaun."

"How do you know? This is why you need to ditch next week and come to class with me. You can confirm. Right now all I know is that he has red hair, red skin, is about four feet tall, and wears nothing but green."

I rolled my eyes, knowing he couldn't see it through my shiny, pink cell phone. "And why would a leprechaun have a PhD?"

"I don't know. Hanging out at the bottom of rainbows got boring, he was tired of clovers, pots of gold lost their sparkle for him—take your pick. But I'm right. In fact, did I tell you that my lab assistant may or may not be a dryad?"

"Wait—aren't they notoriously lusty?"

There was a pause at the other end of the line.

"Oh, you are *not* going to that lab again."

Lend laughed and I closed my eyes, picturing how he would look in front of me. "Trust me, there's only one paranormal I'd like to be notoriously lusty for me."

I sighed. "Okay, but I don't think I can find a hag on such short notice."

He laughed again, almost covering the sound of the bell. I looked around, panicked. A stray paper drifted across the now forsaken hallways.

"Crap, I'm gonna be late! I'll talk to you later, okay?" Flipping my phone shut, I ran for the locker room. At least it was gym and there was a little wiggle room.

Or so I thought. Miss Lynn, that hideous creature, was waiting outside the door, marking off girls as they came in. She looked up and smiled, pleased to have caught me in an obvious infraction. "That's half your participation points for the day, Green. Another tardy and I believe you'll qualify for in-school suspension."

Where was Tasey when I needed her? It took all my willpower to suppress an eye roll as I skulked into the locker room. The faint aroma of sweat and mildew greeted me, and I passed girls in various states of undress to get to my locker. I wasn't nearly as fond of this one.

Carlee pulled on her tennis shoes, already good to go. Honestly, how her boobs could be so perky in a sports bra I'd never understand. Or stop envying.

She shook her head. "You should be more careful. Miss Lynn really doesn't like you."

I sighed, pulling out my gym clothes. What school chooses yellow and brown for their colors? Gross. Just, gross. "The feeling's mutual."

"So how was your weekend?"

"Sucktastic. Lend had to go back to school."

"Lame. I'm sorry."

"How was yours?"

Her face lit up. "Great! So John and I got back together, right? And at first I was all like, awesome! But then Friday night he was supposed to call, and he totally didn't, so then I was like—" My eyes glazed over as I tried to pay attention. I liked Carlee, and appreciated having a friend that wasn't undead, but sometimes the effort it took to keep up girl relationships felt like too much.

"—and then he was like, 'If you don't want to'—"

A scream erupted from another aisle. I didn't know whether to be grateful for the interruption or scared of what could be happening. Carlee and I both darted around the corner and found girls covering themselves and shrieking. "What is it?" I shouted, vowing to never again leave Tasey at home.

One of the girls pointed to the next row and I crept toward it, every muscle tense and my back to the wall. The aisle opened in front of me and I shouted, ready to spring at—

Jack.

Stupid, stupid Jack, standing up on one of the wooden benches that lined the middle of the aisle, hands on hips as he surveyed the empty row like some sort of bizarre conqueror.

"What are you doing here?" I asked, horrified.

He looked down at me. "Oh, there you are. I'm supposed to give you something."

"And you couldn't have given it to me *somewhere else*?" I looked around, exasperated and anxious. Girls were starting to trickle over, past their first shock and now curious.

"What's wrong with here? Here seems plenty nice to me." He patted his pockets, finally muttering, "Aha!" before pulling out a familiar white phone-like device. An IPCA communicator. I'd forgotten how boring they were compared to my supercute cell. He smiled and let it slip through his fingers. I gasped and lunged forward, but he bounced it up off his foot and snatched it out of the air. Grinning, he handed it to me with a flourish.

"Raquel wants you to call so she'll know a good time to talk again, since she doesn't want to disrupt your life."

"And what the bleep do you think you're doing right now?"

A throat cleared next to me and I noticed Carlee standing

there. Her shoulders were thrown back and she was giving Jack a weird look. No, not a weird look . . . a *hey, baby, fancy meeting you here* look. "Who's your friend?" she asked, a giggle following her question.

"Not my friend! So not my friend."

"How did you even get in?" Vicious Redhead Soccer Girl asked. She was eyeing him with a mixture of suspicion and interest. "Do you go here?"

What was wrong with these girls? A psychotic boy appears in the middle of the locker room and they're ready to flirt? Hadn't they watched *any* high school comedies? We should have been whipping him with wet towels at this point, ferocious in our fury to protect the sanctity of the girls' locker room. Instead, they were concentrating on strategic posture shifts for maximum cleavagization.

Honestly, he wasn't that cute. The curly mop of blond hair and too-big blue eyes got on my nerves. Oh, look at me, I'm so adorable and innocent, I can show up wherever I want and screw with Evie's life!

"Okay," I hissed, nervous at the growing crowd. Miss Lynn would figure out something was going on when no one rushed to start stretching. The more zealous were always out earlier to warm up. "Thanks for the delivery, now go! Away! Now!"

"But I just got here." He stuck out his lower lip in a mock pout.

"Quick, before Miss Lynn—"

"Before I what?" a familiar tenor voice asked behind me. My spine stiffened in terror. This wasn't my fault! Surely I couldn't get in trouble for this. Miss Lynn placed one beefy hand on my shoulder, and it was all I could do to stay standing under the weight.

Jack took his sweet time, looking her up and down, his eyes lingering on her linebacker body.

She growled, "And who is your friend, Green?"

I was dead. I was so, so dead. I was going to be expelled and then I'd never get into Georgetown, and I'd work at the diner for the rest of my life and Lend would marry the dryad lab assistant and they'd have half-tree-and-one-quarter-water-thing babies, and no one would know quite what they were, but they'd be beautiful. And I'd serve them French fries when they came home to visit.

Jack looked at me, exaggerated confusion clouding his face. "I don't know her."

"Oh, really." Miss Lynn was trying not to sound amused, but I could hear the glee in her voice. This was way better than marking me tardy.

"No. I came here to see you. I didn't believe the rumors, but after hearing it on so many continents I had to come and see for myself."

"See what?"

His eyes widened in adulation, his voice taking on a reverent tone. "If it was true that Helen of Troy, nay, Aphrodite herself had been reincarnated in gym teacher form."

The room was utterly silent. Except Vicious Redhead's jaw dropping to the ground with a little *plink*. Or maybe I imagined that. And then the class did the worst thing possible: They started giggling. Miss Lynn was going to murder me.

Jack fell to his knees on the bench, his eyes rolling back in ecstasy as he clutched both hands to his heart. "Oh, heavens above, to have seen such beauty with my own eyes! It's more than I ever hoped for. But how can I live now, knowing that you're not mine? Please." He crawled forward to the edge of the bench. "Marry me. Nay, marriage will cost us precious moments together. Let us make sweet, passionate love right here. Let me bear your children."

A primal growl signaled Miss Lynn getting over her shock at being thus addressed. She lunged forward; Jack deftly rolled off the bench, jumping up out of her reach.

"Goodness, I didn't expect you to be quite this enthusiastic about my advances. If I don't play hard to get, how will I ever know whether or not you respect me?"

Another growl, this one sounding like "*you!*" Or perhaps, "*eew!*" because that's certainly how I felt about this whole exchange. Everyone stopped laughing and watched, wide-eyed with horror, unsure whether to stay or distance themselves from the inevitable outcome, which would quite possibly involve Jack's dismemberment.

I didn't know who to root for.

Dodging another grab, Jack used the bench as a launching

point, bouncing off and propelling himself to the top of the row of lockers. If I didn't know for sure he was human, I would have suspected something paranormal behind his acrobatics. He had a future in the Olympics, provided Miss Lynn didn't kill him first.

"How about I call? We'll do lunch." He blew a kiss toward Miss Lynn's increasingly purple face and jumped off onto the next row. I noticed a small flash of light. Panic welled up in my chest, but the entire class had gathered here. No one else saw.

Miss Lynn shoved past me, running to block the exit. "Guard the gym door!" she shouted, eyes blazing as she took up her position and waited.

And waited.

And waited.

But Jack was long gone, having eluded both Miss Lynn and any repercussions for his idiotic actions. She fixed her beady black eyes on me, and my stomach sank with the knowledge that I'd have no such luck.

Thanks a lot, Raquel.

THERE'S NO PLACE
LIKE HOME

What were you thinking, sending that rabid monkey child to my *school*?" I shouted into my communicator.

"Beg pardon?" Raquel asked.

"Jack. My school. The girls' locker room. Ring any bells? If Carlee hadn't sworn to my ogre of a gym teacher that Jack was neither my boyfriend nor my brother, I probably would have been suspended!"

"Your gym teacher is an ogre?"

"Focus! If I get suspended, my grades take a hit. If my grades take a hit, I might not get into Georgetown. And I *will* get into Georgetown."

"I'm pleased to see you finally taking ownership of your education. And I'm sorry about Jack; I asked him to contact you discreetly."

"That boy wouldn't know discreet if it tap-danced on his stupid blond head."

"Still, if this *discreet* were tap dancing, it wouldn't be very discreet, now, would it?"

"Shut up," I said, trying not to smile. I was annoyed. No smiling. "When did you get funny?"

"I'll talk to Jack and tell him not to contact you at school anymore."

"What's his deal, anyway? He's the weirdest person I know, and that's saying something."

"Jack has had a very . . . unconventional upbringing. You two have more in common than you think. His life was disrupted by the fey, too. He's a remarkable boy, though, and a great asset. We're lucky he found us."

I frowned. It made sense that Jack had some connection to faeries with his abilities. "Fine. No more school visits, though. And tell him not to come into my room unannounced."

"So you're certain that you want to help us?"

I hesitated, biting my lip. It felt like I was balancing on a fence. Tip to one side—say no—and I knew exactly what I would find when I fell.

More of the same.

Say yes and tip to the other side, and . . . I had no idea.

But the fence would still be there, and I could always find my way back over. Right?

"Two conditions," I said, practically feeling her relief and excitement seeping through the connection. "One: I am not Level Seven or anything in any system. I am not IPCA. If I don't like a mission, I don't do it. It's totally my call."

"Done. And the second?"

"I want my credit card back." Clearly the unknown I was about to venture into would require a new wardrobe.

"Very well. As long as you reserve it for emergencies."

"Seriously, Raquel, when did you get so funny?"

She paused. "Evie, I'm—I'm very pleased you'll be helping us again."

"I missed you, too." I meant to be lighthearted, but was surprised by an uncomfortable itch in my throat and pricking in my eyes. Good heavens, I was not about to cry on a call with Raquel. After all, my seventeenth birthday was coming up, I was living on my own, independent, strong. I was doing this because I wanted to—*not* because I missed her. That would be stupid.

After a very suspicious throat clearing, Raquel's voice resumed its brisk, business tone. "Excellent. I'll send Jack for you tonight around eight."

"Whoa, tonight? So soon?"

"I wasn't joking when I said we needed help. Lately, it seems as though everything that can go wrong does. And

there have been strange shifts in the paranormal world—
nothing compared to April, but enough that we're forced to
use manpower we don't have to try and track it."

"I guess I can swing it, then." A night free from cow
print and grease? Bleep yes I could swing it. "So where to?
Italy? Iceland? Ooh, I could go for Japan."

"Actually, it's a little less exotic than that. The Center."

And just like that my excitement was replaced by an icy
dread.

I couldn't go back there. The Center was a tomb. In
my mind it hadn't changed since my last night there. Lifeless vamps lined the halls, eerily illuminated by warning
strobe lights that failed to save the mermaid I loved most.
I couldn't handle the thought of revisiting what had been
our home.

"Raquel, I—"

"I'll see you at eight!" The line went silent and left me
staring numbly at the communicator.

Two hours later I was still on my bed, glaring at the ceiling. Not even the familiar contours of Tasey clutched in my
hand made me feel better.

I'd have to tell Raquel the deal was off. There was no
way I was going back there. As soon as I could get my fingers to punch in her connection, I'd do it. But I couldn't
stand to hear the disappointment in her voice. She'd been
excited, genuinely happy about working together again.

Happy wasn't something she did very often. And now I'd have to tell her that I wasn't coming because I was too freaked out.

Lame.

I turned onto my side. The pendant Lend gave me sparkled on the nightstand and I reached out to it, running my finger along the side of the heart.

Why didn't things ever get easier? Sometimes I wanted to take a memory—one perfect memory—curl up in it, and go to sleep. Like my first kiss with Lend. I could live in that memory forever. Just us and our lips and figuring out how well they fit together. If things always felt like that, life would be better.

"Honestly, Evie," I huffed, flopping back to the center of my bed and glaring at the ceiling. "Why don't you whine some more instead of actually doing anything?"

"Talking to yourself is the first sign of madness," Arianna volunteered, leaning on the frame of my open door.

"Yeah, so's seeing things no one else can, but people seem to like that about me."

"Good point. Odds are, you've been crazy for years now. I'm probably nothing more than a figment of your imagination."

"If that were true, I'd imagine you as less of a slob."

She sighed. "Isn't it sad that you hate yourself so much you can't even dream up a pleasant roommate?"

"Not as sad as the fact that you admit how bad you suck as one."

Flashing a wicked grin, she narrowed her eyes. "I'd use the term 'suck' sparingly around me. Don't want to go planting ideas in my pretty, dead head."

I threw a pillow at her.

"Anyway," she said, fixing her spiky red and black hair (far nicer than the strands that clung to her shriveled head under her glamour—*don't look*, I reminded myself yet again), "It's dark out. Let's go to a movie. I'm so bored I could die."

"Too late."

She threw the pillow back and went out into the main room. I sat up on the side of my bed and heaved a sigh. The communicator radiated waves of guilt from its position next to my pillow, but I couldn't call Raquel. She'd figure out I wasn't coming in about—I glanced at the clock—ten minutes.

It was probably for the best.

Oh, bleep, like I knew what was for the best anymore. Shaking my head, I picked up Tasey and walked to my dresser, opening the sock drawer.

"Sorry, friend," I whispered. "Maybe another time."

I heard the front door open, and Arianna shouted. "I'm leaving now. Meet me there if you want to come."

"Yeah, let me get my—"

A light flashed as a hand reached through the wall, grabbed my arm, and pulled me into the infinite darkness.

OLD HAUNTS

I screamed as the tiny rectangle holding the door to my room—my life—winked shut, leaving me in the darkness so thick and complete I could feel it on my skin.

"Whoa, calm—"

I whipped around, slapping my palm flat against the chest of—Jack. Again. Seriously, one of these times I was going to kill him by accident. Or on purpose. And I wasn't going to be sorry. "What's wrong with you! Let go of me!"

He raised his eyebrows and loosened his grip on my wrist. "Really? Okay, if you insist."

If he let me go, I would be lost in this darkness. Alone.

Forever. The only thing you could see on the Paths was the person you were with—there was nothing else there. I hadn't wanted to use the Faerie Paths ever again, and now that I was here the familiar dread filled my entire body. I clutched his arm with my free hand. "Stop it! Why did you grab me like that? Terrorizing me at school wasn't enough?"

He shrugged. "Raquel told me to get you at eight."

"It's called *knocking*, dimwit!"

"I know I make it look effortless, but creating doors between realms isn't exactly simple. Pulling you through was easier than coming in for some polite conversation and perhaps a bit of tea, at which point I would have had to make another door. I didn't know you'd scream like a little girl."

"I did *not* scream like a little girl."

Flashing his dimples, he took a huge lungful of air and burst into an earsplitting—and decidedly little girl-ish—scream. "Like that. Only with crazier eyes and more flailing."

"Shut up."

"Gladly. We're going to be late." He slipped his hand down from my wrist to my hand and started walking. "Heaven and hell, your hands are cold."

I never thought I'd prefer the dead silence of the Paths over anything, but it had to be better than listening to this idiot. And I didn't need any reminders that my hands were cold. Cold, mortal, dying hands. "Can we not talk?"

"But you're such a charming conversationalist. Still, if you'd prefer to simply bask in the glory of my company, I understand. You're probably overwhelmed by holding my hand and want to enjoy the moment."

I rolled my eyes. "It's all I can do not to swoon, but I'll try to contain myself."

"I think swooning is highly underrated. You could bring it back into vogue."

I turned my head to look at him rather than focus on the inky black around us. It was like people on the Paths existed outside anything else. Jack and I were the only two creatures alive, for all you could tell. What a horrible thought.

"Where on earth did you come from?" I asked.

He grinned, but there was a strange tightness to his face. "Telling that story would require talking, which I seem to recall you requested not happen. And here we are!" With a flourish he waved a hand—at nothing.

I watched him expectantly. Nothing happened.

"Can't you feel it?" he asked, his eyes narrowing.

"Feel what?"

"Come on. You've been through here as much as I have. You never tried to figure it out?"

I made the mistake of looking at my feet standing in the emptiness, and now I kind of wanted to puke. "Can we please get out of here?"

"Honestly, Evie, you don't know how to have fun, do you?" He put a hand flat out, and his eyes narrowed in concentration. The darkness rippled, light tearing through it but illuminating nothing as a door formed, opening into a painfully familiar white hallway.

"Home sweet home," Jack chirped, pulling me forward with him. The door shut behind us.

I felt like I had walked into a dream. When I left this behind, I let part of myself believe it ceased to exist. The fluorescent lights buzzing overhead drilled in the fact that the only different thing was me.

We both turned and looked down the length of the hall. A woman I didn't know, dressed in a pin-striped suit, ran past us, screaming bloody murder and swatting at the air around her head.

I sighed. "Yup, home sweet home about covers it."

I looked back down the hall, my attention drawn by the soft tapping of sensible pumps. This time the woman in a suit wasn't insane—or at least, not the running-around-screaming type. "Evie," Raquel said, pursing her lips to avoid smiling.

Another scream echoed; I caught a glimpse of someone running through one of the cross halls. He looked suspiciously like Bud, my tough and gruff former self-defense teacher.

"I leave for a few months and this whole place goes to pieces."

Raquel shook her head, shooting an annoyed look in the direction of the continued screams. "Well, since you're on the clock, why don't I show you to the problem area?"

"Sounds good to me." Being here was like déjà vu. The faster I solved their problem, the sooner I could leave and freak out in private.

"You're welcome." Jack waved cheerfully, got a running start, and did several roundoffs down the length of the hall.

I turned to Raquel. "I think he's broken."

She heaved a *don't I know it* sigh. "Jack's past isn't one that contributes to stability. But he's a good boy."

He nearly got me disemboweled by my gym teacher. Good boy he was not.

More screams rang through the hall. "Seriously, what's going on here?"

"It's the poltergeist. Apparently we've pinpointed its current location."

"Yippee."

"If we can get this little problem taken care of, I'm certain that the other issues will be easier to address. Not only is it nearly impossible to keep employees functioning, important files keep disappearing."

I followed her down the hall, trying not to think about all the times I ran wild here. This wasn't my home anymore. I was here for work. A job. I could be professionally detached. As long as we didn't have to go to—

Central Processing. Raquel stopped right in front of the sliding doors. Of course. Because nothing could possibly be easy tonight.

"Here?" I asked, already knowing the answer. Of all the places in the Center, the poltergeist had to take up residence here. I closed my eyes, picturing her aquarium as it had been—blue-green water; tropical fish; living coral reef; happy, funny, capable Lish in the middle of it all, running the computers and saying bleep.

No matter how hard I tried to hold on to that image, I could only remember the jagged hole in the glass, Lish's lifeless body iridescent in the lights as it lay at the bottom of the pool.

I opened my eyes, realizing that Raquel had been talking for a while now.

"—understand why I can't come in with you."

I frowned. "Uh, sure." I raised my hand to the palm pad and . . . nothing happened. The strangest sense of betrayal and abandonment surged through me. They'd changed the locks?

"Sorry about that," Raquel said, waiting for me to move so she could palm the door. It slid open with a hiss, and she backed up out of view. "I'll leave it unlocked."

Taking a deep breath, I walked in. The emptiness of the large, white, circular room hit me like a blow. The aquarium was gone. No trace left except a faint ring around the middle of the floor. It was like Lish never existed. The door closed behind me, and I slid against it to the floor.

I definitely wasn't ready for this.

A bitter cold breeze tickled the back of my neck.

Something dark darted past the edge of my vision. I turned my head, but nothing was there.

The lights flickered, then went out, except a single dim bulb.

"I've been waiting for you," a low voice hissed in my ear.

A tickle on my arm drew my attention to the black spider with a crimson hourglass belly creeping its way up. The last light died and a death scream ripped through the room as it plunged into darkness.

DEADLY REUNIONS

In the pitch black the only sensation was the spider's eight sinister legs on my arm. "You'll die in this room," a voice whispered in my ear. I wouldn't be the first. My chest tightened, thinking of Lish's last moments. Was she scared? Did it hurt?

The lights flashed back on to reveal my entire body covered by a writhing mass of black widows.

"Oh, piss off," I snapped, standing up. I'm sure I would have been scared, terrified even, if it weren't for the fact I could see right through the scampering little arachnids. Poltergeists' projections are a combination of glamour and manipulating air currents to create the illusion of sensation. Neat trick, really.

There was a pause, then the spiders disappeared, replaced by a howling wind. Blood seeped through the seams between the wall and ceiling, dripping down right in front of my face. I stuck my hand out and let the blood illusion pass right through it. "Maybe try corn syrup and red dye next time?"

A low growl echoed through the room, which proceeded to burst into flames, crackling as they devoured the walls and surrounded me.

"Are you about done yet? Because this is all very impressive, but it's a school night and I've got homework to get back to."

The flames winked out of existence, leaving the room as pristine and empty as before. "I'll kill you," the voice croaked, and something about it triggered a memory.

"Steve?"

The air shimmered in front of me to reveal the translucent image of—yup, Steve the vampire. Or at least, what used to be Steve the vampire. Considering he was *dead* dead now, instead of undead, he wasn't technically a vampire.

He scowled at me. "You aren't any fun."

"Party pooper extraordinaire, that's me. What are you doing here?"

"What does it look like I'm doing?" He raised his

hands and they burst into flame.

"Looks like cheap parlor tricks to me. Seriously though, the last time I saw you—" The last time I saw him, he was so wigged out over being brought into the Center that he bit Raquel, knowing it would trigger an injection of holy water and kill him. Again. But permanently.

His eyes flashed with anger. "Glad to see you remember me."

"Of course. But why are you still here?"

"I'm going to make them pay. All of them. They'll rue the day they ever brought me into this prison." Steve had always had a flair for the dramatic. He should have raised one ghostly fist in the air as he said it, though, for the full effect.

I sat back down, settling against the door. "I guess that's fair enough."

"Aren't you going to try and exorcise me?"

"Nah. Not my department."

"Oh." He bit his lip—or at least tried to, but failed due to the whole incorporeal thing. "Well, what now, then?"

"Ooh, can you make it look like bugs are exploding out of my skin?"

He dropped a few inches in his hovering. "Seriously?"

"Could be cool, right? If you want, I'll even pretend to be scared."

"It's not the same if you're faking." He dropped down to my eye level; this left about half of him beneath the floor, but he didn't seem to notice.

"Sorry. I can't help it."

We sat there for a while, Steve shifting position like he couldn't quite get his ethereal body comfortable.

"I have a question," I asked, finally breaking the silence.

He perked up. "What?"

"I don't get it. I mean, you hated the idea of this place, right? You committed hari-kari just to avoid being locked up here for even a few days."

"Yes. And?"

"I don't understand why, after all that, you'd choose to spend eternity here."

His eyes went out of focus, the outline of his body fuzzing ever so slightly. "I— They need to— I'm making them pay."

"Sure, I get that. But aside from giving them nightmares and being a nuisance, you can't do anything, can you? All you've done is trapped yourself more effectively than they ever could."

His shoulders slumped. Man, poor guy. I kept ruining his afterlives. I reached out to pat him on the shoulder but stopped short. It'd probably make him feel worse if I went straight through him. "Umm, don't worry about it. You're not really stuck, after all." I waved my hand near his arm in a way I hoped was comforting.

He was already starting to lose definition. It's not easy hanging on once you're dead, and if you take the will to haunt out of them, they usually poof right on to where they're supposed to be.

Wherever that is.

But most people couldn't handle sticking around long enough to pinpoint the location for an exorcism, or, in this case, a good old-fashioned chat session. Which was where I always came in on poltergeist duty for IPCA.

Steve nodded. His extremities had already vanished. "You're right. About time I gave being dead a shot."

"That's the spirit!" I smiled encouragingly.

"Thanks. At least one of us will finally be free of this nightmare."

"Oh, I—" I was going to explain that I was free now and it was my choice to be here tonight—or at least, kind of, since Jack hadn't really given me a chance to turn him down—and honestly, I had such mixed feelings about the whole thing, I wasn't sure what to tell Steve, other than that I wasn't a prisoner or even an employee and he shouldn't assume I was—

Before I could form a coherent thought, he had disappeared. For good, this time. I hoped.

"Bye, Steve," I whispered to the empty room.

I sat there for a few seconds, but being alone here was far more frightening than any haunting could have been. This room didn't need dramatics to give me nightmares. I scrambled up, waited for the door to open, and stumbled into the hallway.

"Raquel?" The blank hall stretched out, empty. Great.

I walked toward her office, lost in thought about Lish, and poor Steve, and all the other souls I'd sent out of this life, some quite literally. Where did they go? Did Steve go the same place as Lish? And was it vampire Steve or normal Steve? What exactly happened to the souls when their human bodies died and became vampires? And then when the vampire bodies died?

Hello, headache.

I sighed and put my hand on the door pad. Only when it didn't open did I look up and realize I'd unconsciously gone back to my old unit.

I stared, dumbfounded, at the door. It felt like part of me, old Evie, should break off from the rest, smile and wave, then go through and flop down on the purple couch. Instead, all of me stood on the threshold, barred from a life I said I was done with.

I had thought so many times about the things—actual, physical things—that I'd left behind. A pair of red peep-toe heels in particular plagued me. Now I actually had excuses to wear them, and they were stuck in my unit. I had even composed a running list in my head of all the stuff I would snatch from my room if I ever had the chance.

But I couldn't get in, couldn't go back. I didn't think I wanted to, either. That unit was a tomb for the Evie who had lived there, oblivious to the complexities of the world around her, clueless as to what she really was. I didn't want anything from her.

I turned and made my way carefully to Raquel's office. I needed to get out of here. Now. Claustrophobia had set in with a vengeance, and the sudden panic of realizing I couldn't get out unless they *let* me out made it hard to breathe. I turned the corner and nearly ran into Jack, who looked equally startled to see me.

"Why, Evie, you look like you've seen a ghost."

"Har, har." I felt wrung out, empty. I wanted to go home. "Is Raquel in her office?"

"How would I know?"

"Weren't you just there?"

"Nope."

"Oookay."

"Evie?" I turned in relief at Raquel's voice as she walked up behind me. "How did it go?"

"The Center is officially Not Haunted." At least, not by any poltergeists. If memories were ghosts, it was positively oozing with them. And now I was, too. "Can I go now? I'm pretty tired."

"Of course. Jack, if you'd—"

We were interrupted by a door forming on the wall next to us. A tall faerie with pure white hair and skin the color of a ripe peach stepped through. "You!" Her voice rang like cold metal through the hallway.

I jumped back. "I won't—"

"I didn't do it!" Jack shouted, interrupting me. I looked

at him, puzzled. Did he think the faerie was after him?

She took a step toward us. Jack turned, booking it down the hallway and sliding around the corner, leaving Raquel and me with the faerie. The way her cobalt eyes tracked him, I wondered if maybe she really was after him.

Who was I kidding. With faeries it was always about me.

Raquel recovered faster than I did. She reached into her suit jacket and pulled out a small iron cylinder. With a neat flick of her wrist it telescoped out into a baton of sorts. "I suggest you leave."

The faerie regarded her coolly, then backed through the wall and out of the Center. I looked wide-eyed at Raquel. "Holy bleep, Raquel, you were totally bad—"

"Please don't finish that phrase." She slipped the baton back to its smallest size and tucked it into her jacket. "Now, do you have any idea what that was about?"

I shook my head. "Nope. Reth visited me the other night, but he didn't try and take me again." Well, mostly he didn't try. Had he tried? Stupid Reth. "But that makes three now—the sylph, Reth, and that faerie. And it seems like there are a lot more weird paranormals turning up in town." I remembered the frog woman in the housedress. It wasn't just that they were weird; it was that they were noticing me. Interested in me. I bit my lip, suddenly nervous. It was too much to be a coincidence. Something was going on.

"This complicates things. I'd thought we were past the

faeries' interest in you. I'd feel safer if you stay here tonight."

"I—oh, no. No. I don't want to stay here. Jack can take me home." I turned, but Jack was still nowhere to be seen. Raquel smiled, and I was stuck in the Center.

Again.

BITE MY TONGUE

Look," Arianna snapped. She slammed to a stop in front of my school so fast I was nearly strangled by my seat belt. "If you don't want to hang out with me, fine. But don't just ditch me and then go stay with a friend for two days without even bothering to call." Huge shades covered half her face, but I could read it well enough by now. She was hurt.

"I emailed," I said lamely.

"Yeah. Great. Just—whatever. Get out."

I opened my door and stepped out onto the curb. "Thanks for the—" She peeled out, the forward momentum of the car slamming the door.

Fabulous. What a nice way to start my first morning back. I hadn't meant to abandon her—really. None of this was my fault. I'd practically been kidnapped by Jack, after all.

"Evie, are you okay?"

I looked up into Carlee's concerned face. I hadn't realized I was still standing on the curb, shoulders slumped and head down. "I'm just tired."

That was an understatement. I'd barely slept at all the past two nights on Raquel's couch. Not only was I freaked out at being stuck in the Center, but for such a small woman, Raquel snores like a hippo. Go figure. Jack, the little fink, finally showed up this morning, and I barely made it back in time for first period. One stupid mission and I felt completely sucked back into IPCA—Raquel had even asked me to file reports on unaccounted-for elementals while we waited for Jack to wander back in. I had a sneaking suspicion that she loved every minute of it and that, if she had her way, I'd move back in.

The bleep I would.

"We have fitness testing today in gym—don't forget." Carlee walked ahead of me, her step light and bouncy.

I jostled my way through the student throng. Faerie fears, sylph paranoia, and as always my increasing guilt over not telling Lend he was immortal twisted together in my stomach. Now I could add lying to him about working for IPCA again. That's what made this the hardest—not being able to talk to my best friend about everything.

I stood in front of my locker, hand on the lock. And, for the first time since I got it, I couldn't remember my combination. "Bleep," I muttered. Even my locker was losing its charm.

"I don't think Miss Lynn'll let you be sick again. She hates you," Carlee said.

"I know."

"No, she, like, *really* hates you."

"No, I, like, really know. Trust me."

She sat down on the bench next to me, where I was still contemplating the pile of yellow and brown putridness that was my gym clothes.

"Are you sure you're okay?"

Carlee was my friend. Why not try being honest with her for once? "I'm worried that I'm dying, faeries might be launching another offensive to steal me, and also I can't get this strange tingling sensation out of my hands since I sucked some of the soul from a sylph, which I definitely should not have done."

She blinked. Slowly.

"Kidding." I flashed her a grimace that I hoped would pass for a smile. "Haven't been sleeping enough."

"Oh. That's easy. Drink chamomile tea before bed. My mom totally swears by it."

"Chamomile tea. Will do." No doubt that would solve all my problems.

"So, about the other day."

Oh, Jack. We hadn't talked since she backed me up. "Thanks again, by the way. You saved my butt with Miss Lynn."

"Of course! But who was that guy?"

I rolled my eyes. "A nuisance."

"Because, well, John and I broke up again, and that guy was pretty cute, and I was thinking maybe—"

"NO!"

Her eyes widened in shock. "I'm sorry, I . . ."

"No, really, I mean, he's kind of crazy, you know? Like, unstable. And he refuses to take his medication."

"Really? Bummer. Those dimples . . ."

"Totally psychotic!"

She shrugged, smiling as she stood up. "Better get dressed."

"Green!"

"Too late," Carlee whispered.

Miss Lynn came around the corner of the row of lockers, glaring daggers. No, daggers would be too delicate a weapon for her. Glaring sledgehammers was probably more appropriate.

"What?" I asked with a sigh.

She jerked her thumb toward the door. "Office."

I stood up, sputtering. "I'm not tardy! I haven't done anything wrong today!"

"Family emergency," she growled. "Get out of here."

"I—oh. Okay."

Checked out again? What was Raquel doing? I had the communicator in my bag. She definitely hadn't been trying to get ahold of me in the few hours since I left.

Still, the timing couldn't be better. I threw my gym clothes into the locker and tried to look nervous as I walked past Miss Lynn. Really it was all I could do not to skip. I didn't even care if I was kidnapped again, as long as it got me out of gym.

I threw open the door to the office and stopped in my tracks. No Raquel this time. It was Lend's dad.

Or at least as far as the flirty attendance secretary was concerned, it was my legal guardian, David. She couldn't see straight through the glamour to the clear-as-water-barely-there face of Lend.

He turned and smiled at me with his dad's face, and after a few seconds I was able to replace my shocked expression with what I hoped was a foster-daughterly smile. "Umm, hey."

"Thanks again, Sheila," Lend-as-David said, smiling at her. I didn't know whether to be jealous, mortified, or amused by her googly-eyed grin.

I walked stiffly next to him out into the parking lot, loving that he was here, wanting nothing more than to throw my arms around him and get the hug I so desperately needed today, but not about to do that when he looked like his dad.

We climbed into his car and I looked over, trying to see only *him* underneath his glamour. "What's my family emergency?"

"I've been worried. You haven't answered your phone in a couple of days."

That would be because the underground Center had zero cell reception. "I lost it," I lied, hating myself.

"I figured. Being worried was just an excuse to break you out." He flashed a grin, pulled out of the lot, and drove through the tree-lined streets toward the freeway. "My afternoon class got canceled, and I had a sneaking suspicion you wouldn't mind missing gym."

"Gorgeous *and* smart. I'm a lucky girl. But, umm, it's kind of creeping me out to be attracted to you when you look exactly like your dad. Glamour shift?"

He laughed, his dad's face shimmering into Lend's standard dark-eyed dark-haired hottie. "Better?"

"Definitely. I won't need therapy now. Well, much."

He laughed again, reaching out and taking my hand in his. "Still, it's a nice trick for rescuing my girlfriend from torture."

"I'm not complaining." I settled back in my seat, loving the feeling of Lend's skin on mine. I never got tired of the contours of his palm, the way his fingers laced through mine like they were designed to fit together, or how he unconsciously stroked my thumb with his. *This* was where I belonged.

He pulled off in an unfamiliar area, parking in front of a hole-in-the-wall Thai restaurant.

"What are we doing?"

"We're going to see if we can't finally find something too hot for you."

Ever since he found out a few months ago that I could eat spicy foods—ridiculously spicy foods—without batting an eye, he'd made it his personal mission to find something too hot for my tastes.

"Just because you've got a wimpy tongue doesn't mean I do," I said.

He smiled slyly at me. "Wimpy tongue, huh? I'll have to show you what it can do later."

I smacked him in the shoulder, unable to hold back another laugh. "Oh, I'm a fan of your tongue, no worries there."

"I'd like to get that printed on a shirt."

"At least I know what to get you for Christmas."

We walked into the restaurant, and an hour later walked back out. Lend scowled in frustration. "One of these days I *will* find something too spicy for you."

"Too bad we'll have to go on so many dates while you search."

"Alas, all noble causes require sacrifice."

We drove back toward home, but rather than taking me to the apartment, Lend turned down a narrow road that led into the trees and meandered around until it dead-ended.

My communicator beeped loudly in my backpack and I jumped. Lend looked over, raising an eyebrow. Oh crap, oh crap, oh crap, I was busted.

"Looks like we found your phone."

I let out a nervous bark of a laugh. "Yeah. In my backpack the whole time. Whoops." He smiled and parked while I tried to calm down my heart. Keeping secrets was going to kill me one of these days.

He turned off the engine. "This is our stop." I looked around, seeing nothing but trees. He pulled a couple of blankets out of the back, then opened my door for me.

We walked through the woods and stopped at a tranquil pond. The autumn leaves reflected around the edges, making it look like the water was burning. Lend spread one of the blankets out on the ground and lay back on it, patting the space next to him. I started to cuddle in, then sat up, looking warily at the water.

"Your mom isn't in there, is she?"

He laughed. "No. It's just been too long since I was around water."

I frowned, troubled. Was water calling to him now or something? Or did he simply find it soothing because of his childhood? I lay back down, snuggling into his side with my head on his chest. The hand stroking my hair lost its pigment and I released my breath and smiled, even though I couldn't see his face. He was still *my* Lend. The Lend no one else could see.

"I haven't seen my mom in a while," he said, a hint of worry in his voice.

"You haven't?"

"No. I think this might be the longest she's ever gone without showing up."

Something from one of the forms I'd filed tickled my memory—something about being unable to account for local elementals. I made a mental note to ask Raquel about it, since I couldn't very well bring it up with Lend.

Wanting him to talk, I asked, "What was it like, having her as a mom?"

He shrugged, my head on his chest rising with the gesture. "I don't know—it's not like I have anything to compare it to. I think my dad compensated the best he could, and when I was a kid I didn't know any better. He had to keep me isolated, so I figured most moms were sometimes there and sometimes not, talked funny, and gave their kids presents of tropical fish schools in the middle of a pond in Virginia."

"I think it sounds sweet."

"It was. I love my mom. It was hard for a while, when I realized we'd never really share a life, but it is what it is. And I know she loves me."

"How could she not?" A familiar ache settled into my chest. Even Lend with his water elemental mom at least had that: the knowledge that he was and always had been loved. And always would be, too, since he would live forever just like Cresseda.

"Do you ever wonder, if maybe yours are still . . ." he asked, trailing off, but I knew how he'd finish. Out there. If somewhere my parents (if I even had parents) were living and going about their normal lives. Without me.

"I don't know. I don't like to think about it. What if they really did just abandon me, give me to the faeries? Or what if I *was* made—if the faeries were—are—*I don't know*. It's not worth thinking about."

He reached up and stroked my hair. We'd talked about my family issues before, but what was the point? I wasn't getting any answers, and I didn't like the questions. I'd never had a real home or a mom who brought me schools of fish for entertainment, and I never would. It was fine. *I* was fine.

"It's been too long since we got to be together like this," Lend said after a few silent minutes. His real voice was like a cascade, warm and liquid and so deliciously sexy I could listen to nothing else for the rest of my life and be perfectly content. I let it work its way through me, releasing the tension I'd built up in my shoulders. That stuff didn't matter. This was what mattered.

"Mmm hmm." I closed my eyes and breathed him in. A cold breeze stirred over us, and I felt my hair lift in response, all my limbs feeling lighter, disconnected and more connected at the same time. It was like my body answered the wind.

That was new. I darted a quick glance at the sky, but

there were no signs of sylphs. Lend pulled the other blanket on top, disconnecting me from the breeze. I was both relieved and strangely disappointed at the loss of the new sensation.

"Tell me about school," I said, banishing all thoughts of paranormals. Besides us, of course.

I listened, half paying attention to his excited stories of professors and classes as I enjoyed the rise and fall of his chest. He was always so animated, talking about schedules for the next year, seminars, internships. His goal was to get degrees in biology and zoology, then pursue a masters in zoology, with the end being intensive studies of cryptozoology, studying the creatures on the verge of science. Given what he knew, he had a natural advantage. And really, it was perfect for him. He could be normal but still help the paranormals he loved so much. His main aspiration right now was to study werewolves and try to isolate what caused it—maybe even cure it.

He loved thinking about, planning for, and working toward the future. It made my heart ache. I wondered again how things would change when he found out he wasn't mortal. Would he still be so set on this future he'd mapped out? Or would it feel pointless to him in light of the fact that he had eternity? Would he switch to immortal pursuits like . . . umm, living in ponds and dispensing incomprehensible advice?

I wondered what was wrong with me, too. I didn't have

any goals. Whenever I tried to think of something I'd be happy doing for the rest of my life, I could only worry that the rest of my life wouldn't be long enough to do anything at all. I desperately wanted to go to Georgetown, but that was just so I could be with Lend. My future felt like a huge blank, dependent on variables I couldn't control.

"I still haven't decided whether or not I should go to med school. But where else am I going to study cellular biology?" He sighed, then laughed. "Okay, enough of that. What have you been up to the last couple of days?"

I bit my lip. The whole poltergeist thing wasn't worth mentioning. Or the faerie. Or agreeing to one stupid assignment with IPCA and getting stuck in the Center. It'd bother him, and, really, it hadn't been *that* big a deal. But it would be nice to be able to talk with him about how bad I missed Lish lately, how weird not being able to go in my old unit was, how being with Raquel made me happy and annoyed at the same time.

Too bad I couldn't.

"Oh, you know. The usual. With you gone and *Easton Heights* in reruns, my life is a black hole of boredom and despair."

"So basically you've been doing homework."

"Like I said, black hole."

He stroked my hair while I tried not to think about all the things I wasn't telling him.

"How are you feeling?"

"Snuggly?"

"No, I mean, after the sylph. Nothing weird?"

Arguably the tingles I was feeling right now in the breeze could be from any number of sources, not the least of which was my incredibly hot boyfriend playing with my hair. "Nope."

"What about everything else?"

It was an open question, but I knew what he was talking about. Reth and Vivian, the only ones who understood what I was—an Empty One—had warned me that I'd burn through my own soul fast. I sighed, pushing up onto my elbows. I pulled open the neck of my shirt and looked at my heart.

Liquid gold flames swirled lazily, bright enough to see only when I was looking right at them. "No change, really." I didn't know whether that was a good thing or not. I looked at them so often it was hard to tell whether they were getting dimmer or brighter. Then a bright spark flashed right in the middle, making me grimace. That was new.

Lend sat up, craning his neck to see down my shirt, which I hurriedly pushed back into place. "Last time I checked, you couldn't see souls."

He shrugged, an exaggerated look of innocence on his face. "Still, it wouldn't hurt for me to try, would it?"

"You have got to be the most selfless boyfriend alive."

"Like I said, anything worthwhile is worth making sacrifices for."

"Speaking of which, weren't you going to give me a tongue demonstration?"

All too soon Lend had to take me back to school in time for English. Before we turned onto the main road, he put his usual glamour back in place. I bit back a wry smile, remembering how weird it had been to see him as his dad. And then it hit me, the solution to the whole immortal problem.

Lend *never* needed to know.

EXTRACURRICULAR ACTIVITIES

I hummed in the shower; not my usual attitude on a Monday morning, but things were fantastic. Ever since last week, I felt better about everything.

I didn't have to tell Lend!

How had I not seen it before? His glamour showed whatever he thought it should—which meant that he would age (or at least, appear to age) right along with me. And he couldn't ever really see what he looked like, so he wouldn't know he wasn't getting older. We could go our whole lives together and he'd never need to deal with the fact that his wasn't going to end.

After all, Lend was planning for a future. A very human future. Telling him now would confuse him, make him question his decisions. He didn't need that. I'd tell him someday, sure. When we were like eighty and I was on my deathbed. Assuming my soul lasted that long.

But the tingle in my fingers reminded me that there were ways of making it last. Innocent ways. After all, the sylph wasn't dead, or even really hurt. In fact, I was sure the sylph would be happy to know it contributed to my ability to live a long, happy life with Lend.

"Hey." Arianna stuck her head into my room as I finished drying my hair. "You wanna do something after school?" She said it in her usual annoyed tone, but there was a hint of hesitancy. She'd barely acknowledged my existence since she thought I'd stood her up for the movie; it was like a dark cloud hung over our entire apartment.

"Sure! I've got work at seven but I'm free after school until then. What do you want to do?"

Her shoulders relaxed. "Mall? I haven't been around true evil for a while."

"And the mall is the best place for that?"

"Have you *seen* what the average populace is wearing? I may have to kill the next person I see wearing pants that unzip into shorts. Also, Uggs over tights are a crime against humanity. No one with a pulse should be willing to wear this stuff. I haven't had a heartbeat in twenty years and even I can tell you that."

"But what if they're *pink* Uggs? Surely—" My communicator beeped from my nightstand drawer and my stomach dropped. Bleep. I'd forgotten that Jack was coming this afternoon for a quick vamp-tracking job. "Oh—I—just remembered, I have a . . . study thing. After school. With Carlee. For a class."

Arianna's eyes narrowed and her shoulders tightened back into that strange protective stance. "Fine. No big."

"But after work we could—"

She turned with a wave of her hand. "Whatever. Don't worry about it."

Great. Now I was ditching my vampire friend to go tase a vampire. Wouldn't Arianna and Lend be thrilled if they knew? Still, I wasn't doing anything that his dad's group could get mad about. No werewolf persecution, and only neutering violent vamps. Whatever David and his group thought, Arianna was *not* typical.

I sighed heavily going down the stairs to the bus. I would figure this out—balance it all—school, Lend, being there for Arianna, side jobs for IPCA. After all, weren't extracurriculars a must for college applications? Next week's trip to Sweden to track down a troll colony and rescue the humans they'd kidnapped would look pretty darn impressive on my Georgetown application.

Yeah, I should probably join the chess club, instead.

After a long day I didn't even mind the humiliation of

climbing on the old, yellow bus with its cracked seats. I was the only senior without a car, but none of them were going on international, human-saving missions after school. Suckers. Plus, I calculated my going rate for IPCA, and with eight years of back pay (a stipulation Raquel put in, bless her heart), I'd be able to pay for college *and* buy a car by the end of the school year.

"Arianna?" I yelled, dropping my backpack by the door. I'd hoped she'd be home so we could talk, but there was no sign of her. I'd make her go out with me that night, maybe buy her something pretty. Or, well, something depressing and black. She'd like that. It'd fix things.

Having a plan made me feel better, so when I walked into my room to find Jack sitting on my bed flipping through my pink journal, I didn't even yell at him.

Much.

Once I finished smacking him over the head with said journal, I put away my school stuff and pulled on a warmer coat. "So." I zipped up my coat and wished I had a cute, fuzzy hat to go with it. "Vamp job. You know where you're going, right?"

He jumped off my bed (literally, bouncing so high prejump he nearly hit the ceiling), and nodded. "Sure." His dark blue knit cap made his eyes look impossibly big and bright, and his blond curls stuck out along the edges. I guess I could see what Carlee saw in him. Too bad he was a lunatic; they would have made a cute couple. I could see the double dates now . . .

No, I so totally could not.

I waited as he made the door in my wall, then reached out and took his hand. He stepped forward and I followed— but as soon as I met the border between my room and the Faerie Paths, a horrible, burning weight slammed into my chest, knocking me back onto the floor.

I gasped, staring dizzily at the ceiling. "What happened?"

Jack's face loomed into view; he frowned down at me. "What did you do?"

"Nothing! That's never happened before."

He unzipped my coat and reached down my shirt before I could get away.

"Back off, perv!"

"Aha!" He pulled my necklace out from under my sweater. "Iron."

I slapped his hands and grabbed the pendant. "So?"

"So, how long have you worked with faeries? Heaven and hell, you don't know anything, do you? The reason faeries don't like iron is that it ties them too strongly to this world. The Paths aren't part of this world—you can't take iron there. It won't let you."

I frowned. "You do realize that makes no sense."

"Unlike being able to open a door in the wall and take you to another hemisphere in a matter of minutes? How odd. Everything about Faerie is usually so rational."

I couldn't hold back the smile, and he rolled his eyes.

"Take it off so we can get going. This is boring."

I reached back to undo the clasp, hesitating. It felt like a small betrayal, taking off the necklace Lend gave me to do something I knew he wouldn't approve of. Still, I was doing good. There were people who needed me. And I'd put it right back on as soon as I got home.

I stood and tucked it into my sock drawer, fingering the heart one last time before turning back to Jack.

"Any other iron on you?" he asked impatiently.

"Just my tongue stud."

His look was a mixture of curiosity and horror.

"I'm kidding, you idiot. Let's go."

He opened the door and took my hand as we walked through. I tried to ignore the oppressive darkness. "So, how come I can take Tasey through the paths?"

Jack shrugged. "All IPCA technology was specially developed to be compatible with faerie magic."

"How do you know about all this?"

"I just happen to be smarter than you is all."

I pinched his hand as hard as I could, then decided to change the subject. It kind of bothered me that Jack knew more about this stuff than I did—shouldn't *I* have been the expert?

"Where's this vampire again?" I was a little surprised that Raquel was pulling me for a basic vamp bag and tag. They really were strapped for help. Sure, I was about a thousand times more efficient because I didn't have to bother with mirrors and holy water, but anyone who knew what they were looking for could conduct an efficient stakeout.

Oh, I kill myself.

A sly smile spread across Jack's face. "Vampire? Who said anything about a vampire?"

"Umm, you did? I thought Raquel wanted me to bag and tag a vamp."

"Who said anything about Raquel?"

"What are you talking about? Where are we going?"

"I thought you and I deserved to have a little bit of fun." Jack stopped, his grin spreading as he opened a door. I watched, more nervous than I cared to admit, to find out what, exactly, lunatic boy considered fun.

VIRGIN DREAMS

I shook my head in disbelief at the creature standing in the middle of a dappled, sunlit meadow, gazing at me with its doleful brown eyes. My most cherished childhood possession (growing up in foster care, I didn't have many) had been one of those felt-and-marker posters I colored in myself: a unicorn rearing in front of a rainbow and waterfall. I'd given it a multicolored mane but kept the coat pristine white, as all unicorns ought to be. I daydreamed more often than was healthy that I'd somehow been transported into that velvet-lined fantasy, the unicorn *mine*, and together we'd ride off to a home behind the rainbow, happy and strong, and we'd never be alone again. That unicorn was power, and magic, and beauty incarnate.

Apparently this unicorn hadn't gotten the memo. It was ugly. Like, seriously ugly. Coat a mottled brown and gray; horn a dingy, stubby thing; hair a matted mess. It looked more like a goat than anything else, with a small, filthy beard and square pupils.

Oh, and the stench? Skunks have nothing on unicorns.

The dang thing kept trying to nuzzle me while I did my best to dodge it. So much for dramatic images of knights on unicorn stallions, too. This creature couldn't carry a child, much less a man in armor. Its head barely came up to my chest, which added a whole new level of discomfort to its continued nuzzling attempts.

Jack hung upside down from a limb of one of the surrounding trees. I couldn't place where we were, but it was warm enough that my coat was uncomfortable, and the sun filtered through the leaves in a green and gold haze. Really, the meadow itself was almost magical, if the bleeping unicorn weren't screwing up the idyllic setting.

Jack laughed at my attempts to avoid being felt up by a mythical beast. "Apparently you're a virgin."

"Shut up! Like that's any of your business!"

He shrugged, the motion less effective upside down. "Unicorns love maidens. Haven't you done any research at all?"

"What, you have?"

He flipped off the branch, startling the unicorn so badly it bolted from the meadow. Thank heavens. "The Center's iron filing cabinets? Not really an issue if you can open a door through any wall and aren't a faerie."

"So what, you read secret files?"

"Among other things. Someone really ought to tell Raquel to modernize. Paper is so medieval. Now." He held out his elbow in a disingenuously gentlemanly gesture. "How about we go and have some real fun?"

"What, shattering my one remaining fantasy wasn't enough?" Faeries didn't have wings and bordered on evil; pixies were dirty, feral, and tended to bite; and mermaids had neither glorious hair nor seashell bras. Now this about unicorns. Sometimes reality sucked.

"You can always chase the unicorn, if you want. Take it for a ride."

I shuddered at the thought and sat down, leaning my back against the tree and unzipping my coat. "No, thanks. But let's stay here for a while. It's warm."

Jack flopped down next to me, lying flat with his hands behind his head. "I can always find warm."

"That must be nice."

He laughed. "It comes in handy."

"Where are we, exactly?"

"A sort of supernatural preserve for wild paranormal animals that were threatened with extinction. The unicorns are the most common. Stinkiest, too."

"No kidding. So, what other secrets do you know?"

"If I told you, it'd ruin all the fun. I like surprising people." Despite his innocent face, something in his expression made me nervous. I was full to bursting with secrets, and recognized the same thing in Jack.

"Please don't tell me our next trip will take us to bigfoot."

"Nah, according to Raquel's stuff, they went extinct around the turn of the century."

"Which century?"

He frowned. "Good question. Too bad I can't ask her for clarification, considering I'm not supposed to know."

I shifted my back to get comfortable and closed my eyes, trying to soak in the sun. "Do you come here a lot?"

"Sometimes."

"Where do you go when you aren't at the Center?"

"Home."

"Where's that?"

He sighed. "Isn't that the question? Where's your home?"

"Umm, the room you seem to make a habit of violating?"

"No, think about it. When I say 'home,' what's the first thing that pops into your head?"

I frowned, images flitting before my eyelids. It used to be the Center, but my recent visit had erased any lingering sense of home I might have felt there. My pink closet bedroom felt more like a placeholder—somewhere I was staying before I left for somewhere else. Lend's house felt like *a* home. But not mine. "I honestly don't know. Nowhere, really."

"Something we have in common, then, besides the world's most perfect hair color. We were both raised by no one and live nowhere."

I squirmed, opening my eyes. He had a point, but not one I especially liked. I was connected to people, to places. Wasn't I? There was something in Jack that I related to, though, on a level I didn't quite understand. Here and there, when he wasn't being an idiot, there was this sort of . . . desperation. Like he was trying to find something, but he didn't know what it was yet. It was a feeling I knew all too well. Vivian understood it, too. Lend never could. But being with Lend made that feeling fade, like the unknown question wasn't as important as it used to be, and maybe someday it wouldn't be a question at all.

Jack still hadn't answered any of my *actual* questions, though. "But what did you do before you started working for IPCA?"

"Survived."

I grabbed a fistful of grass and tossed it at him. "How about a real answer?"

He smiled. "I'm from Oregon, or at least that's what I think I remember. But, alas, it doesn't pay to be a beautiful toddler when stray faeries wander through town. Now I'm from that dark dreamscape, beauty and terror eternally intermingled, blah, blah, blah."

I frowned at him, puzzled.

"Hey, they need entertainment and slaves even in the Faerie Realms."

"Wait—you—you *live* in the Faerie Realms?"

"For now."

That wasn't possible. Faeries had a nasty habit of kidnapping mortals and taking them to their Realms. It was a one-way trip. Once you were taken there and tasted faerie food, you could never come back. Even if you somehow found a faerie willing to bring you back to Earth, human food would never satisfy you, and you'd waste away to nothing. Ah—thus Jack's apple-spitting at Lend's house.

"So the faeries raised you?"

He barked out a laugh. "I wouldn't call it that, no."

Vivian had been raised by faeries, but as far as I knew they never took her to the Realms. She talked about it sometimes, how the faeries took her wherever they wanted to go without any care for how she felt. Once she almost froze to death because they decided to have a ball on a glacier. Excellent caregivers, the fey.

I'd only been to the Realms a couple of times, both when Reth forced me, and it was so strange and alien, I couldn't imagine growing up there. How Jack could navigate both worlds, even survive in the Faerie Realms, was beyond me. Was he a specific faerie's servant? Maybe he was a sort of contract faerie employee, like I was for IPCA, and they taught him how to use the Paths.

Finding out more about Jack only made him a bigger enigma. "How, though? I mean, I'm sorry, but plenty of people are kidnapped and taken to the Realms, and I've never heard of them coming back. How do you do it? Did they teach you?"

"Living there, well, it changes you. And, besides, if you were constantly being left places by yourself with no way to get out of them unless a faerie happens to come along and find you—which sometimes takes a very long while indeed—you'd get a little innovative, too, wouldn't you? It's amazing what one can learn if it means not starving to death. Faeries aren't as mystical as they want you to think. I'll teach you some tricks one of these days."

I set my head back against the trunk. "I'll pass, thanks. I've had enough faerie for a lifetime. Several, actually."

Jack's stomach growled loudly. "I need food."

"I have a shift at the diner tonight. I could probably hook you up with a free dinner." The words were out of my mouth before I realized that would mean bringing Jack—from my secret job—to my real job. Not a good idea. Besides which, I wasn't sure how much I wanted him in my life, anyway. There was that connection we had, yeah, but it made me more uncomfortable than anything else. I felt in Jack so many of the things I didn't like about myself—the lying, the evasiveness, the selfishness. He seemed completely at ease with those traits, though.

"Yes," he said, "and I could probably vomit the putrid food back up all over you. I live in Faerie, remember?"

I grimaced. "Oh, duh. Sorry."

"I'll go grab something quick. You wanna come with me?"

"There is not an ounce of me that has any desire whatsoever to set foot in the Faerie Realms ever again."

"Boring. I'll be right back then." He jumped up and was gone before I had a chance to tell him he could drop me off at the diner first. I looked warily around the meadow, hoping that the unicorn would keep his personal space issues far, far away from me. Relatively certain that my maiden self was safe, I closed my eyes. Maybe Jack wasn't so bad, after all. Weird feelings aside, this afternoon had been pretty fun. He seemed to be good at fun. I liked that.

I got in a decent nap before Jack came back. "So, what should we do now?" he asked, positively buzzing with energy on a full stomach.

"Now," I said, rubbing my neck where it had stiffened up because of my position, "we should take me back so I can work my shift at the diner."

"Who cares about the diner. Anyone can move dishes around and be grouchy at customers. How about we find some dragons? Or spit off the top of the Empire State Building? Ooh, or there has to be a movie premiere somewhere we can crash."

"Oh, shut up. I *have* to work."

"Why?"

I shrugged, holding out my hand. "It's part of my life."

"Yet again I ask, why?"

Because I couldn't admit that I had another source of income and no longer needed that job. Because I had to keep up appearances that IPCA wasn't part of my life again. Because I felt like I owed it to David for taking me in. "Because it is. Let's go."

"Admit it. You like wearing those stylish little uniforms."

I laughed, smacking his shoulder. "Nothing's hotter than cows. But, wait, when have you seen me in uniform?"

He held up his free hand as he concentrated on opening a door in a wide tree. He had a knack for not answering questions. A door appeared and we squeezed through. Jack always needed a surface to open doors, but I had seen Reth open doors in the middle of the air before. I wondered if that was harder.

"Pick up the pace, Evie. If we want to get you to work on time we've got to *mooooove* faster."

I groaned, laughing. "That has got to be the worst pun I've ever heard in my life." I was still laughing when Jack opened a door and we walked out into my room—nearly bumping into Lend, whose eyes took in the faerie door, Jack, and our clasped hands in a single sweep.

Bleep.

OH, SO BUSTED

I stared openmouthed at Lend. What could I say? How could I talk my way out of this?

"Hey-oh! Glad there are no frying pans handy tonight!" Jack grinned, then looked from Lend to me and back again, shoved his hands in his pockets, and backed up through the door. "Uh, good luck with that, then," he said as it closed.

I half expected Lend to start yelling, which he had never done to me before, but he just stood there. Anger and hurt bled together on his face, and it killed me.

"Look, Lend, I can explain. We—"

"How long?"

"What?"

"How long have you been working with IPCA?"

"I haven't done much, really! Something with a poltergeist in the Center. And just now I wasn't even working for them!"

"So, what, you two were hanging out?"

"I—no—I thought— Jack said something about a mission, but then there wasn't one." Lend *couldn't* be jealous of Jack. It might look bad, but he had to understand there was no one else for me. Jack was fun, cute even, but there wasn't anything in me that was attracted to the little maniac.

Lend shook his head and looked up at the ceiling, avoiding my eyes. "The two days I couldn't get ahold of you. You didn't lose your phone, did you?"

"No," I whispered.

"Where were you?"

"I got stuck in the Center after the poltergeist thing—it wasn't a big deal."

He looked at the door. "Thought I'd surprise you and come hang out while you worked. I've got to—I'm going to go now."

"Lend, wait!" I grabbed his arm. "Listen! I missed Raquel, and she needed my help, and I'm not doing anything that's dangerous or would hurt paranormals. Besides, they're paying me, which means I have enough money for school now, so your dad doesn't have to try and help me. It's really not a big deal!"

"It *is* a big deal! You lied to me. You've been lying to me this entire time. How is that not a big deal?"

I felt the tears build in my eyes and fought them back. "I didn't want you to get mad."

He let out a strangled laugh, started to say something, then shook his head and walked out. I followed him desperately down the stairs.

"Can't we talk about this?"

He paused at the door to the diner kitchen and took a deep breath. "Yes. But not right now. I've *always* been honest with you, and it kills me that you don't trust me enough to be the same. Even if you think it's going to bother me. *Especially* if you think it's going to bother me."

"Lend, I—"

He shook his head. "I'm too mad to talk right now and I love you too much to say anything I'll regret."

"Okay," I agreed, my voice wavering. I didn't want to push it, but I needed to know that we were going to be okay, that we'd get over this. He hesitated, then leaned over and kissed me roughly on my forehead.

"I'll call you later." He opened the door and looked back at me. "Is there anything else you're hiding?"

"No!"

He nodded and walked into the kitchen. And swore loudly. I scrambled after him.

Reth stood with Nona and Grnlllll near the stoves, filling the kitchen with his radiance. He looked up at us and beamed. "Lovely to see you again, Evelyn."

I pointed at him, looking at Lend as my voice rose at least an octave. "I did *not* know he was here!"

"Nona?" Lend asked, tensed as though he wasn't sure if he should fight Reth or turn and leave us all behind.

"Calm yourself, child. The faerie's business is his own."

"He's dangerous."

"And leaving." Reth dipped low in a mocking bow, then winked at my livid boyfriend. "Well met, as always." He left through a door in the wall, the kitchen positively exploding with silence in his absence.

Lend turned his scowl on Nona. "Does my dad know you're working with faeries?"

Nona smiled at Lend, swishing by and patting him on the shoulder as she moved to go out front. "Don't worry yourself. She will always be safe here. Evie? We need you on the register tonight."

"I—seriously? After that, *him*, here, you still expect me to work?" Nona kept that same insanely calm smile on her face. I glared at her; I'd always trusted her, but to see her talking with Reth like it happened every day . . . I didn't know. Maybe she was just telling him to leave. And he was gone, after all. I turned to Lend. "Will you wait?" I asked, desperate to fix this.

"You really didn't know Reth was here?"

"No! Are you kidding? I hate Reth. You know that."

Lend rubbed his eyes wearily. "I need some time to work

through this. I'm gonna go. I'll see you this weekend."

I nodded, biting back everything I wanted to say to him. He needed time to process. We'd talk soon. It'd be okay.

Three hours later, my feet aching, I scowled at Kari and Donna, a pair of selkies still hanging out in the corner booth, taking their sweet time with their watercress sandwiches. Kari and Donna weren't their real names, and I was never sure who was who, anyway, but since their actual names came out as yips, barks, and an awesome kissing sort of noise, it was easier for everyone to use their nicknames. Their huge, round, watery brown eyes were almost entirely iris, with barely any white showing. They were strange in that they didn't put on a glamour to look human—they actually removed their seal skin. But besides a faint haze that always clung to them (and that only I could see), there was something off. The way they used their fingers was clumsy, and they often laughed as they tried to pick things up, resorting to using their whole hand like a flipper. I guess they were new to the area—David hadn't even known they were here until I pointed them out.

Normally I didn't mind the selkies, since they were pleasant and playful and decidedly vain, always showing me new tricks for doing my hair, but tonight I wished they'd hurry the freak up. What was it with paranormals and not paying any attention to the time?

A luxury of immortality, I suppose.

Finally they finished and I closed shop, dragging myself

upstairs to curl up in a ball of misery and stare at my phone, willing Lend to text me.

He didn't.

I let my head rest against the diner window, watching cars pass and wishing Lend were here. We'd pick a number, say four, and the fourth car to pass was ours. Somehow I always ended up with beaters. Lend usually got minivans, so that evened it out a bit.

But he wasn't here.

"Okay, so we need birth certificates for Stephanie and Carrie, Patrick needs another license because he looks way too young for his birth date now, and that new werewolf family needs cages installed in their basement." David looked up from his agenda.

Arianna slouched down further in the bench next to me. "I'm on the official documents. New guy at the county record's office. One look at my mesmerizing eyes and oddly enough he's willing to do anything I ask . . ." She tapped the saltshaker, bored, like talking about her vamp ability was the same as any other job skill. *Excellent typist, always on task, can compel others to do my bidding.*

"Excellent. Evie, I was wondering if you could meet with a couple of vampires who want to sublet the apartment next door, just make sure everything's on the up-and-up. They can't compel you, so you'll be able to tell very quickly if they're lying about anything."

"Sure." I stabbed sullenly at my eggs. Normally I liked my weekly meetings with David and Arianna. Since paranormals weren't running scared from Viv anymore, things had calmed down, but there was always something that needed to be done in their little operation. Today, however, it felt pointless. It all felt pointless. Lend still hadn't called. It had only been two days, but it felt like a lifetime. We'd never gone this long without talking.

I wondered, too, whether or not he'd told his dad I was back with IPCA. David hadn't said a word, had greeted me with his usual warm smile and a side hug. Not that it was any of his business, either. He was my legal guardian, but, as Raquel pointed out, there really wasn't much that was legal about it. Still, he'd taken me in when Lend and I broke out of the Center, trusted that I wasn't going to betray their secrets, and always did whatever he could to help me out. I didn't like feeling as though maybe I'd betrayed him, too.

I didn't like any of this.

I scowled out the window again, directing my foul moods at the innocent bystanders walking down the sidewalk. A mom and dad walked by with a little girl between them, all holding hands. For some reason it made me want to cry.

A car honked loudly, drawing my attention away from the family to a woman, calmly walking down the middle of the street as though she owned the place. She wore a flowing purple dress, had shiny brown hair, and—

Yelping, I ducked beneath the table.

"What the—? Evie?" David asked.

"Faerie!" I hissed. "Outside!"

Arianna leaned toward the window. "Where?"

"The woman in purple! No, don't look! I mean, you won't be able to tell—she's glamoured! But don't draw her attention here."

After a tense minute that felt more like an hour, Arianna kicked me. None too gently. "She's gone. You can get up now."

I peeked hesitantly out, scanning up and down the street to make sure the faerie really was gone, then sat down. My heart was racing.

"Did you know her?" David asked, frowning.

"No! Never seen that one in my life."

"I wonder what she was doing here."

Reth's warning about my safety flashed through my mind. "Looking for me?"

"I dunno," Arianna said, tracing patterns into a thin sheen of ketchup she'd poured onto the table. "She didn't really look like she was searching for anything. She just sort of walked down the street casually, not even looking from side to side."

"It can't be a coincidence. How many faeries do you get here?"

David shrugged. "I have no idea, actually. For all Arianna and I know, she could be here constantly. She looked like a normal person to me."

"Hotter, though," Arianna added. "So should we tell

you any time we see someone who's really hot?"

I glared at her. "Yeah, that'd be really helpful, thanks."

"Still, you're right. This is unusual." David frowned thoughtfully. "I'll ask Nona about it."

"Fat lot of help she'll be."

"Why?"

I shrugged. "There've been a lot of weird paranormals in here lately. And Lend and I caught her talking with Reth in the kitchen the other night."

"Really? That . . . that *is* weird." Scratching at his stubble, David stood up. "I'll go talk with her right now. Been meaning to, anyway. I still haven't been able to see Cresseda, and Raquel was saying something about missing fire and earth elementals." He gazed at a spot on the wall, lost in his own thoughts, then shook his head and smiled reassuringly at me. "I always want you to feel safe here, Evie, and you know I'll do whatever I can to make sure that's possible."

"Thanks."

Brilliant. Just what I needed—further confirmation that something was going on. And even less of an idea what it was. I stood and turned to go up to the apartment, only to find Grnlllll standing by the counter, black eyes staring intently at me. Then, she did the creepiest thing I'd ever seen her do.

She smiled.

Something was *definitely* up.

GRIM PROSPECTS

I'm not sure I should go."

Jack rolled his eyes, stepping into my room all the way and letting the door close behind him. "Is this because of your jumpy boyfriend?"

Lend had texted me a couple of times since Monday, but he wouldn't get here until tomorrow night. It felt like I was betraying him again, going out on a mission Thursday afternoon. On the other hand, he knew I was working with IPCA. And I hadn't told him I'd stop.

"I don't know," I muttered.

"Look, if you don't want to come, no big deal. I'm sure

those families being held captive as troll slaves will totally understand that you're moping because of your stupid relationship problems."

I glared at him. "Fine." I'd agreed to this troll mission from the very beginning when Raquel asked me to come back, and they'd finally pinned down the area of the city where they thought the trolls were. Jack had been there with a faerie the day before to scope out sites to make a door. It'd be low impact, in and out. I didn't have to confront anyone or anything, just see a troll, note the location, and report back to IPCA. I was helping people. It was important.

Feeling grouchy and sick to my stomach, I stood up and took Jack's hand. I resisted the temptation to close my eyes as we entered the Paths. Maybe if I pretended not to be scared, I'd get over it. Jack seemed unusually eager, pulling me along.

"Your hand is all sweaty," I complained, wishing I could take mine out of his to wipe it on my pants. "Nervous or something?"

He let out a quick, high laugh, but didn't answer. After a few minutes he slowed, frowning in concentration as he held a hand up and felt around the nothingness.

"Lost?"

A smile broke through his focus. "Nope. Here we are. I give you Trollhättan, Sweden." A door opened in front of us and I saw a glimpse of green trees and cloudy skies. I let go and stepped through.

Right into a free fall.

My scream was extinguished as I plunged into bitterly cold, dark water. It flooded my senses, finding its way into my eyes, nose, ears, mouth. Everything was gray and green and cold.

I gagged, struggling to push my way to the surface. My coat was soaked through, and I could barely drag it through the fetid liquid. I looked frantically through the murk for Jack, but he hadn't splashed down next to me, or maybe in the shock I missed it. He could be right by me and I'd never know it.

My lungs burned, but a glimmer of light above my head drew me. A few more inches and I broke the surface, swallowing a lungful of air, grateful and desperate. I was about twenty feet from the dirt banks of the evergreen-lined river. I turned my head and saw, to my horror, some sort of gate on the narrow, walled end of the waterway lifting. Lifting, and flooding my portion of the river with a torrent that spun me around and tumbled me back under, directionless.

I fought, kicking wildly, but I didn't even know which way was up. I was going to drown—oh, bleep, I was going to drown alone in Sweden—when a hand reached out and grabbed my arm.

Jack! If I could have, I would have cried with relief. I turned to face him and found myself looking at a strangely beautiful person. He matched the grays and greens of the water around us, with eyes that took up nearly half his face.

Soulful eyes. Hungry eyes. His full lips parted in a smile, and I smiled back.

His voice moved through the water, achingly sweet and lovely. I closed my eyes, lost in the melody. I'd never heard music that powerful, that alluring. He pulled me forward and put his cold mouth to mine, his song somehow continuing as he gently parted my lips and kissed me, drawing my breath into himself.

We sank together, twirling languidly, until my feet rested against the soft, shifting silt at the bottom of the river. Between his lips and his song, the burning in my lungs faded into the distance, barely noticeable. I opened my eyes, sleepy and deliciously content, to see his eyes staring at me.

I pushed back, a scream bubbling out of my throat. Because now that I looked, I could see he was both this beautiful man and a horse—a horse with razor eyes, needle teeth, hair like wire weeds. The hair whipped forward, wrapping itself around my wrists as he pulled me in close again.

The melody had changed, becoming a haunting lullaby, filled with longing, sadness, and finality. Sleep. Cold, soaked, eternal sleep. I shook my head, terrified, but the beautiful man-horse smiled again, cradling me to his chest.

His mistake.

I slammed my palm against him, the channel between us opening with a flood more powerful than the river had ever been. Now his eyes were the ones opened in terror as he released me and struggled backward. I kept my hand to his chest, the roaring in my ears echoing through my whole body in an overwhelming deluge.

A stray current smashed into me and disconnected us. In an instant he was gone, and I was pissed. I screamed my rage into the water. He had tried to kill me—turnabout was fair play, as far as I was concerned. What a poor sport.

The water didn't bother me anymore. The currents were no longer forces working against me, but rather living things I could read and understand. I let them pull me up until my head broke the surface once again. I took a reluctant breath, a strange part of me wanting to sink back down and discover what mysteries the river had to whisper to me.

Instead I half swam, half let the water carry me to the bank. Climbing up, I collapsed onto the side and stared at the cold, gray sky. The air's bite was foreign and empty; it lacked the caress and touch of water.

"Evie!" Jack's voice drifted toward me. He knelt next to me, concern twisting his features. It was a new look for him. "Evie, are you okay? I didn't know! You stepped out too soon, and then I had to find a door to the bank, and I couldn't find you. Are you okay?"

I sighed, my sodden coat chilling me to the bone. "Peachy. Made a new friend."

He pulled me up by the hand, unzipping my coat and yanking it off me. "Shirt, too, please."

"No!"

"It's only fair. I seem to recall you making me strip the first time we met. Besides, it's going to get a lot colder, and we don't have time for a costume change."

Already trembling, I dropped my coat on the ground and peeled off my shirt, almost too cold to feel self-conscious of my barely there cleavage in a purple bra. Jack gave me his coat and I wriggled into it, grateful for the leftover body heat. I glanced at the water—it would be warmer in there, wouldn't it? Maybe just a quick swim.

What was wrong with me?

Jack frowned. "There's nothing we can do about your pants—mine probably wouldn't fit, and it wouldn't do for me to go around pantsless, much as it would be the best day of your life."

"It's fine." My teeth chattered violently and my sinuses sloshed like half the river had hitched a ride in them. "What is this place?"

"The Göta älv river. It's a lock system, with gates that change the level of the water. It has a rich history of trade and aided Trollhättan's industrial revolution."

"Let me guess: Raquel's got you in tutoring, too?"

"Only when she can catch me. You want me to take you back? We can try again tomorrow."

I shook my head. I was sure if I stopped to think about things, I'd have a meltdown, but I didn't want to have to come back tomorrow. Or ever, really, with Jack as a guide.

Besides, tomorrow I'd be with Lend, and I'd make things okay. I just needed to finish the job and go home. I could lose it then.

"It's only a little way to the city," he said. "I can try another door, if you want."

"No! No, I'm good with walking, thank you very much."

We were quiet for a bit, picking our way through the evergreens and gray rocks. It was beautiful. Or it would have been, were I not soaked to the bone and freezing.

"What were you saying about making a new friend?" Jack asked.

A rush of cold swirled through my heart and veins, like an injection of river water. Maybe it would extinguish the tingling in my fingertips.

"Umm, yeah, if by friend I mean someone who tries to drown me. Ever heard of a fossegrim?"

He shook his head.

"Kelpie? Nix? No? All variations of the same lovely type of paranormal who hangs out in the water and drowns people for kicks." I'd learned about them from Lish. Different areas of the world had different breeds, varying from horselike creatures to dragonish things. Judging by the beautiful-man appearance and music, I'd run into a fossegrim. Supposedly you could kill them by saying their name but a) how would you find it out in the first place, and b) it's a little hard to talk when your lungs are slowly filling up with water. Still, legend had it they were occasionally benign, giving music lessons and even marrying mortals every now and again.

I didn't get the impression this one had any intentions of taking vows.

"So you aren't going to be best friends."

"I dunno—he could be fun at a pool party. Assuming you hated everyone you invited."

We walked in silence for a while, both of us hunched against the evening's chill, until we entered the outskirts of a city that was far too beautiful and charming to be mistaken for anywhere in America. The buildings were red brick and wood, with a classical feel that made the cars parked out on cobblestone streets look ridiculously out of place. I half expected a horse-drawn cart to come prancing down the street, followed by villagers in braids, singing and dancing. Or maybe I watched too many musicals.

"The neighborhood is a few blocks this way," Jack said, after reading some street signs to get his bearings. Lamps flickered on and I added Trollhättan to the list of places I'd like to visit for fun someday. I could totally see myself in a traditional Swedish outfit, my hair in ribbons, walking hand in hand through the streets with Lend.

How would he look in lederhosen?

Come to think of it, no one here was wearing lederhosen. That didn't mean Lend couldn't, though. . . . Of course, first he'd have to forgive me for sneaking around behind his back. A celebratory trip to Sweden would be a nice way to make up, right? Tucking that idea away for a later date, I started looking—really looking—at the people we passed on the street as we got closer to the potential troll district. For once I blended in well, a much better fit in Scandinavia than most other countries.

"Anything?" Jack whined after we had been wandering for close to half an hour. It was nearly dark now, and we were both shivering. Blisters already claimed every available surface of my wet-socks-and-shoes-clad feet. If I didn't see something soon, this whole trip was a bust. I hated to think that the poor people kidnapped and forced into slavery by the trolls would have to wait until next week to be rescued, but there wasn't anything more I could do tonight.

"Nope. Not a—"

A young girl darted across the street in front of me. Cute thing with a pug nose, ruddy cheeks, blond hair, and . . . a little tail sticking out from under her skirt.

TOURIST FRIENDLY

I grabbed Jack's arm and pointed to the girl. He looked at her, then shrugged. "Does that mean we're done?"

"Come on. Let's check to be sure we know which house." We trailed her down the streets, winding through shopping areas and into a residential district. The brick-and-wood homes were neat and well tended, the streets clean under warm lights. The window boxes were empty now, but I imagined how charming this place would be in the spring and summer, lined with flowers.

I tried to keep a discreet distance from the girl. My only job was to figure out where she was staying and report back. No contact of any kind, which I was more than fine with. I hadn't even brought Tasey along—a fact I was now grateful for, since my little swim wouldn't have been good for her.

We passed a few people sitting on porches. When I made eye contact, I smiled, and they nodded back hesitantly. If they only knew what was in the midst of them. One woman in a pretty red wool coat stood next to a lamppost, dialing her phone. She glanced up, a small look of surprise on her face as she met my eyes, probably because my hair was still dripping wet. She winked at me and I gave a small wave. The Swedes totally deserved their friendly reputation.

Another corner and the little girl bounced up steps and into a nondescript house. "Bingo." I was about to tell Jack we could finally go when a throat clearing sound behind us made me turn.

Every single person we'd passed on the way here, including the woman in the red coat, stood behind us, forming a semicircle. A distinctly menacing semicircle.

"Umm, Jack?" I tugged on his arm.

He glanced over his shoulder, then looked back at the house, pulling a communicator out of his pants pocket. "What?"

The crowd moved in closer.

"Jack!"

He turned around, shooting me an annoyed look. "Let

me call it in already. I'm cold."

He couldn't see them. Which meant they were invisible. Which meant they were trolls.

Trolls who knew I could see them.

"Oh, bleep," I muttered. How had I forgotten about their invisibility glamours? Now that I looked I could see a hint of distortion around their faces—my stupid sight piercing straight through the invisibility. They'd known something was up the second I saw them on the streets. I waved to the trolls. "Umm, we were just leaving." I grabbed Jack's arm, startling him into dropping the communicator, and started to back up—bumping into a particularly large guy, whom I now noticed had an unusually flat nose. And a tail. We were surrounded. He clamped one huge hand onto my shoulder. I bit his thumb, twisting out from under his hand.

"Run!" I darted through the growing crowd, but Jack, unable to see them, stood there like a big oaf. I stopped, torn. They had him surrounded. There was a slight shimmer, as though a wave of heat had come up from the cold streets, and by the look on Jack's face I knew they were visible to him, now, too.

They closed in, backing Jack up to the wall. The woman in the red coat glared at me. I wanted to scream in frustration. After everything I'd already been through today, now I had to go face a horde of angry trolls to save Jack.

Jack. Stupid, crazy Jack.

I walked back, my feet feeling like they weighed a ton. Jack darted a look at me to say—*what?*—and I shook my head. Of course I wasn't going to leave him.

I reached the edge of the circle and the big troll grabbed my arm, carefully staying out of reach of my mouth.

"Evie, you idiot," Jack said.

"I had to come back for you!"

"No, you really didn't." It was then that I noticed his hand on the wall, which opened into blackness. Jack grimaced at me, then slipped through and was gone, much to the trolls' surprise.

"You little fink!" I shouted at the now solid wall. Here I'd come back so he wouldn't die alone, and he abandoned me. *After* dropping me into a river and nearly getting me killed.

If I ever saw him again, he was going to get a proper introduction to Tasey.

The trolls whispered a conversation in a guttural, harsh-sounding language. I squirmed, but Big Troll Guy's hand wasn't going anywhere. After a moment they pulled me into the nearest house and shoved me onto a floral couch.

There were at least twenty of them now, and they blocked all the escapes. The room wasn't exactly what I expected of a troll den. Instead of gnawed-on bones and trash, it was spotlessly clean with warm paint tones and tasteful prints. I wondered where the family that really owned it was, how long they'd been held prisoner. And whether or not I was about to join them.

I'd be okay, though. Jack knew where I was. He'd get help and bring it back . . . just like when he'd disappeared and left me stranded in the Center for two days.

I was so screwed.

I watched the trolls warily. Many of them were making phone calls—since when did trolls use cells?—but the others were glaring at me. Now that I looked closer, there were the obvious differences between them and humans, other than the tails. Flatter, wider noses, close-set, small eyes, all of which were slate gray. Most of them had one patch of hair that was wild and uncombed, at odds with their downright professional dress. I should have recognized the look before, invisible or not, but I hadn't dealt with trolls since I was twelve.

Finally, the woman in the red coat, hair bundled into braids like spun gold, stood in front of me with hands on her wide hips as her tail twitched rapidly from side to side.

"We know who you are." Her English was heavily accented but clear.

I raised my eyebrows. Apparently even after several months out of the IPCA game my fame had spread. "Then you know you should let me go." Bluffing was my only option at this point, so I sat up straight and maintained eye contact.

She let out a bitter laugh. "So you can slaughter more of our children?" My jaw dropped, then I sighed, exhausted.

When would paranormals stop accusing me of murder?

A TEETH-GNASHING
GOOD TIME

The trolls glared at me, waiting for a response. A strange creaking, scraping noise came from my left; I couldn't place it until I realized the large male troll next to me was grinding his teeth, every muscle in his considerably muscled body tense.

Not good.

I held my hands up. "First of all, I don't kill kids. Or anyone for that matter. Who do you think I am?"

The woman in the red coat narrowed her eyes. "If you aren't the foul creature, how did you see us?"

"What kind of foul creature are we talking about here?"

I asked, swiftly changing the subject. My abilities weren't something I wanted this crowd to know about.

"Vampire," an ancient troll near the door spat, his lips quivering with rage.

"I am so totally not a vampire." My chest lightened considerably. This would be easy enough to prove—and to solve.

"Give me a mirror. Or holy water. I'll drink it, even!" I gasped as someone threw water on the side of my face. "A little warning next time would be nice." I wiped my cheek with the sleeve of Jack's coat and watched the faces around me shift from murderous to confused.

"Who are you?" Red Coat asked.

I didn't know whether or not to lie, so I opted for a combination. "I'm with IPCA."

The old troll spat again. Charming, that one.

Red Coat shot him a look, then turned back to me. "How could you see us?"

I shrugged. "I'm talented. I've been trained to pick out most paranormals."

"And what interest does IPCA have with us?"

"All IPCA wants is to free whatever humans live here."

She shook her head, then gestured to the door and said something in the guttural language. Most of the trolls except Hulking Teeth Gnasher and Old Man Saliva left. Red Coat sat down in an armchair across from me, folding her hands in her lap.

"What is your name, child?"

"Evie."

"I am called Birgitta. And now that we have shared names, let us be honest with each other. This IPCA of yours does not only want whatever precious humans we nasty, murderous trolls have taken."

I squirmed under her unwavering gaze. "I don't know what you're talking about." The lie tasted heavy and acrid on my tongue. I knew all about the forced relocation and monitoring. When I'd helped IPCA identify a troll colony before, Lish was processing them for weeks afterward. I wasn't sure where they removed the trolls to, but they definitely wouldn't let them stay in the stolen houses. "I was only supposed to find you."

"And what if I told you there were no humans?"

My eyes widened in horror. "What did you do with them?"

She looked up at the ceiling, her face a picture of exhaustion. "There never were any. We bought all these houses. We have lived by your rules, in your world. And now we are to be removed for doing so?"

"Wait, you didn't push people out and take their stuff?" That was kind of what trolls *did*. They took over homes— sometimes whole villages—secreting the people away to their underground lairs as servants. And they were notorious thieves: food, gold, cattle, even babies. Very sticky fingers along with the tails.

"It is not always trolls that thrust humans out of homes. Over a century ago we lived on islands in and under the river. We had our . . . disagreements . . . with the local humans, but were separate and happy to be so. Then they dammed the river with their locks and gates, and drowned the colony we had spent centuries building. Our homes flooded, some called for vengeance. But most of us were tired of working against the tireless onslaught of humans. We decided to stop fighting. We took our gold and bought our way into human society."

"You own all this stuff?"

She raised her chin proudly. "Why do you think this city flourished after building the locks? By increased trade with *us*. We do not have the same mechanical skill as you humans, but we manage nearly every business here."

"So you aren't hurting anyone at all." Well, crud. This made things more complicated. A lot more complicated. If she was telling the truth—and she had no reason to lie to me—then IPCA didn't have any business with them. The whole point of IPCA was to keep paranormals from harming humans, and these weren't doing any harm. But I didn't think IPCA would see it that way. Trolls were trolls to them.

I rubbed my face, tired and cold and wishing the world were black-and-white again. "Okay. I can—I don't know. Let's pretend like none of this ever happened."

Old Man Saliva grunted something at Birgitta and she

nodded. "You work for IPCA. Your job is to find but also protect paranormals, is it not?"

"Yeah, I guess it could be interpreted that way." If you thought monitoring, detaining, and controlling were the same as protecting, which IPCA did.

"Then you must help us." She stated it as fact. "You see things no one else can. You will find the vampire plaguing us."

"I didn't—"

"Find a paranormal to take back to IPCA and protect those of us doing no harm. This is your job." Her slate eyes bored into mine, softening around the edges. "Please—our children, the little trollbaerns. We have so very few and they are more precious than any life we have built here. Help us."

How could I say no? I stood. "Alrighty. Let's go bag a vamp."

Thirty minutes later I was wandering the evening streets with Hulking Teeth Gnasher by my side. Birgitta had told me about the vampire stalking them. Trolls only have children once or twice a century, and the trollbaerns don't learn how to use invisibility glamours for several decades, leaving them vulnerable. Already two had been killed and another seriously hurt.

The whole thing made me sick to my stomach. These were the vamps I knew. This was why IPCA still needed to be in the world, no matter what Lend thought.

The trolls had set a trap for the vamp, which I unwit-
tingly triggered by following the little troll girl bait. Now
it was my job to freeze my butt off and find their sleazy
stalker. I didn't know how I'd find anyone under these
circumstances, though. Gnasher's breathing was so loud I
could barely hear my own footsteps. It was cramping my
style.

"I think I'll have more luck by myself." I smiled so he
wouldn't take it the wrong way.

He frowned, his brow almost covering his close-set eyes.
"Not safe."

"Trust me, I've been around the block a few times. I can
handle a vampire."

"Invisible." He gestured to himself. I shook my head. A
vampire would still smell him, which was no doubt why
they hadn't had any luck trapping it.

Glaring dubiously, he hesitated, then turned around and
went back the direction we had come. I let out a relieved
breath. The trolls in this town might be innocuous, but that
didn't make them any less intimidating.

Hands jammed into my pockets and thighs already chaf-
ing from too much time walking in damp jeans, I wandered
the streets, picking directions at random. There was a lot to
think about. The strange liquid sensation that kept drifting
over me, for one. The way the breeze seemed to follow me
like a little lost puppy. The English test I was going to be

way, way too tired for in the morning. What I was going to say to Lend to make everything better. How I was going to find a ride home with no communicator. How hard I was going to hit Jack for abandoning me.

That last one warmed me up a bit.

I kept thinking I heard footsteps shadowing mine, but no matter how many times I whipped around, no one was there. When I'd gotten myself completely lost, a soft voice with a hint of an accent drifted from a dark stoop next to me. "I think you're in the wrong part of town." I could hear the smile through the dark.

I stopped, facing him. "No, I'm pretty sure I'm in the right part."

He stepped forward into the light, white eyes gleaming dully beneath his glamour and fangs bared in a pleasant smile. Yup, exactly where I needed to be. Bring it on, dead guy.

LIKE A BAD MOVIE

Still smiling, the vampire shook his head. "You should be careful where you go in this city, *Liebchen*. Monsters walk with human faces."

I snorted. "You don't say." This was the first time since I was eight that I had faced a vampire without either backup or Tasey. Still, I wasn't going to back down. I could *so* take a solitary vamp.

His hair was dark and curly, longer than most vamps wore it, giving him an almost artistic air. Well, minus the corpse he was rocking underneath the glamour. He put his hands in his pockets and shrugged. "There are things in this world you're better off not knowing. Go home and leave the night its mysteries."

"Wow, melodramatic much? You vampires always take yourselves *so* seriously." His eyes bugged out in surprise. "Yeah, I know you're a creature of the night. Bringer of death, sucker of blood, needer of tans, so on and so forth. And oddly enough, I'm still unimpressed."

He narrowed his eyes. "How do you know what I am, child?"

What is it with paranormals and calling me "child?" I'd be seventeen in December. How about a nice "ma'am" or something? "I know because it's my job. It's also my job to tell you this whole troll-stalking thing you've been doing is over."

He threw back his head and laughed. I felt like I'd walked into some cheesy vampire movie. Finally done with his little show of sinister confidence, he focused on my eyes. "You will take me back to the trolls."

Vampire mind tricks are dependent on their glamour, and with my nice view straight to his white corpse eyes, he just looked silly. I let my face go blank and nodded slowly. "Yes. The trolls. Back. With me. Cannot form. Complete sentences." I shook my head. "Yeah, so not happening."

He considered me, annoyed and at a loss for what to do next. "I don't kill humans."

"Me neither! See, common ground already."

"Then I suppose we should both be on our way."

I put my hands on my hips. "No, we shouldn't. I'm not going to let you murder any more troll kids."

He sighed. "Then I'm afraid we'll have to lose our common ground." Flashing his fangs, he lunged forward. I drew my arm back and punched him full in the face.

"Ow!" we screamed in unison as he clutched his nose and I shook my poor, poor hand. Why didn't anyone ever tell me punching faces *hurts*?

"You hit me!"

"You were trying to bite me!"

We glared at each other, his intensity somewhat diminished by the hand he still held to his nose. "So what now?" he asked, smooth voice muffled.

"I haven't thought that far ahead yet." I wasn't going to let him go, but I had neither the weapons nor the inclination to kill him. After another tense minute, he crouched down on the porch stoop. With a heavy sigh I sat down next to him, wrapping my arms around my knees in a pathetic attempt to ward off the chill. It felt like the blisters on my feet had coupled off and started forming little blister families. Tonight sucked.

I turned to the vampire. "You don't bite humans, huh?"

He leaned back, staring into the night. "Not for a long time now."

"Why?" I knew a lot of vamps like Arianna who didn't drink human blood—but they didn't drink trolls' blood, either. This was the first time I'd ever heard of paranormals being targeted by a bloodsucker.

"Because, *Liebchen*, I remember what it felt like to have a heartbeat, a pulse. I remember what it was like not to be a monster. I am content to watch humanity swirl around me, growing and aging and changing in ways that I never will."

"Fair enough, but if you're such a pacifist, why murder troll kiddos?"

He turned to me, the weariness he'd displayed while talking about humanity replaced by an almost palpable anger. "Because I am eternal, and blood calls to me. It calls to me everywhere I go, begging for me to take it, crippling me with thirst. What made me this way? What else in the world is untouched by time? These creatures, and others like them. If I am a monster, I will play my part. But I will prey on my fellow monsters, and someday I will find out how they corrupted human life to make vampires, *and I will kill all of them.*"

I shivered, and it had nothing to do with my wet clothes. When Viv was on her spree, at least she thought she was helping paranormals by setting them free. This vampire—he simply hated. I resisted the urge to scoot farther from him. "Why do you get to decide? It wasn't like the troll kids chose to be here. It's outside their control, like your, uh, change was. You're punishing them for being what they are. How does that make sense?"

A smile colder than the dark night spread across his features. "I have had four hundred years to think this through. You're very sweet, but when you've been a monster as long as I, 'sense' stops having any influence."

I squirmed, my butt going to sleep against the concrete steps. What had I gotten myself into here? My communicator was still in my wet coat, which I'd stupidly abandoned on the riverbank. Maybe I could knock him senseless and find Hulking Teeth Gnasher and the other trolls. But they'd probably kill him. Didn't he kind of deserve it, though? And did thinking that make me just as bad as him?

"I should have stayed home and studied," I muttered.

He let out a low chuckle. "Indeed. It would appear we're at an impasse. I will not stop, and you're committed to stopping me, no?"

I shrugged. "It's my job. Sort of."

"I ought to let you in on a secret, then."

"What's that?"

He leaned toward me. "You don't smell entirely human."

That did it. Vamp guy was going *down*. How hard could it be to beat a corpse senseless? I stood up, balling my hands into fists. "Tell me something I *don't* know."

He stood, too, a cruel smile twisting the rotting, desiccated remains of his real face. "Something you don't know? Very well. I've found that paranormal blood has added benefits over human blood."

Before I could move, he reached out and grabbed my wrist. I tried to jerk it back, but couldn't break his far-too-strong grasp.

Oh, *bleep*.

I LIKE THE NIGHT LIFE

I pulled against the vampire's grip again; he didn't budge. This wasn't happening. This couldn't be happening. Vampires weren't strong!

Seeing my growing panic, he smiled. I wanted to kick his rotting teeth in, I was so sick of that smile.

"Not what you expected? I did warn you."

I threw a wild punch with my left hand, only grazing his head. He pushed forward and tripped me on the porch stairs. I fell back hard, cracking my tailbone against the blunt corner of a step, and let out a sharp cry of pain. He put his hand over my mouth. His hand that close to my eyes made me dizzy, unable to focus on his glamour or his real body. Smooth skin, dead skin, smooth skin, dead skin—I swallowed against the nausea.

"Hush, now, we don't want to draw any extra attention. I'll make it quick, my little monster." He shoved my head to the side to expose my neck.

Screaming my frustration, I bit down as hard as I could on his fingers. He jerked back and I gasped air, gagging at the thought of what I had just put in my mouth. I ducked to the side and stumbled out of his reach. As soon as I had my balance, I took off running, my breath ragged. I raced down the street, turning a corner as I looked behind me, and nearly ran into a wall. Swearing, I flipped around—too late. He already blocked the way out, leering confidently.

"You don't want to do this," I said, holding up my hands.

"I really do."

"No! I—" The chill breeze pulsed through me, and the tingling in my hands grew stronger. I could feel the air swirling in tiny eddies around me, connected to it in a new way. Suddenly my tired and aching body felt light, insubstantial but powerful. And I could feel the vampire's soul, too, in front of me. Calling me. I could even see it, the faintest glow around his heart.

I shut my eyes, fighting the urge to close the distance between us. "Please," I whispered. "I don't want to hurt you."

He laughed. "Are you confused, *Liebchen*?"

My eyes snapped open. Something in his expression changed when he saw the look there, his predatory sneer replaced with fear. I clenched my hands into balls. Not again. Not unless I had to. Holding myself back took all my strength, and my voice came out low and aching. "You should run."

I hoped he wouldn't.

He frowned, then backed slowly out of the alley, never taking his dead white eyes off me. When he reached the street, a baseball bat swung out of the night and cracked into his skull.

Jarred out of my horrible desire, my view opened up. Jack grinned and smacked the bat into his hand. "Fancy a quick game?"

My gaze drifted to the vampire lying on the ground. He was helpless now. Completely helpless. Which meant there was no excuse to drain him anymore. I took a shuddering breath and tried to clear my head by focusing on Jack.

Jack! "Where have you been, you miserable little creep?"

He raised his eyebrows, a look of mock hurt on his face. "This is the thanks I get?"

"Give me that bat and I'll show you how grateful I am, coward!"

"Hey-oh, let's not be hasty. What good would it have done us if I had been snatched, too? Besides, I came back. Right on time, by the looks of it." He smiled, but something in his eyes was intense, accusatory, almost as if he knew what I was about to—no, what I *might* have done. "But you had it under control, right?"

I yanked the bat from his hands. "Do you at least have anything useful? Ankle trackers? A spare communicator?"

He made an elaborate show of checking his tight, long-sleeved shirt for pockets, then shrugged. "They're all in my coat."

I looked down at Jack's tailored wool coat. The coat I'd been wearing the entire time. I slipped my hand inside and, sure enough, in a hidden pocket near my heart, was a thin communicator and a single ankle tracker.

Figures.

"'Be prepared,' that's my motto." He smiled smugly at me. "That, and 'Sleep whenever possible.' Oh, and 'If you don't notice it's gone, what's the harm in me taking it?'"

"Call it in," I said, weary beyond belief and wanting to be as far as possible from this vampire. I tossed the communicator to Jack and bent down, my fingers twitching as I attached the tracker. I wouldn't look at the vampire's heart. I wouldn't touch him. I put my thumb on the tracker to activate it, but nothing happened.

"Looks like they don't trust you with trackers. Wonder why?" Jack leaned down to take over.

Maybe their distrust had something to do with the fact that I'd freed Lend? Or that I was responsible for releasing nearly every werewolf they had? I probably wouldn't trust me, either. I took several steps back and leaned against the wall, looking up into the cloudy night sky, trying anything to take my focus off the vampire.

Jack stood. "They're on their way." He tossed the communicator lazily into the air and caught it behind his back. "Where are the trolls?"

Ah, crap. The trolls. How was I going to lie my way out of this one? I wasn't about to turn them over to IPCA. As far as I was concerned, they'd earned their lives here. This vile creature on the ground in front of me was the only threat that needed to be eliminated.

I opened my mouth to spin a story, when a door opened in the wall across from us and two men in black turtleneck sweaters stepped quickly through, their faerie escorts remaining anonymous in the dark. They looked in both directions before walking forward and kneeling down next to the body.

One addressed me, his yellow wolf eyes glowing beneath brown ones. Huh. Guess IPCA didn't lose all their werewolves, after all. "The trolls?"

I grimaced in what I hoped was a regretful way. "Long gone. They were tracking the vampire, some sort of blood vengeance. Tribal thing. But when they found out I was with IPCA they cleared out rather than be caught. I was following them when I met the vamp."

"They don't have a base here? No humans have been taken?"

"Nope. Just passing through. They took me to an empty

warehouse, where they were camped. No sign of any people at all."

I could feel Jack's eyes on me and deliberately avoided looking at him. I was going to sell this lie. The only one who could contradict me was the vampire. Maybe I *should* have drained him . . . But, no. Raquel would take my word over his.

The werewolf nodded, then helped his partner haul the vampire up by his armpits.

"Be careful. He's really strong. Like, stronger than you."

The werewolf eyed me dubiously.

"No, really. He kills—" I stopped, my stomach sinking with the realization of what that information could do if it were spread around. "I'd better talk to Raquel. Make sure he doesn't wake up until you have him in Containment. An ankle tracker's not gonna do it with this one." They nodded, half carrying, half dragging him back through the door. I caught a glimpse of one of the faeries, but I didn't recognize her. Just as well.

Sighing, I slid down the wall to sit on the ground and winced as pain stabbed through my lower back, radiating outward from my tailbone. A few painful shifts and I was comfortable, in a not-going-to-die-right-now-but-maybe-later sort of way. A movement at the end of the street caught my eye. Birgitta, invisible to anyone else's eyes, nodded at me, then disappeared back into the shadows. At least I'd done something right today. Maybe. Probably.

"So." Jack sat next to me. "A fossegrim, trolls, and a super vamp all in one night. I've changed my mind—you really *do* know how to have a good time."

On the verge of tears, I leaned over until my head was resting on his shoulder. "You have no idea." I couldn't get the desire—the need—I had felt to drain the vampire out of my head. My empty stomach churned with guilt. But I hadn't done anything. I wouldn't have, either, even if Jack hadn't saved the day. My fingers tingled, disagreeing with me, and I balled my hands into fists. No.

We were quiet for a while, Jack tense under my head, uncomfortable but nice enough not to move. I felt strangely close to him right then, like we were the only two sane ones in a world swirling with madness and murder. I could feel the threads from that world, threatening to pull me in, and I'd take whatever anchor I could get. Even if he was a blond nightmare.

I lifted my head to look at him. "How did you find me?"

"Just lucky." The answer was smooth, but it felt like he blurted it out a little too easily. I narrowed my eyes, but he continued. "Why did you lie about the trolls?"

"I didn't." We sat there looking at each other, two seasoned liars, until I couldn't take it anymore. "Jack?"

"Hmm?"

"Thanks." My voice cracked a little. "If you hadn't shown up . . ."

"If I hadn't shown up, you would have been fine. No

need to get sappy on me when I've decided you might be some decent fun after all. Now, you happen to be wearing my nicest coat. I'd like very much to get it back, so let's take you home, shall we?"

I couldn't argue with that.

HONESTLY A LIAR

Raquel frowned at me over the top of her black coffee. "Just looking at your drink is giving me a cavity."

"Good thing IPCA has excellent dental." I smiled and used a candy cane to stir my double whipped cream hot chocolate. The coffee shop was small, with warm yellow walls and poofy chairs in dimly lit corners, the scattered patrons hunched over laptops typing out caffeine-fueled works of dubious genius. I had picked this place because they stocked Christmas flavors ridiculously early (in spite of the various spiders and bats hung in honor of Halloween), and because it was thirty minutes by bus outside my town, so there was little chance of running into someone I knew. I doubted any of my werewolf or vampire buddies would recognize Raquel, but I preferred to avoid finding out.

"This is nice." She wiped at a spot on the table, again, and glared at a couple making out in the corner opposite us. At least she'd agreed to meet me here. Mostly because I'd flat-out refused to go back to the Center to debrief about the mission.

Well, to lie about nearly everything, if you want to be technical.

We'd already gone over my story about the trolls passing through. I resisted the urge to ask if the vampire had said anything about them. If he had and I was caught, I'd know. I hated keeping secrets from Raquel, but some things called for it. Jack had mentioned the near drowning, so I fed her some nonsense about how the fossegrim hadn't killed me because a stray current separated us and let me get out of the water. No reason to give her more to worry about. The uber-vamp was information overload enough for one visit.

I shivered at the memory of his grip on my wrist and what I had wanted to do to him. "You're not letting him out of Containment, right?"

"Of course not. He's far too unstable for even the most basic assignment. But you were right not to tell anyone else why he's so strong. It's a disturbing development. I've never come across a vampire who targeted paranormals, and the fact that it helps him overcome natural vampire weaknesses—well, it's best kept strictly under wraps." She heaved a *things are never simple, are they?* sigh.

"Good. Guy's a psychopath, even by vampire standards. And that's saying something." I leaned back, trying to find a position that didn't hurt my bruised tailbone. I'd have to figure out how to hide it from Lend when he came tonight.

No. No more hiding.

"Hey, what about the elementals? Do you think maybe the vampire—" I felt slightly ill, worrying about a repeat of Viv's spree. I didn't think I could handle more paranormal deaths that I had to figure out.

Raquel shook her head. "No, I don't think it's related. There haven't been any deaths or bodies. Nearly every elemental we've identified and have contact with has disap- peared, but elementals are unusual—you understand. We've only been keeping track of them for a couple of decades now, so for all we know, this is common behavior."

I nodded, relieved. No more violence. I'd have to tell Lend, make sure he knew that it wasn't just his mom who had disappeared. Of course, I wasn't sure if that made it sound better or worse.

Raquel took a sip of her drink. "It's too bad about the trolls, though."

I gulped my hot chocolate, scalding my throat. "Yup. Too bad. Still, I brought in a dangerous paranormal, which was always the goal, right?"

"Of course, and you did well. I'm sorry it wasn't as easy

an assignment as I promised."

"Yeah, well, get Jack a GPS or something. He's a step above faeries, but only just. At least *they* never dropped me straight into a river. Don't give me any assignments near cliffs, okay? I shudder to think where Jack might toss me out."

"Next time let him step out first."

I laughed, shaking my head. "Good idea."

To my surprise, she asked me about school, and it felt both surreal and perfectly natural talking with Raquel about my big *Dracula* essay, the English test I'd fallen asleep during that morning because of the troll adventure, and my complaints about Miss Lynn. I flashed back to all the times I used to pretend Raquel was my mom, daydreaming about doing something like this with her.

It was nice.

"And how is Lend?"

I looked down into my dwindling hot chocolate. "Not so great. I, uh, kind of didn't tell him I was working with you again."

She raised her eyebrows. "And he found out."

"Yup. You can imagine it didn't go over very well."

She nodded sympathetically and took my hand in hers. "Lend and I certainly didn't start off on the right foot"— only Raquel would refer to Lend punching her and then us imprisoning him in an IPCA cell and interrogating him as being the "wrong foot"—"but he's always been good to you, and I have no doubt you two will be able to work this out."

"Thanks. I—"

But her communicator beeping shoved us out of our little snippet of normalcy. She read the message and gave her *there aren't enough hours in the day* sigh, then looked up at me to apologize. I waved my hand.

"No worries. You go save the world. I'm gonna finish getting a cavity."

She paused. "I really am sorry, Evie. Sometimes I worry that pulling you back in was the wrong thing to do. Perhaps it was selfish on my part. But I can't tell you how much I appreciate it." She smiled, patting my hand. "I'll be in touch."

"I know."

"Let me know if you need any help on that essay. And if I can help with the Lend situation."

When she left, I felt warmer inside from more than the cocoa. In spite of what a mess the last mission had been, things worked out. And having Raquel back in my life meant more to me than I'd ever imagined it would. That was worth a few near-death experiences in Sweden, right? Lend would understand. I'd make him understand.

One bus ride and three hours later I was exhausted from trying to figure out how to do just that. Lend hadn't given me a specific time when he'd be there, so I lay on the couch with my phone, shifting positions until I found one that didn't hurt my tailbone.

The previous night's adventures caught up to me, and I dozed into fitful sleep. A gentle hand brushing the hair away from my face woke me up. Lend crouched on the floor, eye level with me. "Hey," he said, his voice soft.

"Hey!" I sat up quickly—too quickly, and squeaked from the shock of pain.

"What's wrong?"

"Noth—" I stopped myself. "I bruised my tailbone pretty bad last night."

"How?"

"I fell down on a step."

"Where?"

"In Sweden."

Some of the concern dropped off his face and he sat back on his heels. "Oh. And what were you doing in Sweden that made you fall down on a step?"

"Fighting with a vampire?"

His face went stony. "So you're totally safe working for IPCA again. Great. Are you going to come back with broken bones next time? See, this is exactly what I was talking about! IPCA gets you in its clutches again; and you're lying to me, hiding things, *and* you've already been trapped in the Center and hurt! Why were you fighting with a vampire?"

I shook my head. "It wasn't supposed to be about a vampire, I was just supposed to—"

"No! It's never what it's *supposed* to be. I can't believe

Raquel sucked you back into doing their dirty work for them."

And suddenly I went from desperate to explain to full-on pissed. "You have no idea what you're talking about. You think because the vampires around here play nice that they do everywhere else? What good does David's little experiment do to protect people from the paranormals that don't want to discover their own better nature? Some of them *are* monsters, Lend. You know that! Yeah, IPCA sucks sometimes, but at least they're doing something! I'd love nothing more than to sit around this town serving pancakes, but guess what? You aren't the only one who wants to help paranormals! I might not do it the same way you do, but don't you dare accuse me of doing IPCA's dirty work. Your precious vampire? He was stalking and murdering troll kids! And if it weren't for me, who knows how many more he would have killed?"

"Troll kids?"

I scowled. "Yeah, I went to Sweden to track down a troll colony."

"You found them?"

"Of course I found them. Because that's what I do, and I'm good at it. The trolls asked for my help, and because they weren't bothering anyone, I protected them from the thing hurting them. And, before you ask, no, I didn't turn the trolls over to IPCA, but, yes, I did turn over the psychotic vampire. So maybe they are using me, but I'm using them, too, and I'd appreciate you not acting like I'm an idiot who does whatever anyone tells me to."

He was quiet for a minute, and I braced myself for his next argument. "I'm sorry."

"I— Wait, what?"

"I'm sorry. You're right. I don't get why you feel like IPCA's the best way to go, but I've never been able to be impartial about them. I don't like it, and I'm not going to like it; there are too many ways you can get hurt. But if you feel like it's important, then I can deal with it. You're not an idiot—I know that—you're the brightest, best person I've ever known."

"So . . . we're okay?" Hope fluttered in my chest, releasing some of the anxiety that had been tearing me apart this whole week.

"Just promise me you're done lying. I hate that IPCA is still a part of your life, but I can accept it if you stop hiding things from me. That bothers me more than anything else, that you feel like you can't be honest with me. You see me like no one else does—the real me—all the time. I want the same thing with you."

I nodded, tears in my eyes. He was right. He couldn't hide from me. It wasn't fair for me to hide things from him.

"So no more lies?"

I swallowed hard. *You're immortal, Lend.* "No more lies," I lied.

He sighed, relieved, and sat next to me, cautiously

putting his arm around me and resting his head against the back of the couch. "So, umm, what do you want to do now?"

I wished I knew.

LIES, LIPS, AND LUNATICS

I can't do it," I whispered, sick to my stomach.

Lend put his hand over mine, wrapping his other arm around my waist. I leaned my head back against him, grateful for this. For us. Things weren't back to normal, but they were getting there.

"Sure you can." He pushed my finger down on the Enter key, and, just like that, I'd applied to the one and only school I wanted to get into.

"I'm going to throw up."

"Well, in that case, please use the bathroom, because I have to sleep in here tonight." He laughed, lightly kissing my neck.

I flopped back onto his bed, rumpling the familiar blue comforter. Being together in his dad's house felt like old times, when we first broke out of the Center and I was living here. "I should have read over my essays one more time. And what about my SATs? My math score could have been better. It should have been better. And my stupid English grade." I covered my face with my hands. "I can't breathe. Could you breathe when you applied? Is this normal?"

Lend sat down next to me, his weight sinking the bed enough that I rolled into his side. "It's normal. I felt the exact same way. But if it helps, you look much cuter freaking out than I ever did."

I peeked out through my hands. "But what if I don't get in?"

He wrapped his arms around me. "No more worrying about it. You'll get in."

"Good. Someone needs to keep an eye on you and that dirty little dryad of a lab assistant."

He laughed, squeezing me until I couldn't breathe. "Why would I ever want a lusty tree nymph when I could have a hyperventilating Evie?"

I worked my arms free and jabbed his sides, tickling him until he released his grip. And then, unable to resist how adorable his mouth was when he laughed, I kissed him, letting my stress melt away in his lips. Good heavens, the boy even *tasted* good.

Just when I was relaxing into a good make-out session, we were interrupted by raised voices downstairs.

"Were you guys expecting visitors?" I asked, sitting up.

Lend disengaged his fingers from my hair. "Not that I know of."

The voices got louder, obviously arguing. "Wait a sec— that's Raquel." Great. Of course she'd show up just when things were feeling okay between Lend and me again. I didn't need IPCA drama right now to remind him of my lies. We hurried down to the kitchen. David was backed up against the counter, his face a strange mixture of anger and sheepishness. Raquel faced him, pointing a figure at his chest and punctuating each sentence with a jab for emphasis.

"Don't talk to me about trust, David Pirello! Don't you *dare* talk to me about trust! If you know something about where they are and you haven't—"

David cleared his throat loudly, and Raquel turned around to see us standing there. Her face was flushed with emotion, something I'd rarely seen. She looked pretty, with rosy cheeks and shining eyes. The scowl diminished the effect somewhat, but she quickly shifted to a neutral expression.

"Oh. David didn't tell me you two were here." She smoothed out her skirt as though that could release the emotion she'd pent up again as soon as we entered the room. "Evie, I wanted to ask you about how your college search is going."

I smiled suspiciously, positive that wasn't anything close

to why she'd come. "Dandy. Finished applying for early decision to Georgetown about five minutes ago."

"You should get applications ready for at least three others, to be safe."

I resisted the urge to glare. My school counselor kept saying the same thing, but as far as I was concerned, there was only Georgetown. "Good advice. Thanks."

"What are you doing here?" Lend asked.

"There have been some recent developments that I wanted your dad's opinion on. Sadly he wasn't helpful." She shot David a glare. He looked grumpy. "Evie, let me know how the applications go." Smiling at me, she walked past us and out the front door.

"Since when does she use normal doors?" Lend asked.

"She's being polite." I frowned, feeling protective of her.

"What did she really want?"

David shook his head. "More elementals and location-specific paranormals slipping out of their network. Anyway, it's not our concern. IPCA creates problems; they can handle them, too. More power to anyone who gets past them."

I shifted awkwardly on my feet. I had no idea whose side I was on in this particular case. Probably both. Or neither. Lend was quiet, and I racked my brains for something I could say to fill up the ever-expanding silence.

My cell phone rang in my pocket. Thank heavens. "It's Arianna—just a sec." I opened the phone and walked into the other room. "Arianna? What's up?"

"Is there a reason there's a blond boy jumping on your bed, or should I kill him?"

"Don't bother," I growled. "I'll kill him myself." If I had to deal with Jack screwing around in my life again . . .

Lend walked in as I snapped my phone shut. "Something wrong?"

I put the phone in my pocket, carefully avoiding his eyes. This wasn't an IPCA job. And we were having a happy afternoon before Raquel showed up. No reason to strain things.

I sighed. The truth. I'd tell him the truth whenever I could to make up for when I couldn't. "Jack's at the apartment bugging Arianna."

Lend scowled. "What's wrong with him?"

"No idea. I've got to get back for a shift, anyway." I'd really been slacking at the diner lately. I didn't need the money anymore, but they still needed the help, and I felt guilty about ditching. Plus, working was an easy way of keeping an eye on Nona. I hadn't spotted any more faeries, but that didn't mean nothing was going on.

"Want me to come help out?"

I smiled at him, grateful he wasn't freaking out over Jack. No doubt it was taking some effort. "You should pick out a movie. That way we don't both have to stink like greasy food. I need a nice date to look forward to."

"I meant help with Jack."

"Oh. No. He's just a little unbalanced and lonely."

He put his arms around my waist, frowning. "Can't he be lonely and unbalanced around someone else's girlfriend?"

"I'll suggest it. Pick me up at eight?"

He leaned down and kissed me softly. "Yup. Call me if you have any problems."

I doubted I'd call Lend, but had no doubt that where Jack was, problems would follow.

ALTERNATIVE LIFESTYLES

Jack was mid-jump when I burst into my room. I snatched his ankle, flipping him horizontal. He crashed down hard to my bed and rolled off onto the floor.

And laughed.

"Let's do that again! But this time I'll jump even higher."

"No! No, you won't! What are you doing here?"

He sat up on the floor and shrugged. "I was bored."

"I don't care! I'm not your babysitter!"

His blue eyes twinkled. Honestly, whose eyes actually twinkle? Then his face crumpled, his lower lip jutting out. He blinked his ridiculously long eyelashes at me. "I thought we were friends."

"Oh, knock it off."

"Come on." He jumped up and grabbed my hand. "Let's do something fun."

"I can't! I have to work, and then I have a date."

"Frying-pan boy again? I thought you guys broke up."

"No! Why would we break up?"

Jack shrugged. "Dunno. He didn't seem thrilled last time I saw him. Whatever, though. I wanted to check and make sure you were okay. Looks like you are, although I still say he's boring. Can he take you to see krakens?"

"No way! Really? Those are real? I've always wanted to—" I stopped, taking a deep breath. "Seriously. I'm busy. With my *boyfriend*." This time I thought I saw a flash of something genuine in his disappointed expression. Great. Another person I was letting down. I knew where he was coming from, though. If all he had to choose from were the Center and the Faerie Realms, well, he deserved a friend. "Can I take a rain check? Weekends are busy for me."

He shrugged, his perma smile back in all its dimpled glory. "You'd probably figure out a way to nearly get killed, anyway."

Arianna cleared her throat loudly from the doorway. I'd charged in right past her without explaining, and no doubt I'd have to do so now. Problem was figuring out *what* to explain.

"Oh, umm, Arianna, this is Jack. He, uh, well, what did he tell you?"

She rolled her eyes, the kohl-rimmed, chocolate brown glamour ones mimicking the actions of her milky white corpse eyes. "He said he was here to inspect the beds. I figured he was one of your old *friends*."

"No, he's not—well, kind of. He's not a faerie, he's human, but, uh—" I hadn't told Arianna about my new arrangement with IPCA. Lend was already mad enough about it; I didn't want my roommate being annoyed with me, too.

"Jack." He flashed her his most melt-worthy grin and stuck out a hand. "Definitely human, but—" he took her hand and pressed his lips to it "—I might be willing to try out an alternate lifestyle if it meant getting to know you better."

"Umm, eew?" Arianna pulled back her hand, her face disgusted but a smile tugging at one corner of her mouth. "Eternal life is bad enough without giving it to pests like you."

He sighed heavily. "Girls are mean. At least faeries simply kill you if they don't want you around." He put a hand on the wall, leaning against it and tapping his foot impatiently.

"Where are you going?" I asked, feeling guilty for not being able to hang out with him.

"To find a faerie to kill me, of course." He winked at us,

then pretended to fall straight through when the faerie door opened. Even Arianna laughed as the door closed behind him.

"Where did you find that one?"

"I have no idea. I'm a magnet for crazies, I guess."

"They must be able to sense a kindred spirit."

"You're one to talk. Don't you have more hordes of the undead to lead in a glorious revolution?"

"Zombies, not undead. There's a fine distinction. And no. Right now I'm scouting new talent. The glorious revolution comes tomorrow."

"Good luck with that. Hey, you want to hang out? Lend's here the whole weekend."

She shrugged. She'd been more and more withdrawn lately. But, short of a faerie apocalypse, I *definitely* wouldn't bail on her this time. "Sure. Yeah. *Easton Heights* marathon?" Bonus to that was, since Arianna didn't sleep, we could watch DVDs the entire night, which meant I didn't have to be apart from Lend at all. Excellent plan in my book.

I nodded and smiled enthusiastically. "Party!"

"Lend'll whine."

"He's cute when he whines."

"There's something wrong with you," she said.

There were a *lot* of things wrong with me, but loving Lend was definitely not one of them.

"Oh, hey," she said, pointing to some thick folders on the

desk. "I ordered materials from a few other DC schools."

"Why?"

"Backup plan. You know, just in case."

I scowled. You'd think *she* was the one sneaking around with Raquel. "I don't need a backup plan."

She rolled her eyes again. "Don't be an idiot. Sometimes things don't work out. You should always give yourself options. You're lucky you have them."

"I don't need options. I'll see you later." I shut the door behind myself rather louder than was necessary.

When I got downstairs I ducked into the kitchen to find Nona and Grnlllll standing next to each other and leaning over something on Nona's arm. I squinted my eyes, sure I was seeing it wrong. It looked like they were talking to some sort of glowing orange gecko or salamander, which couldn't be right.

Then again, Nona was a tree. So pretty much nothing she did was weird. Or everything was. There really wasn't a standard for normal here.

"Hey, Nona?"

She straightened, pulling her arm protectively behind her back with a stern look. I frowned, wondering if I wasn't supposed to see that, or if she was just pissed at me for not working much anymore. "You need me on tables or register today?"

"Neither, Evie. Thank you. You may go."

"O-kay . . ." There was definitely a strange vibe there.

Between her hushed conversations with Grnlllll and meeting up with Reth, Nona was seriously creeping me out. And there was this certain way she watched me when she thought I wasn't paying attention—like she was just, I don't know, *waiting*. For something.

I was pretty sure I didn't want to know what.

As I walked through the diner to go out, I swear every pair of eyes in there, not a single one of which were human, watched me. Fighting off a shudder, I pulled out my phone to call Lend for a ride. No way I was walking outside under the open sky today.

My head drifted dangerously close to my desk. The even, smooth slab of plastic faux wood was inviting, and the even, smooth drone of my English teacher's voice in the background seemed to have hit on a previously undiscovered cure for insomnia.

I couldn't remember the last time I'd been this bored. If only I were officially accepted to Georgetown. Then I could relax. Right now I couldn't afford any more slipups, just in case they checked on my grades.

Which was why I was doing yet another extra-credit fun run during lunch today for Miss Lynn. "Fun run" indeed, what a misnomer. That'd be like saying "calm gremlin" or "pleasant hag." Or "entertaining history textbook." It was my third fun run this week, and I was positive I was sacrificing years off my already shortened life for a bleeping grade. Still, at least running was so exhausting I couldn't be bored. Unlike right now.

I stifled a yawn. I wanted something—anything—to happen. Maybe Lend would come and rescue me again, and we could go on another magical date and get over the tension that still seemed to linger between us in the quiet moments. Resting my head on my fist, I stared at the door.

What if a zombie came in, reeking of death and decay? He'd totally go for the Vicious Redhead Soccer Girl sitting right by the door. I could take a zombie. That ruler on the teacher's desk looked like a sharp edge, and how cool would my classmates think I was? Especially if I had Tasey.

I sighed, leaning my head back and staring up at the ceiling. It would never work. No ruler would be sharp enough. Besides which, I never bring Tasey to school. And even if I saved everyone in the class, I'd probably still be expelled due to the school's zero tolerance policy on violence.

I'd just have to live without the everlasting appreciation and admiration of my classmates. Truth was, most of them barely noticed me. They had their established cliques, and while they were friendly enough, I didn't socialize with anyone outside school. Part of that wasn't my fault, what with all the time I spent working at the diner and devoting my weekends to Lend.

But if I were being honest, mostly it was because, as much as I wanted to, I didn't fit in here. Their dramas revolved around who was going out with who and who said what to who and who got in where and so on and so forth. My dramas mostly involved whats—as in, What on earth is that horrible creature about to rip out my throat?

Or at least they used to. I'd been on edge all week. Raquel hadn't needed me for anything, which left way too much time to stress about everything. There was nowhere I could go where I felt safe or calm. The diner was all paranormals, and even though Nona acted the same as always, I got the creeps every time she looked at me now. Arianna was like my own personal poltergeist, always home, always infecting the apartment with her moods. Outside made me too nervous—the breeze that followed me everywhere, constantly having to watch the sky for sylphs and the crowds for faeries. I had nowhere to go that was mine.

It was like Jack said: I was homeless.

But right now I was just bored. So, maybe a stray vampire came to the school and . . .

A paper slapped down on my desk and it took me several seconds to realize what I was looking at. My test. My last test! My test with a—

No, that couldn't be right.

I stared in disbelief at the letter gracing the front page. C+? *C+?* Didn't he know how much time I spent studying for this stupid, pointless test? Didn't he know I'd spent half the night before taking it battling the forces of evil? *Didn't he know I needed to get into George*freaking*town?*

The C+ sat there, mocking me. It was probably a good

thing I didn't have Tasey in my bag, or I would have burned that heinous letter right off the page. Class was over before I could register any parting instructions the teacher gave us, and Carlee was standing next to my desk.

"A C+? Nice!"

"Nice doesn't get me into Georgetown," I moaned, perilously close to tears. Please, please let them check my transcripts *before* my new grades were posted.

"You'll get in for sure! You're so smart. Don't worry." She put her arm around my shoulders as we walked together to lunch. "Let's talk about happy things. What should I be for Halloween? I can't decide between a sexy vampire or a sexy fairy. I've got a whole tub of glitter body gel for either costume, if you want to be the one I'm not!"

Faeries and vampires were glittery now?

Honestly.

CARAMEL-COATED COMPLICATIONS

I groaned, holding my stomach. "*Easton Heights* never covered this. Cue dramatic voice-over: 'On the next all-new episode: Halloween gone dangerously wrong. Carys consumes lethal amounts of sugar. Will she live to see Homecoming? And, more terrifying, *Will anyone ask her now that she's gained three pounds?*'"

Arianna frowned as she pinned my wig into place. "No one *made* you eat an entire bag of Tootsie Rolls. Hold still."

Getting ready would be easier if we could use a mirror, but Arianna hated them, so I was sitting in a chair in the middle of the tiny family room. I couldn't complain too much, since there was no way on earth I could have come up with a costume this good on my own. Sometimes it paid to have an undead-former-fashion-school-student for a roommate.

"Okay." She stepped back, admiring her work with a firm nod. "You're good to go."

I jumped up and checked myself out in the bathroom mirror. "Oh, Arianna, this is awesome!"

My red wig and wide purple headband complemented my purple dress, pink tights, and green silk scarf. I always loved the *Scooby-Doo* gang. They were like my exact opposites. They hunted monsters that were revealed to be humans; I got to see humans that were actually monsters. I think they had a better deal. And they got a groovy van out of it, too.

"Fits then?" Arianna called from the other room.

"You are an absolute genius! I'm the best Daphne ever!"

"And so humble, too."

I walked back out to her. She was already at the computer with her game.

"Do you want to come with us?" I asked.

"I don't do Halloween."

"Oh, come on, Halloween is your night!"

She looked up and gave me a dead stare. "Thanks, I'll pass."

I hesitated, feeling guilty. I'd spent hardly any time at all with her lately. I even fell asleep thirty minutes into our all-night marathon the other week. I didn't want to admit it, but that stupid uber-vamp in Sweden had brought all my vampire loathing back to the surface, and I was having a hard time looking directly at Arianna. Plus, the past few weeks she seemed to be really withdrawn and antisocial.

Well, *more* withdrawn and antisocial, at least.

But she'd taken the time to do this awesome costume for me. The least I could do was make her get out. "Come on. It'll be fun! Besides, vampires are hot this year, so you're automatically cool! You don't really want to spend Halloween holed up in this stupid apartment, do you?"

Her eyes narrowed. "That's exactly what I want to do, thank you ever so much. Besides, I'd hate to force my company on you when you clearly don't enjoy it. I don't want your pity, Evie."

"That's not it at all!"

She sighed, turning back to her game. "It's fine, whatever. I get it. I wouldn't want to hang out with me either."

I was about to contradict her when a horn honked outside. I put my hand on her shoulder, but she shrugged it off, not even looking at me. When Arianna got in one of her dark moods, there was no talking her out of it. I tried to shake off the guilt as I raced down the stairs and through the diner. Lend got out of the car as I walked out, a special trip home this Thursday just for me. I frowned. "You didn't dress up!"

He grinned, opening my door for me. "Sure I did. I

dressed up as the non-invisible man!"

I smacked him in the chest. "Lazy."

"Hey, I wear a costume every waking hour. You only dress up once a year, which I believe makes *you* the lazy one. However, you look really hot in pink tights, so I'll let it pass."

"How noble of you." He kissed me, lingering on my lips, and I was filled with warm happiness. We were going to be fine.

I watched out the windows as we drove to his dad's, thrilled to see the first groups of tiny trick-or-treaters. I vaguely remembered trick-or-treating when I was little. One of my foster families made a big deal out of it; we got to carve pumpkins and everything. The woman who ran my last foster home didn't think it was safe, so we had to stay inside and watch some Charlie Brown cartoon three times. I've never liked beagles to this day.

Raquel, of course, thought the holiday was a load of nonsense, with people running around pretending to be the things we protected them from. Plus, she always worried about offending our "coworkers" by making light of their existence. Judging by Arianna's mood, maybe Raquel had been right about that one.

I turned to Lend. "What's on the agenda for tonight?"

"First, pumpkin carving. I've drawn up some designs. We're gonna cream my dad."

I smiled, excited to see what he had drawn. Most of his

sketches lately were for his human anatomy class. I much preferred it when he did it for fun. "Awesome. Then what?"

"We make caramel apples and man the door. The only people who trek out to the house are the local werewolves with kids, so it's always fun to see them."

"Oh. Great!" I said it like I meant it but was disappointed. This was my first normal, teenage Halloween. I had my heart set on something a little more exciting than passing out candy to werewolf pups. Carlee was having a party tonight—her annual Halloween bash—and even though I didn't hang out with anyone who would be there, I was kind of curious. The only real parties I'd ever seen were on TV. Or at the Center, but those were lame. It was always awkward mingling with paranormals that I had personally bagged and tagged. Plus, no one ever spiked the punch.

However, being with Lend trumped everything else, and he hated parties. He was a bit of a homebody, since he'd had to be secluded when he was little before he could control his shape-shifting. And even though when he got older he had the potential to be quite popular (read: hello, hottie), he felt like no one could ever know the real him.

Until me, that is. Which made me all sorts of happy.

Lend looked over at me and smiled. "You are so bad at faking excitement. That's not all we're doing."

I perked up immediately. "Yeah?"

"Well, you're already dressed for it, so I thought we

could go . . . disco bowling."

"Disco bowling? Seriously? Is there such a thing?"

He laughed. "I've never been, but you mentioned bowling a few weeks ago, and I figured tonight of all nights I could go ahead and impress you with my mad lack of bowling skills. Besides which, you look way too hot to waste on trick-or-treaters. They have a costume competition— you're a shoo-in."

I laughed, giddy, and grabbed his hand to kiss his knuckles. I knew he'd rather stay at home, but he planned tonight around making me happy. And he wanted to show me off, which appealed to my vanity more than I cared to admit. Best. Boyfriend. Ever.

"Pictures, please? And if we're going disco bowling, you have to dress up."

He pretended to sigh, but his glamour hair grew out into a massive 'fro and I squealed with delight. Then it shifted into shorter hair with a yellow-blond side part. "I figure with an ascot and blue pants I can do a mean Fred to your Daphne, right?"

Tonight was perfect.

"Aren't those for, like, preschoolers?" I couldn't stop laughing as Lend pulled out bumpers for our gutter. The entire place was lit in neon lights, with a giant disco ball throwing spangled reflections everywhere. Music pulsed so loud we had to shout to be heard, but everyone was having a good time. We even saw Kari and Donna a couple of lanes down, their barking laughter reminiscent of the seals they usually were. They waved happily to me, ignoring the large queue of guys trying to flirt with them.

"Yeah, bumpers are for preschoolers or two teenagers who couldn't stop throwing gutter balls if their lives depended on it. Which, fortunately, they don't. Because we'd be screwed."

I grabbed my glittery hot pink ball (which I was seriously considering buying) and imitated the perfect form a Mohawked guy next to us was using. Instead of shooting straight down the lane and knocking over all the pins, my ball inexplicably went flying backward toward Lend.

"Okay, now we're getting dangerous." Lend brought my ball back and, wrapping himself around me, we threw it together. After pinballing off the bumpers on both sides, it knocked down a whole three pins.

I jumped up and down, screaming. "That's like, practically a strike, right?"

"Good enough for me!"

For Lend's next round he squatted, throwing the ball with both hands from between his legs—and into Mohawk guy's lane. He wasn't nearly as amused as we were, but Lend grinned and apologized, charming his way out of it.

"It's a good thing we're pretty to look at," I said as Lend sat down on the orange plastic seats next to me. "Because we don't have much else going for us as bowlers."

"So you think the blond looks good?"

I ran my fingers through his ridiculous hair. "Really, really not. I like you tall, dark, and handsome. Well, my favorite is tall, invisible, and handsome, but still."

An announcer stopped the blaring disco music to declare the beginning of the costume contest. Lend pulled me up and we started over, when I felt my purse buzzing. My phone! I pulled it out and was surprised to see Carlee's name on the caller ID. Oh, crap, did I forget to tell her I wasn't coming to her party?

"Carlee? What's up? Sorry I couldn't make it!" I shouted over the noise, pulling Lend over to the double doors by the entrance where it was a little quieter. I didn't want Carlee to think I'd ditched her. Even though I had.

"Evie! Evvvvvvie!" She drew my name out, and behind her I could hear the chatter of way too many hyper teenage voices. "Girl, you came through for me! I owe you one!"

"What?"

"Your friend! You told him about the party, you sly little brat."

"What friend?"

"Jack, of course!"

HAPPY FREAKING
HALLOWEEN

I put a finger to my free ear to hear the phone better, angling myself away from Lend. "Wait, what? *Who* is there?" Carlee couldn't have said what I thought she said.

"Jack, the cute one! Thanks for telling him to come. I'm so over John! And so glad I went for the slutty angel costume! Can you give me any hints? His likes, dislikes, whatever?"

"He's— Jack is *there*? Now?" Lend turned his head sharply, suddenly focused on the conversation.

"Yeah, he's—wait—" A girl screamed shrilly in the background, and then loud cheers erupted. Carlee swore, laughing. "He flipped off the second floor balcony and landed in the foyer!"

I put a hand over my eyes, trying to figure out a way to make this better. Jack couldn't be there. My worlds were not supposed to mix like that. How did he even find out about it? And, knowing Jack, he was bound to get them into some sort of trouble. It's what he did. Besides which, the thought of Jack and Carlee making out made me feel vaguely ill, and I knew it wasn't because of the caramel apples I'd overdosed on at Lend's house. What happened when he disappeared and broke her heart? I'd lose the only normal friend I had. And if he told her about his real life—well, she'd probably think I was crazy by association. I didn't want to spend the rest of my senior year totally friendless.

"Can you put him on the phone? Carlee? Put Jack on the phone."

She was laughing, shouting something that I couldn't understand over the background noise. "Okay, I've gotta go—everyone's heading to the cemetery! Thanks again— full dish tomorrow, girl!"

The line went dead. "Oh, *bleep*." I flipped my phone shut, momentarily paralyzed. This had disaster written all over it. Jack wasn't exactly the picture of discretion—or sanity, for that matter—and if he told her my secrets . . .

"Jack, huh." Lend's voice was flat, carefully controlled.

I shook my head, hating Jack for shattering our perfect evening. "I guess he showed up at Carlee's party."

"Oh." Lend didn't say anything. I couldn't fight down the rising panic over what Jack would do or say. The lights strobed as the costume parade started. We were missing it.

"I should— They're all going to the cemetery. I should make sure Jack doesn't get into trouble."

"If you think so." Again with the flat voice. Lend trying not to betray any emotion was a lot worse than him being openly annoyed about something. "I have to go back to school tonight, anyway. I can drop you off—it's on the way. Will you have a ride back?"

"Yeah, I can get one with Carlee." Even if I couldn't, the cemetery was only about a mile from the diner. It'd be easier to walk back than asking Lend to either wait or come with me. Our night wasn't supposed to end like this. Suck, suck, sucktastic.

"Are you sure?"

"I'm sure. Thanks."

The drive was painful, and every minute that passed in strained silence made me that much more determined to wring Jack's neck. My phone rang when we were nearly there and I flipped it open.

"Carlee? What happened?"

"It's Arianna."

"Oh. What's up?"

"I can't stay in this apartment another minute. They're doing a slasher flick marathon at Crown Theater. Where are you guys?"

My heart sank. Perfect. She'd pick now to want to socialize. "Umm, actually, I'm going to a party thing, and Lend was gonna head back to school. But I can maybe meet you later?" I waited for her response, but the line went flat. "Great," I muttered, throwing the phone into my purse.

Lend pulled up in front of the wrought iron fence that lined the perimeter of the cemetery. It was a beautiful spot—and, trust me, I've seen more than my fair share of cemeteries. Massive ivy-covered trees shaded the entire thing and gave it a sense of privacy. Narrow, paved pathways wound throughout, lined periodically with stone benches. During the day it was peaceful, lovely, as nice a spot for an eternal resting place as you could ask.

At night? Yeah, kind of creepy. You couldn't see more than twenty feet in any direction thanks to the trees, and the whole thing was poorly lit by the occasional pathetic lamppost.

"Do you have Tasey?" Lend asked.

I let out a nervous laugh. "I don't usually bring her on our dates, oddly enough. Besides, this is your dad's territory. It's probably the safest cemetery in the world." The vampires here were almost militant in their regulation of one another. There's no way they'd let someone mess around in their area and draw attention.

"You have your necklace, though?"

I smiled at him and pulled it out from under my dress.

"Yup. I'll be fine. And if I had Tasey, I'd probably just use it on Jack."

I hoped for a laugh, but Lend sighed and nodded. "I'll see you tomorrow night then."

"Yeah." I leaned in and was rewarded with a quick kiss, our lips barely brushing. Stupid, stupid Jack. I climbed out of the car and Lend waited until I was through the gate and down the path a bit before I heard him drive away.

A shout and some distant, nervous laughter drifted through the trees, and I gritted my teeth. After several twists and turns, I found the group, gathered around one of the benches. They seemed to be focused on someone standing on the bench in the center. I got closer and narrowed my eyes. Jack—of course. He did a standing backflip off the bench to applause.

Then he noticed me and grinned as though seeing me was a welcome surprise. "Evie! You made it!"

"Yeah, funny thing, that. *I* was actually invited. How did you get here?"

"Evie! Yay!" Carlee threw her arms around me. She had to be freezing in a tiny white sleeveless dress, go-go boots, and wings. "Isn't this awesome?"

"Oh. Yeah. Totally. Love cemeteries. Let me guess— Jack's idea?"

"Yes!" She giggled. "I don't know why we didn't think of it sooner!"

Jack's eyes were bright, almost feverish in his excitement.

"Isn't this fun? I haven't been to a party like this, well, ever!" I still hated him for dragging me out here, but part of me was jealous. This was the exact thing I'd always imagined for a Halloween night party, but I had to play Miss Responsible now and get him away before he did any damage. Then again, this didn't look anywhere near as fun as the bowling had been. It was mostly just cold, and half the students looked like they were working up to being good and drunk.

"Hey!" A lanky, dark-haired guy I recognized from the hallways at school stood on the bench to get everyone's attention. "Hide-and-seek! Feel free to hide in pairs." He gave a leering wink, then jumped down. Carlee turned to Jack, way too excited, but the guy slapped her on the shoulder. "Carlee's it!"

With shrieks, everyone scattered into the darkness. Carlee stuck her lip out in an exaggerated pout. "Don't hide too hard, okay, Jack?"

He winked at her. She giggled. And I threw up a little in my mouth. He turned to run into the trees and I was forced to follow him. If this was what parties were, well, lame. Although I probably wouldn't have thought it as lame if I were with Lend.

When I caught up, I grabbed Jack's arm. "What are you doing here?"

"Hiding! That's how you play the game, right? I thought the title hide-and-seek was fairly self-explanatory. Then again, you are blond."

"So are you, idiot. Again, what are you doing *here*?"

He shrugged. "I thought it would be fun. I found the invitation on your bed the other week."

I hadn't seen Jack since I got the invite. Which meant he was in my apartment when I wasn't home *and* snooping through my stuff. "What were you doing in my room?!"

"I stopped by to make sure you were okay. You've seemed kind of down lately."

I frowned, taken aback. I'd expected a glib answer, but he seemed sincere. "Oh. Well, don't mess with my stuff. And you shouldn't be here."

"Come on. What's wrong with what we're doing? Not everything is life and death. A little party never hurt anyone." He turned and ran deeper into the trees, and I followed him with a groan. I needed to get him out of here, even if he did genuinely seem to be having a good time and hadn't caused any damage that I could see. So far. But how dare he accuse me of not being able to have fun? I'd been having plenty of fun before he ruined it.

My phone rang and I pulled it out. Lend. "Hello?"

"Did you find him?"

"Yup. We're leaving."

"He's coming back with you?"

"No! I'm just getting him away from the innocent high schoolers." Someone screamed close by and I stiffened, all senses on alert, but then the scream melted into laughter and playful shrieks.

"Probably a good idea."

I bit my lip, scanning the darkness for Jack. I'd lost him. "Yeah." I struggled for something else to say.

"Call me when you get home, okay? I want to make sure you get back safe."

"Sure, of course."

He sighed heavily. "I should have stayed. I'm turning around."

"No, really, it's okay. Jack's my problem, not yours. I'll call you when I get home, and you'll be back tomorrow night."

"Alright." The static silence between us felt like the miles were stretching, deepening. "Talk to you soon then?"

"Yeah. Bye."

I hung up the phone, staring sadly at it for a moment. Then I looked around, determined to find Jack and get him out of here so I could call Lend back. I was deeper into the cemetery than I'd ever been—in fact, I wondered if I was even still in it or if there was no fence separating the outer boundaries from the surrounding woods. The hairs on the back of my neck rose. It felt like I was being watched.

Something grabbed my arm, and I screamed, dropping my phone.

"Hey-oh, aren't you jumpy tonight?" Jack grinned at me.

I kicked him in the shin, then leaned down and picked up my phone. I pocketed it and turned back toward Jack. "Let's go."

He perked up. "Where to? If you're bored here, I'm sure I could find us a more entertaining party in New York." He held out his hand, and although it was too dark to see his dimples, I could practically feel them. "Come on."

I shook my head. I couldn't hang out with Jack, even if he would take me places I'd never see otherwise. It'd be too much of a betrayal of Lend. "I'm going home."

A velvet voice bled out of the darkness. "So soon, *Liebchen?*"

UBER–BLEEP

I froze, terrified, as a shadow detached itself from a nearby tree and walked forward.

"Are you surprised to see me, little monster?" His voice was soft, the trace of a German accent low and subtle.

I swallowed hard, nodding before I could think better of it. What the bleep was Uber-vamp doing here? And how was I going to get out of this?

He smiled, his perfect white glamour teeth shining over his blackened, dead ones. "If it makes you feel any better, I am pleasantly surprised to see you, as well."

"How did you get here?" I asked, taking a small step back

as I tried to think of a way to stall, to call for IPCA help, to do anything. Vampires had no business being strong. It made things so much more complicated. And scary.

"That is the question, now, isn't it?" He considered me calmly, not moving forward. "I was in my cell in that hateful institution when someone attacked me from behind, and then I woke up here. And now you are here, too. It would appear that this is a night for strange coincidences and monsters in the dark."

"Wait—someone jumped you from behind? In your locked cell? And you didn't see them?"

He nodded, nonplussed. "Where are we?"

I frowned, ignoring his question. There was no way this was a strange coincidence. Someone knocked him out, got him out of the Center, and brought him here—somehow knowing exactly where I would be. There was only one type of someone who could pull that off.

Faeries. Of course. It had to be a faerie. The question was, which one? Was this some sort of joke on Reth's part? He had deliberately put me in harm's way before when he brought Vivian to the Center. But I couldn't see any point to this.

Then again, there was a whole dark court of faeries who hated me, not the least of which was Fehl, who was nearly killed by Vivian last spring. And there was that faerie who showed up at the Center. She hadn't seemed very friendly. Plus Nona, who was definitely in contact with at least one faerie that I knew of. And if what Reth had said was true, I was supposed to do something for his group of faeries. When I chose not to, I kinda screwed up all their big, prophetic plans. So basically, you'd be hard-pressed to find a faerie who *didn't* want to hurt me. The sylph, the fossegrim, now this—there had to be someone behind it. Someone out to get me. The same someones who had always been out to get me.

"Bleeping faeries," I muttered darkly. Why couldn't they leave me alone?

Uber-vamp's eyes lit up. "Faeries? Do you know where I can find one?"

I rolled my eyes. "Trust me, if I could, I'd set you loose on the whole race."

Someone screamed and giggled close by, and Uber-vamp and I both snapped our attention to the direction of the sound.

"Friends of yours?" he asked, and ice spread through my stomach.

"Humans."

"Pity. I'm so very thirsty. Still, you and I have unfinished business, *Liebchen*."

I pinched the bridge of my nose. I didn't want to be around him, be reminded of how badly I'd wanted to take his soul that night. "Look. I'm tired, and things haven't gone the way I wanted tonight. I'd really rather not deal with you right now, so what do you say we let Jack here escort you back to the Center. I'll visit you soon, and we can have a nice, long talk then."

He laughed. "I think not."

Something clicked and I grinned at him. "Well, it doesn't really matter anyway, since your ankle tracker tells IPCA exactly where you are, and they'll be here any minute." Oh, bless you, IPCA technology.

He looked around, his movements slow and unconcerned. "And yet here we are, still, and *they* are nowhere to be seen."

I frowned. He had a point. They should have been here almost instantly. Why weren't they?

"Umm," Jack said, reminding me that he was still standing behind me, "any ideas, Evie? I seem to be fresh out of baseball bats." Uber-vamp directed a chilling glare in Jack's direction. I inwardly cursed the idiot boy for bringing it up and putting himself in danger, too.

"I'm guessing you didn't bring your communicator."

"In hindsight, not a clever move on my part."

So we were on our own, then. I reached for Tasey before remembering I'd left her at home, safe and sound in my sock drawer. Not good.

We all stood there, the tension palpable in the darkness. Uber-vamp feinted forward and I shouted, aiming a kick at him. He darted to the side, dodging me, and I bent down and grabbed a solid stick from the forest floor. Bless Jack's unintentional foresight in bringing us back here. I broke it in half over my knee and held it out, ready for his next charge. I'd never staked a vampire before—the thought made me sick—but I'd make an exception if it meant not dying. Hopefully he was weakened from not drinking paranormal blood during his time in the Center.

Suddenly someone came skipping out of the darkness next to him.

"Jack! There you are!" Carlee squealed.

Not her! "Carlee, run!"

"Come here, my dear," Uber-vamp said, his voice low and commanding. I ran forward but was too late. She looked up into his eyes and that was all it took.

"Course," she murmured, her voice sleepy, happy, and downright dopey. She leaned into him and he put his arm around her, looking up at me with a gloating smile. Great. My clueless, sweet friend was now under the thrall of the strongest vampire alive, and it was my own stupid fault for being a murderous-paranormal magnet.

"Let her go."

He stroked her neck with his dead hand as she nestled happily into his shoulder. "Drop the stake."

I clutched it, trying to think of any way out of this. I could rush him. If I went fast enough, he wouldn't have time to dodge.

"I'll break her neck," he said cheerfully, anticipating my thoughts.

Taking a deep breath, I shook my head. I didn't want

my hands free. I didn't want to have to make this choice. Not now. Not him. My fingers had already started tingling, my veins rushing, and I was hyperaware of the night air, almost nudging me forward. In the darkness I could see it, that hint of light around his heart. "Trust me," I whispered, "I'm safer armed."

His fingers squeezed Carlee's neck, digging into the skin. Her breath caught, but if anything she looked happier. "Now, please."

I dropped the stick, and losing that weight in my hand felt like losing my last defense. There was nothing between me and the vamp's soul now. I looked up at the night sky, clouded over without a hint of stars. Why couldn't anything ever be easy?

"Do something," Jack prodded from behind me.

I shot a glare back at him. This whole thing was his fault. No, it was the faeries' fault. Still. I should have been winning a costume contest with Lend, not fighting for my own soul and Carlee's life. I let out a frustrated growl. "I am so *sick* of moral dilemmas!"

Uber-vamp frowned. "Beg pardon?"

"Don't make me do this. You remember in the alley? You knew then. I saw it—your instincts kicking in, telling you to be afraid of me." I leaned forward, my hands balled into fists and trembling at my sides. "You should listen to your instincts."

He smiled, licking his sharp teeth. "I'm afraid I'm rather

more curious than frightened. I want to taste you, find out what kind of monster you are."

"Good luck with that." I narrowed my eyes, stretching out my fingers. No choice. I had no choice. This wasn't my fault. I was out of options.

He laughed, and before I could react he threw Carlee at Jack, knocking them both to the ground. My eyes still on them, I wasn't ready for him to barrel into me. We flew through the air together, landing hard on the ground with him on top of me. He snarled, baring his teeth, and went for my throat.

His fangs pierced my neck. I screamed and shoved my hand against his chest. This time when the channel opened I was ready. Anger coursing through me, I threw it open wider, pulling as much as I could, as fast as I could. Forget defending myself. I was going to end this. His back arched but he was too shocked, in too much pain to get away.

Then someone shouted and slammed into Uber-vamp, knocking him off me and breaking the connection. My heart raced and I gasped for breath, body swirling with energy, foreign and delicious. I wanted the rest of him. I pushed up to sitting, wanting to find the vampire, drain him completely.

That's when I saw Lend, on top of Uber-vamp, punching him again and again in the face until he was sure the vampire wasn't going anywhere. And then what I'd done—what I was going to finish—came crashing down on me. I dropped onto my back and put my hands over my face.

I would have killed him.

I *wanted* to.

GUILTY IS
AS GUILTY DOES

*L*end didn't take his arm from around my shoulders, hugging me as much as holding me up. Even though I buzzed with nervous, guilty energy, I felt hollowed out, like I could collapse at any moment. Raquel paced back and forth in front of us, her pumps snapping twigs. After David called her she'd wanted to take us to the Center to talk, but Lend refused.

Jack appeared, out of breath. "Told everyone the cops were coming; the cemetery's cleared." Luckily Carlee didn't remember anything from being under the vampire's compulsion; she just felt a little dizzy and suspected someone of spiking her drink. If only. Jack had taken her back to the group, none the wiser.

He looked at Lend and glowered. "I was just about to save her. You didn't need to come."

I glared at him. He hadn't saved me. Lend had. He thought he'd saved me from being drained, but really he'd saved me from draining the vampire. I wondered what he'd think if he knew he'd attacked the wrong monster.

No. I wasn't a monster. Uber-vamp deserved it. And Lend saved me from myself. It was fine.

"Look," I said, "it doesn't make sense. There's no other explanation besides the faeries!"

"But why would a faerie take the vampire from the Center?"

I forced my eyes not to roll. "Umm, to kill me? Because they hate me? They sent Vivian after me before. This is probably just the Dark Queen's new tactic. There've been too many faerie coincidences and weird attacks lately."

"But only the transport faeries even knew about the vampire being in the Center."

"It only takes one, now, doesn't it?" Lend said.

Raquel sighed; I was too tired and edgy to even try and interpret. "I checked our logs, and both transport faeries that handled him were on assignment and accounted for the entire night."

"Then how do you explain his ankle tracker being deactivated?" I asked.

She rubbed her eyes. "I can't. It could have been a data entry error. We couldn't tell if the tracker's locator had ever been properly activated, which shouldn't have been a problem, since he was never supposed to be released from Containment."

"I'm so comforted."

"We've got him in our high-security section now, and I promise there's no way even a faerie can get him out."

I folded my arms. I knew I was being petulant, but it was late, I was tired, and my sugar high had crashed in the worst possible way. I hated tonight. I hated what I'd done. I hated that I didn't hate it, and part of me felt like it was totally justified. There were enough unanswered questions in my life; I didn't like having to wonder whether or not I was a good person.

"Fine. I'm going home. And if I'm tardy for school because I sleep in, I expect you to call and excuse it."

Patting me on the hand, Raquel checked my neck again, then Lend took me home. He came upstairs with me and held me when I burst into tears as soon as we got to my room.

"I'm so sorry, I never should have let you go alone. If I hadn't come back . . . I can't even think about it. Evie, I'm so, so sorry."

I shook my head, burying my face in his chest. He had no idea. "It's not your fault. Thanks for . . . saving me."

He stayed with me until two or three. I wasn't crying

anymore, and after checking my neck wound again and making me swear to call him if I needed anything else at all, he headed back to school for his early morning lab.

I lay in bed, fully dressed in my stupid costume, exhausted but unable to stop my mind from spinning in angry circles. Of course it had been a faerie who set Uber-vamp loose on me. Apparently now that I was dangerous, they were sending other paranormals to do their dirty work. Typical faeries— devious *and* lazy. It was their fault I'd lost control and nearly drained the vampire all the way. Their fault, not mine.

I didn't know I'd fallen asleep until I realized Vivian was sitting next to me on a grassy hill.

"What's wrong this time?"

I startled, looking at her and biting my lip. I hadn't talked with her since the sylph. She was the person most likely to understand what I was going through, how bad I felt about what I'd done, but how justified it was, too.

She was also the last person on the planet I could talk to. Because if I did, then I admitted I was as weak as she was. No. I wasn't like her. I was defending myself!

But then again, it wasn't really her fault, was it? "It's all the faeries' fault. Everything. You shouldn't be here, like this."

She narrowed her eyes thoughtfully, then looked down at the grass she was sitting on, pulling some out between her fingers. "I made my choices, Evie. They were the wrong ones."

"But the faeries forced you! They tricked you!" It was their fault everything was wrong, their fault Lish was dead, their fault I couldn't be happy.

She sighed. "Listen. I did what I did. And I can't make it right. No faerie made me kill those paranormals. I *liked* what I was doing." I opened my mouth to argue with her, but she put her hand over mine. "No. I know you're trying to forgive me, but don't rationalize it. You owe your friends more than that. I didn't kill them because faeries made me—I killed them because I was desperate and alone and I wanted to. I thought I was doing them a favor, but, more than that, I liked the way it made me feel. And that's the worst part. It was always, always about me. And if you hadn't stopped me, I'd probably still be doing it."

Her words hung heavy between us. An ugly darkness, cold and empty, seeped through my own sad little soul. I wanted her to blame the faeries. Why did she have to bring all this stuff up when I wanted to forget it? And why the bleep did *her* confessions make *me* feel guilty?

"But the faeries," I said, a whine creeping into my voice. "They ruined your life. They won't stop making mine a mess. Without them, we could have—everything would be different. Easier."

Vivian laughed, her voice hard. "Screw the fey—they can't touch me now. And I can't touch them, more's the pity. I'd kill every single one of them if I could for what they did to us. But I'm pretty sure that without them neither of us would exist. It's probably better I'm stuck here in dream-land so I don't have any more souls on my hands. Literally."

She grinned wickedly and elbowed me. I let out a pained laugh, but really I wanted normal sleep tonight, sleep free from conversations that hurt my head and made me ache.

I closed my eyes and opened them to my dark room. For a minute I thought I was still asleep, that Viv and I had switched locations, until I realized the person sitting on the edge of my bed staring at me wasn't my crazy sister.

MATTERS OF LIFE AND UNDEATH

I sat up in bed, my heart racing, and swallowed the scream just in time as I recognized the spiky hair. I flicked on the lamp by my bedside. "Arianna? You scared the crap out of me. What's wrong?"

She wasn't staring at me but rather right past my head, at a blank spot on the wall. Her glamour eyes looked as dead as her real ones. "I don't understand it. Any of it."

"I'm sorry?"

Her eyes focused on me, and she shook her head slowly. "Lend told me what happened. About the vampire. Evie, I don't want to be one. This isn't me, this thing, this living, endless nightmare I've become. I shouldn't exist. I wish I didn't." Her voice was low, even. It was scarier than if she were upset or crying. "Did you know my name isn't Arianna? It was Ann. I hated that name. Plain and boring, like me, and my life, and my family. I hated my family, too. They were WASPs, as middle-class and conventional as possible. My mom did crafts and worked on the school board, and my dad was an accountant. They wanted me to be blond, and happy, and on teams. They were always pushing teams—swim, cheer, track, it didn't matter. They wanted me to fit somewhere. That was the last thing I wanted.

"My mom and I used to fight over what color my hair was, my newest piercing, my music. When I dropped out and left for fashion school, I didn't say good-bye, or thank you, or I love you. I was glad to leave them. They told me I was being stupid, moving to a big city where I didn't know anyone and barely had enough money to live. I didn't care. I was finally going to figure out who I was, find somewhere I could be different.

"Then I met Felix, and he was dark and delicious and everything my family wasn't. He told me I belonged with him, that our love would last forever, that he saw who I really was, who I could be. He promised to show me the world. I never noticed that his world was always night.

"And then he bit me, and the first time I liked it. But

then he did it again, and drank my blood, and I passed out. When I woke up, he told me what he was. I didn't believe him, thought he was crazy. I'd let him in too fast, and he knew where I went to school, where I worked, where I lived. I didn't feel safe anywhere. So I went home. I got there at night, pulled up in front of the house. I could see my parents through the bay window, reading in the living room, and it was light, and warm, and safe. I started up the walk, and then Felix stood from where he was sitting on my porch, waiting for me.

"My parents found me there the next morning, dead."

I fought back tears. I'd never heard her talk about how this happened to her. Vampires had always made the least sense to me—how could a human become an immortal paranormal, and why did they have glamours? Werewolves were weird, sure, but they didn't have immortality or glamours. Raquel had never been able to explain where vampires came from. All she knew was that in order to become one, you have to be bitten more than once over the space of a month or so, and the vamp has to leave you alive just enough for the change to take place before your heart stops. It's not easy, and for the most part vampires have no interest in swelling their ranks. Good thing, too, because if all it took was one bite, the world would have been overrun by bloodsuckers centuries ago.

Arianna always seemed so tough, so jaded, sometimes I even wondered if she had sought out a vampire and been changed on purpose. In spite of her emotionless tone, my heart broke knowing the truth—she was just a girl trying to find a place to fit in. It sounded familiar.

She continued. "Of course, I don't remember them finding me. The next thing I knew, I woke up in a morgue. Felix was there, waiting for me, with this look on his face. He was so excited. He thought he'd done something wonderful."

"Where is he now?" I whispered.

"I went with him, because I had nowhere else to go and no idea how to live as a vampire. Then he picked out a lonely, artistic girl, we stalked her, and he lured her into an alley for us."

My stomach clenched. I didn't think Arianna had ever killed a person. Did David know about her past?

She closed her eyes. "And when Felix lulled her into bending her head to the side and offering us her neck, I killed him."

"Wait—you killed *him*?"

She looked at me for the first time since she started her story. "I was already this thing, this mockery of life. He took away everything that I was, everything I could have been. I wasn't going to let him do that to anyone else."

I sat, dumbly, with no idea what to say. She and David were total pacifists when it came to dealing with other paranormals, but she'd killed another vamp to protect an innocent girl. Did that make what I did okay, then? Because

Uber-vamp would have hurt other people. Carlee, the other kids. I know he would have. I shook my head, focusing. "Arianna, I'm so sorry."

She smiled sadly. "Doesn't matter. Eventually I found David, and here I am. And here I'll stay, because eternal life is no life at all, and I have no idea what to do about it. Ann's dead, and I'm stuck here, dead and alive and neither."

I put my hand on her shoulder. "You're alive! You're still a person."

She looked at me, her eyes sharp once again. "Don't lie to me, Evie. You can see exactly what I am."

I cringed, wondering how bad a job I'd done all these months of pretending like I wasn't horrified by the way she looked under her glamour. "That's not you, though!"

"I know what I am. I just don't understand why." She stood. "I shouldn't have woken you up. Sometimes I like to watch you sleep, though. I wish I could sleep. Sleep and never wake up."

Before I could say anything she walked out of my room and out of the apartment. I sat, stunned, then flopped back onto my bed.

Why had I ever thought life would be easier out of the Center?

TREE HUGGER

Lend sat, touching me from our shoulders down to our feet, in the diner booth. One perk to being attacked by Uber-vamp was that Lend had been distinctly silent on the issue of IPCA's containment methods. Seeing firsthand what some paranormals did made IPCA's standards a lot less suspect.

Unfortunately that was about the only good thing to come out of last night. It was all I could do not to bounce up and down, my fingers tapping out a nervous pattern on the table. I felt keyed up, full to bursting with anxious energy. I didn't want to think where it came from. I hoped it wasn't Uber-vamp's soul inside me. It was just . . . I don't know, leftover nerves. That was it.

I jumped as Nona set our plates down on the table, then swished back to the kitchen.

"Are you sure you're okay?" Lend asked.

"Fine. Fine. I'm fine." I reached up to scratch my neck but stopped. It was sore but already healing. If it scarred, Uber-vamp was going to pay.

Then again, he already had. My stomach soured, the grilled cheese sandwich in front of me suddenly inedible.

"Hey, kids." David slid in across from us, worry creasing his forehead as he looked at my neck. "How are you, Evie?"

I waved a hand dismissively, bouncing my knee up and down under the table. "Just tired. Skipped school today to sleep. I'll be okay. Where's Arianna?" She hadn't been home this morning. She was *always* home. The way she talked last night, I couldn't help but wonder if maybe she was tired enough of eternal life to do something about it. Poltergeist Steve flashed through my mind and I struggled not to panic. Whatever else Arianna was, she was my friend. I couldn't lose her.

"She texted, said she couldn't make the meeting today."

I wasn't sure whether that was a good sign or not. At least she was still in contact with David. I'd have to get her alone, talk to her, do something to make things better. If only I could figure out what.

"Raquel called this morning, too."

I looked up, surprised. "Do you two talk a lot?"

David gave a noncommittal shrug. "She wanted to make sure I was checking up on you. She's worried. You think the attack last night was related to the fey?"

Lend gently removed my hand from where I was unconsciously peeling at the bandage. He kept my hand in his, stroking it with his thumb. I stopped bouncing my knee and took a deep breath. Focusing on Lend's hand helped me calm down.

"Yeah. I do. There have been too many weird things. First the sylph, then the fossegrim—"

"But wasn't that random? Jack dropped you in the water."

"Oh." I frowned. I hadn't thought about that. How would the faeries have known I would hit the water there, then? Maybe my luck just sucked. Then again, I already knew that. "But Reth's been here a couple of times, and then there was the faerie I saw walking down the street, plus a faerie showed up at the Center when I was there and Raquel had to get rid of her. And then the vampire. No one but a faerie could have pulled that off."

"True." David rubbed his eyes wearily. Lend did the exact same thing when he was worried. Sometimes their similarities, the way they laughed at old jokes I would never get, the warm playful ease they had with each other made me hurt. Lend was so lucky to have a dad like David. I wished it were my dad rushing here to check up on me instead of my boyfriend's.

I felt eyes on me and looked up to see the same froglike old woman that had ahemed at Lend and me kissing on the sidewalk what felt like an eternity ago. She was outside the diner, staring in through the window. At me. I narrowed my eyes, but then the woman looked past me at something and abruptly turned around and walked away. I whipped around to see Grnlllll, making a furious shooing motion with her small, pawlike hands.

"What was that about?" I asked, but the gnome ignored me entirely, going back behind the counter where she couldn't be seen. Kari and Donna were sitting there on barstools, halibut plates untouched as they watched me with their huge, round eyes. They broke into identical playful smiles. Mischievous smiles . . .

"Maybe this isn't *just* the faeries, though," I said, suspicion rising. I stood and walked straight back toward the kitchen. Grnlllll jumped out in front of me, trying to block my way and grumbling something, but I stepped over her and burst through the door.

Nona was back there, leaning over a large, intricately carved wooden bowl.

And *talking* to it.

". . . under our care. Continue the gathering. Things will be in place when the time is right, and—"

Nona looked up, surprised to see me. "Who are you talking to?" I demanded, rushing over. Before I could get to the bowl she swished her hand in it, and when I leaned over all I saw was rippling water. "What are you doing?"

Her beautiful lips broke into that same infuriating smile. "Nothing, child."

"Liar!" I shouted. I heard the door behind me open again.

"What's the problem?" David asked.

"She is!" I pointed an angry finger at the tree spirit. "She's lying! She was talking to a bucket of water. Something is going on, but she won't tell me what. First she was meeting with Reth, now there are all the weird new paranormals in town, and they watch me! I know they're watching me!" I turned my glare back to her. "You're working with the faeries, aren't you?"

Nona's face went serious. "No, child. I am not. The fey are no friends of my kind. And I promise you what I have always promised—you are safe here. I will never let harm befall you while you are under my care."

"But I'm *not* under your care!"

"Evie," David said, his voice even as he put a hand on my shoulder. Lend stood protectively on my other side. "I've known Nona for a long time now. And huldras can't lie. She isn't trying to hurt you."

"Please excuse me," Nona said, picking up the bowl and carrying it out the back door.

I was left fuming. "How do you know they can't lie? Besides, what is she even doing here? Why would a tree spirit want to run a diner?"

David shrugged. "A lot of elementals and paranormals mix with humans every now and again. It's entertaining, I guess." Was that how he viewed Cresseda's relationship with him? He entertained her for a bit? I didn't understand how he lived with that kind of pain and rejection.

I shook my head. "I don't buy it." My head hurt. My neck hurt. My brain hurt. My whole *life* hurt today.

"If Nona wanted to harm you or turn you over to the faeries, wouldn't she have done it already?" Lend asked. "I mean, you've lived here for months now. I know weird things have been happening, but I really don't think Nona's behind them."

I sighed. He was probably right. "But what about the staring? They're always staring at me!"

"You are rather nice to look at, you know."

"Har, har."

"Seriously, though, they're probably just curious. Most of them don't know what you are, but they know that you know what *they* are. It's not normal. Simple curiosity."

"Fine," I mumbled. Maybe I was being paranoid.

Lend put his arms around me, resting his forehead against mine. "Believe it or not, I worry more about your safety than you do. And if you're really worried about it, let's get you out of here. You can move back in with my dad. Right?"

David nodded. "If it'll make you feel better, of course."

I shook my head. I didn't want to live with David again

without Lend there. I liked him, but, awkward. And I really didn't want to leave Arianna alone. They were right. I was probably overreacting about Nona. This was faerie mischief, not hers.

Still, I knew when I was being lied to. And I was never taking the trash out for that ratty little gnome again.

VAMPTASTIC

I was going to go crazy. Why couldn't early decision be, well, early? All this beginning-of-December nonsense was infuriating. How long did it take to look through a sheet of grades, a couple of test scores, and some pointless essays? Images of a stack of papers with my entire future inside just sitting on someone's desk tormented me while I listened to teachers drone on about something that couldn't possibly matter as much.

When the school deemed my head acceptably full of hypotenuses and chemical bonds and metaphors, I was set free. As per my new ritual, I begged Carlee to give me a ride home so I could get to the mailbox sooner. She shook her head as I bounced nervously in my seat.

"If they said the beginning of December, it's not going to be there yet. If anything, it'll probably be late."

"I know." She was right. I knew she was right. But I couldn't calm down until I was *sure* she was right. I watched the trees fly by, for once not terrified of Carlee's erratic, speedy driving. Faster, faster!

"Besides, you haven't been waiting that long. My cousin had to wait, like, four months for her acceptance to VU."

I sighed heavily. "It's been *forever*." I had been patient—really, really patient—for so long after I sent in my application. Being attacked by Uber-vamp and attempting to talk to a completely unresponsive Arianna after her little midnight chat were distractions (not necessarily pleasant ones), and I'd been trying to focus on other things. Still, I didn't think I could take much more of the waiting. How could I think about anything else? Say what you will about zombies and their hygiene issues, at least they kill you fast. College acceptance boards? They like to draw out the torture as long as possible.

"So, have you heard from Jack lately?"

I fidgeted guiltily in my seat, forced to think of something besides Georgetown. Carlee might not remember Uber-vamp throwing her around on Halloween, but she did remember flirting up a storm with Jack.

"No, he kinda dropped off the face of the planet. He does that."

"Oh." She nodded but looked disappointed. I wished I knew some nice, normal boy to introduce her to so I could make up for putting Jack in her world. But I only had one nice boy in my life, and he was far from normal. Also, all mine.

We pulled up in front of the diner and I almost fell out of the car, barely gasping good-bye to long-suffering Carlee as I dashed for the mailbox. I knew it was irrational, but I had a strange feeling about today. Anticipation had been building all afternoon, and now it felt like I was ready to burst. It was only two weeks until the date they gave us. Plus, it was a Tuesday, which meant they had Monday to catch up and mail it, so if I got it now I'd call Lend and he'd come home early to celebrate and we'd plan our lives together and—

The mailbox was empty.

I let off a string of curses that would put even the boy's locker room to shame, ending with an emphatic kick to the mailbox post. And the worst part was of *course* it wasn't there yet. My weird nerves all day were pointless.

I stomped upstairs, ignoring Grnlllll's barked order to do something or other. Raquel hadn't needed me the last two weeks (I suspected she felt guilty over Uber-vamp and the fact that I'd only met him because of a mission she sent me on), so I'd been making up shifts. Although there were still an unusual number of new paranormals in town, I hadn't seen any more faeries, and Nona continued to defy my attempts to catch her doing something suspicious.

Today, however, I had better things to do than help in the kitchen and worry about paranormals. My plans revolved around going into my room and stewing for several hours.

I flopped onto my bed and tried to burn a hole in the ceiling with my glare. It was a good thing, not getting the letter today. If they were going to reject me, they would probably do it early. Those beautiful, thick acceptance packets took time to put together. No doubt they placed every sheet, every paper with personalized love and attention.

I would get in. I had to get in. But why, oh why, couldn't they just tell me and release me from this agony?

My communicator beeped mutedly from its honored place in my sock drawer. I was shocked to realize how much time I'd managed to stew—it was already dusk. Anxious for something, anything to distract me from application purgatory, I flung my socks across the room, digging out the communicator. The message read *Vamp job, immediately, yes or no.*

Okay, maybe there were things worse than waiting. Stupid vampires. Still, it had to be done. I punched in a quick yes and had barely taken off my necklace and holstered Tasey when a light flashed on the wall and Jack held out his hand.

I grabbed it before the door closed and he yanked me through. "Hallo, Evie. Having a nice day?"

I scowled. "No. Let's get this over with. And if you drop

me into another river, I swear this time I am taking you with me."

He laughed, the idiot boy, and we hurried through the emptiness together. I tried to focus on my anger and annoyance and not think about facing a vamp again. I would *not* be tempted to drain another paranormal. Not ever. Lend and I were in a good place, and I was doing better. I didn't feel weird most of the time. The breeze still trailed me, I was spending more time than usual in the bath and seemed to sense running water whenever I was near it, but this new nervous energy was just stress. That's all. I figured I hadn't really taken that much from Uber-vamp, and the more I thought about it, the more I was sure it had been the right choice.

Still, having to confront another vampire made me edgy.

We came out in a dirty, narrow alley between two brightly painted wood buildings. "And no sudden plummets to your death, even!" Jack sounded way too pleased with himself. Loud screams echoed at the end of the alley— which made sense, since we were at a cheap carnival, teeming with hordes of people and dark corners. Vamptastic.

I checked to make sure Tasey was easily accessible. "Stay here; I'll be right back. This shouldn't take long."

I turned toward the carnival, but Jack grabbed my arm. "You can't tag, remember? Which makes me the other half of our fabulous bagging-and-tagging duo."

I bit back a snotty remark, knowing it wasn't his fault I was stressed. "Fine. Try to keep up." I stalked out into the crowds, not trying to absorb the atmosphere like I used to. I didn't need to grasp at glances of humanity anymore. I got plenty of it in the halls at school.

After a frustrating half hour, I finally caught sight of a glamoured corpse head in the middle of a crowd waiting for the Ferris wheel. He had his arm around a pretty young thing in an incredibly weather-inappropriate outfit that showed off her very slender, very blood-filled neck. She stared at him in that vapid, intoxicated way employed only by women under a vamp's control. Or the way I sometimes got when faced with cupcakes.

Mmm. Cupcakes.

Narrowing my eyes, I unbuttoned Tasey. No doubt the vamp was planning on taking her up for a ride she'd never forget—and never get off. He'd probably bite her at the top, a sick flair for the dramatic, then act like she was drunk as he dragged her off to some dark corner to finish. Rage flared inside me, thoughts of innocent Arianna flashing through my mind. IPCA vampire protocol called for me to lure him to a secluded spot so that no one was any wiser about the murderous creatures walking among them.

I pushed through the crowd, tapped him on the shoulder, and tased him.

His eyes went wide with surprise before he collapsed, twitching, onto the ground. His would-be victim stared at him for a few seconds before she let out a small scream. The crowd edged away from us, forming a sort of circle around the unconscious bloodsucker.

I rolled my eyes at Tasty Neck Girl. "Oh, get over it. Would have been the shortest relationship of your life." Jack walked up behind me, smiling sheepishly at the crowd as he bent down and attached the ankle tracker. I grabbed the vamp's wrist and dragged him unceremoniously out of the circle and toward the alley.

People—clueless, clueless people—stood there, staring in confusion as they tried to figure out what kind of show I was doing and whether they should clap or call the police.

"Call the transporters," I said, dumping the vampire at the mouth of the alley. Thanks to Uber-vamp, new regulation called for all vampires to be detained immediately without being read their rights or directed to a processing facility.

Jack pushed the button, then looked at me. "That was . . . subtle."

"Screw it," I muttered. If the general populace was finally clued in to the fact that the supernatural was alive and well among them, was that really such a bad thing? By protecting them from knowing about these things, we were also creating victims like Arianna.

Besides, luring the vamp would have taken too much time. And facing the vamp alone . . .

It wouldn't have tempted me. I wanted to go home is all.

As soon as the transporters got there, I shoved Jack toward the wall. "Home, now." He mock bowed, escorting me through a door and the darkness, back to the familiar comfort of my room/glorified closet. We walked through and the first thing I saw was a letter.

On my bed.

A white letter.

With a return address I'd wanted to see for weeks.

In an envelope that was far, far smaller than it should have been.

GOING NOWHERE,
GOING SOMEWHERE

Evie? Evie! Ouch!" Jack yanked his hand out of mine, shaking it and glaring at me. "I need these fingers later."

I couldn't move. My future was lying on my bed—how did it get there? Why wasn't it in the mailbox?

Grnlllll. She had been trying to get my attention when I came in from school. She must have gotten the mail, which meant she knew my letter was here. Arianna probably knew, too, since Grnlllll didn't climb stairs. Arianna would have been the one to put it on my bed.

My eyes burned with tears and shame, my stomach already twisted up in a sick knot.

Maybe it wasn't a rejection. Maybe they were jumping on the whole "green" bandwagon, and it was an acceptance with directions to access the information I needed online.

Maybe.

Please.

Please, please, please. I grabbed my necklace off the dresser, clutching it like a talisman as I walked forward, each step making my stomach hurt a little more. I picked up the envelope, trembling. Why couldn't they have waited another two weeks to send it to me?

"I can't do it," I whispered.

"Can't do what?" Jack asked, curious enough by now that he'd let the faerie door close behind himself.

"I can't open it." Squeezing my eyes shut, I held it out to him. "You do it."

For once he didn't make a stupid comeback, just took the envelope from my hand. Each sound of tearing paper ripped a piece of my soul away. Maybe it wasn't a rejection. Maybe it wasn't a rejection. Maybe it wasn't . . .

"Dear Miss Green, blah, blah, blah, like to thank you on behalf of blah, blah, blah, regret that at this time can't accept—" He stopped, and so did my heart.

I couldn't open my eyes. I wouldn't. I wasn't going to Georgetown. That was it. Everything I'd worked for, everything I'd chased since leaving the Center, gone. I'd work in the diner for the rest of my life, sneak in pointless odd jobs for IPCA, and Lend would get bored with me and marry the lusty lab assistant, and they'd be happy and beautiful forever, and I was

never

going

anywhere.

My future was a gaping void, worse even than the Faerie Paths, because at least they always had a destination. I had no destination now.

"You're scaring me," Jack's voice finally cut through, and I opened my eyes, barely able to see him. "Okay, good, yes, breathe. Breathing helps one stay alive, I've found. What on earth is so bad about a stupid school saying no?"

"My life"—I gasped—"is over. It's over. Everything."

He frowned dubiously. "Who would want to go to a place called Georgetown, anyhow? Ridiculous. Now, I could understand your devastation if it had a distinguished name like, say, Jacktown, but as it is, you're overreacting. Why do you want to go to more school? I went once for a few hours and nearly lost my mind."

"But, I—it's all I had planned, and—"

He waved his hand in the air as though swatting away all my pesky dreams. "Make new plans. You don't really want that anyway. You might think you do, but that's not your world." He smiled at me, his blue eyes the only thing coming in clearly through my tears. I cried even harder.

Sighing, he shuffled awkwardly from foot to foot. "Do you want me to get Raquel? Or your jumpy boyfriend?"

"No!" I couldn't face Lend, couldn't tell him that I wasn't good enough. Raquel, either. She'd be disappointed in me. I'd tried to be normal, tried to make a home for myself in this world, and failed utterly and completely. Why could Lend be so good at both worlds but I couldn't manage in either? Why was I so bad at life?

Jack threw back his shoulders. "It would appear, as usual, that everything is up to me. Good thing I'm always ready for a challenge." He took my hand in his and opened a door, pulling me through. I was crying too hard to protest when Lend's necklace was jarred from my hand. I looked back as the door closed, the necklace gleaming in a crumpled heap on the floor of my life.

"Jack, I—" My breath came in gasps now, and I couldn't manage to get out more than a few words at a time. "I don't—want to—please—"

He stopped dead in his tracks, frowning at me. Raising one eyebrow as though considering a particularly puzzling problem, he put his free hand behind my neck and hesitated for a moment.

Then he kissed me.

Shocked out of my shock, I registered his lips on mine, but it wouldn't process. They were full and warm enough, but the strange mashing motions he was making were far from the kisses I'd so often enjoyed with Lend.

And . . . it was Jack. *Jack.* Of the many things I'd considered doing to him, most involved violence. None of them involved lip-on-lip action.

I jerked my head back, but it wasn't hard to get away, since he pulled back at the same moment.

He wrinkled his nose. "Well, that was . . . interesting. Always wanted to try it, but now that I have, I'm pretty sure I never want to again."

Furious, I smacked him in the shoulder with my free hand, hating that we still had to have one clasped so I wouldn't be lost forever. "You"—*smack*—"little"—*smack*—"freak!"—*smack*. "What was that?!" *SMACK*.

He dodged another volley. "And I had been under the impression that afterward was a little less"—he winced as I connected hard—"painful."

"Listen, creep, if I wanted you to kiss me, I would have asked! And I didn't. And I wouldn't! And if you *ever* try that again, so help me, I will find that fossegrim and throw you to a watery death!"

And then—as if his awkward, terrible kiss weren't bad enough—he started *laughing*.

"SHUT UP!"

He shook his head, grinning smugly. "See? Two goals accomplished. One: try out kissing. Miserable failure, no doubt your fault, but a noble effort nonetheless. I should find your friend Carlee. She's probably better at it than you are."

Why couldn't my glamour-piercing eyes have a laser function? I wouldn't kill him. I'd just burn the word "freak" into his forehead.

"Aren't you going to ask me what my second goal was?" He batted his eyelashes at me.

"No, I'm not."

He nudged me in the ribs with his elbow. "You aren't crying anymore, are you?"

I'd have to let go of his hand to throttle him. So that option was out. "Being so mad I'd like to kill you is better?"

His smile tightened. "Being angry is *always* better than being sad. Another of my mottos, in fact. Now, do you want to go cry by yourself in your room, or do you want to have an adventure?"

I hesitated, wary as always of Jack's idea of an adventure but not wanting to go home, either. And he had a point—at least I wasn't sobbing anymore. I knew as soon as I walked back into my room with that letter, I'd lose it. Even thinking about thinking about it was making me tear up, and . . . forget it.

I squeezed his hand harder than necessary. "What did you have in mind?"

He narrowed his eyes and smiled, cherubic face suddenly wicked. "Let's go play." He dragged me along behind him as he sped through the Paths. He kept changing direction, altering his course to the right or left as though following a constantly shifting trail. I'd never seen anyone go anywhere but straight ahead before.

"Do you know where you're going?" I asked, increasingly

nervous. I wasn't keen on the idea of being lost in the Faerie Paths with Jack or anyone else. And the longer we were stuck in the dark, the more I had to fight the panic.

"It changes. Never in the same place twice. Makes it rather difficult to find, especially when one is being nagged, but now we—" He stopped, triumphant. "Here. Put your hand out. Tell me what you feel."

Rolling my eyes, I put my hand out next to his, against the emptiness and—there was something there. Or not something, even, but the *idea* of something. It wasn't tangible, and I wasn't sure how I was feeling it at all, other than the slight stirring under my fingers, the recognition of place in the midst of nowhere. I imagined it was akin to amputees feeling phantom limbs, only in this case it was a phantom door. There was nothing there, but there *should* be.

Jack watched me intently. "You can feel it, can't you?"

I shook my head. "I think so; I don't know. It's weird."

"There's no reason I can do it and you can't. In fact, you can open a lot more than just doors. This would be easy if you'd put your busy little mind to it instead of worrying about grades and schools and kissing. Especially kissing. Nasty thing, that."

"Yeah, nasty when it's with you. But how can you do this?"

"I think the faerie food changes you a bit. Besides, if you watch long enough, and want something badly enough, you'd be amazed at what you can do. What you will do.

The Faerie Paths meant freedom for me."

My heart twisted sadly in my chest, reminded of Jack's life with the faeries. Like Vivian, but Jack seemed so sure of himself, saner than she had been. Which wasn't saying much, but still. He wasn't completely unbalanced. "I'm so sorry about your childhood, Jack. That must have been hard."

He grinned, a baring of teeth. "Ah, but look at what a fine young man I've grown into. I have no one but the faeries to thank for who I am today."

"You can leave, though! Why do you still go to the Faerie Realms at all? Why not come back to Earth entirely, leave it behind?"

"Come back to what? Besides, you know that once you've tasted fey cuisine, you never go back. *Can* never go back."

"Couldn't you bring a lot with you or something? Store it?"

He shook his head. "I'm afraid one way or another Faerie and I are linked. I'm not done with them yet."

His smile seemed to me a more thorough glamour than any I'd ever seen. Just when I thought I was learning something about him, that smile would crop up, wiping away any real emotion. How could I ever read what was underneath it?

"Moving on," he said. "The door. You can feel it."

"What am I feeling, exactly?"

He traced his fingers almost reverently along the space where the door waited for us, staring at the blackness. "You know when you're on the edge of wake and sleep, and the dream you're leaving feels more real to you than anything the world has to offer? When you open your eyes, it's as though part of you stayed, and you know you'll never feel things quite as deeply, experience them quite as truly as you had in that tiny space of awareness between darkness and light. We're going into that." I held my breath, and he snapped out of whatever state he was in. Winking, he opened a door. "Welcome to the Faerie Realms."

MATCHMAKER, MATCHMAKER

Before I could tell Jack no, we were through the door and into the Faerie Realms. The only times I'd ever been there had been with Reth, in rooms of golden rocks, swirling meadows, and way-too-fancy furniture. I never thought I'd want to go back, but I'd take Reth's rooms in a heartbeat over this.

The sky above was crimson red, a vast expanse broken by pinpoints of glimmering black, like the absence of stars. Although I could see clearly, the air was thick and heavy as a summer night, carrying a hint of charred cinnamon. We stood on the pitch-black banks of a massive lake, silver but completely unreflective in defiance of the sky. Hulking rocks broke the monotony of the plain around us, scattered as if by violence, twisted and tortured things. The entire scene was mesmerizing, beautiful but wrong.

"Jack," I whispered, pulling on his hand. "We shouldn't be here."

"You're right," he said, and I let out a relieved breath. "Forgot the supplies." He put his hand out and we slid sideways, the air shifting as the nightmare landscape was replaced by a room. I swayed dizzily.

"Sorry about that." Jack let go of my hand and went to a table in the corner. "Once you're actually in the Realms it's easier to get from place to place. Takes some time to get used to, though. Mind the rug if you're going to vomit."

I clutched the edge of a couch for balance and looked around. This had to be the strangest room I'd ever seen. The walls were pale green rock and lit by an unseen ambient light, the furniture similar to what I'd seen with Reth, scrolling woodwork and rich velvets. However, scattered through all the faerie finery were dirty socks, discarded pants, and dingy sneakers.

Leave it to a boy to make the Faerie Realms look like a dump.

Jack lifted a tattered cardboard box and set it on the oak table, then grabbed a luminous fruit from a bowl. It looked like a peach, if peaches were blue and made from pieces of heaven. He closed his eyes as he bit into it, a rapturous, ravenous expression on his face. I'd never tasted anything as good as that fruit looked. I breathed through my mouth, trying not to smell it. After he finished, he offered me the bowl. "Want one?"

"I'll pass, thanks."

He shrugged. "You have no idea what you're missing. Ah well. I work better on a full stomach. Now that we've got supplies, we can get back to it."

"Whoa, not so fast. What was that place? I don't want to go there again." Jack's room at least was contained, closed off. On the banks of the strange lake we'd been completely exposed. I didn't want to be in Faerie at all, but I really, *really* didn't want to be there.

"Sorry, no time to lose. We've got a boat to catch." Jack balanced the box against his hip and grabbed my hand before I could yank it away. With another stomach-churning shift, we were back on the shore of the lake.

But this time we weren't alone.

A great ship, gleaming black as obsidian, silently passed us. The silver water was undisturbed in its wake, not even a ripple extending outward. I shrank back, but the boat went on without incident, coming to a stop against the next curve of bank. An arching bridge descended from the side. I was terrified to see who was going to get off.

"Jack?" I whispered urgently.

"Oh, right. We shouldn't be seen. I don't *think* they'd kill us, but one never knows."

"*I'm* going to kill you!" I hissed as we ducked behind one of the horrible boulders. Jack peered around the edge. I cowered. I'd spent too long running from faeries to come here on my own, practically offering myself to them. "Let's go!"

"You should see this."

"No! No, I really shouldn't, and you shouldn't, either! Let's get out of here."

"Look." Jack yanked me over until I could see, too. The procession was as silent as it was eerie. Faeries, beautiful and terrible at the same time, descended the bridge, their steps carefully measured. They had every color of hair imaginable—from black to blinding white—but their faces were sharp, cruelty etched into perfection. Their clothing, a singular shade of deep purple, floated around them on an imaginary breeze. Following the last member, the faeries all turned to face the boat. I held my breath in anticipation.

The next figures appeared, and I bit my lip to keep from crying out in horror. People—humans—crawled on all fours, their heads shaved, completely naked save for brilliant silver patterns painted on their bodies. Supported across their back was a finely wrought platform, all scrolling silverwork, and they crawled in perfect uniformity so as not to disturb it. Without any signal they stopped, waiting. I fought back the bile building in my throat. Far worse than their stripped bodies, lean and sinewy, was the look on their faces.

They were happy.

More than happy, they were enthralled, their expressions bordering on ecstasy. "What are they for?" I whispered, but Jack cut me off with a quick glare.

I didn't have long to wait. A woman, taller than the rest of the faeries by at least a head, glided forward. And in that moment I knew beauty and terror were one and the same, inseparable. How could anything less consuming than true terror ever be beautiful? Her hair swirled like black oil, dark rainbows undulating as it cascaded down her back. Her eyes were pure black against the alabaster of her skin, her violet lips full, cruel, flawless. Anything that fell from those lips would be pain and pleasure, inescapable, irresistible.

Here, then, was eternity. I would go to her—I had to go to her. In a world ever shifting, ever dying, she was an absolute, she was gravity, she was everything. I wanted to be lost in her forever.

Jack pinched my arm, twisting the skin between his fingers. Gasping, I turned to glare at him. He rolled his eyes. "Newbie. Try not to throw yourself at the Dark Queen, okay?"

I shook my head, trying to get the remnants of the desire, the need, out of my head. That had been close. Too close.

I hate faeries.

I turned back, determined not to lose myself to her pull again. I focused on anything other than her, watching her slaves instead. In unison the people dropped to their stomachs and she stepped onto the platform. Raised seamlessly into the air on their backs as they resumed crawling, she stared coldly past her entourage.

The faeries formed a line behind her and she was carried forward across the plain. The farther away she got, the easier it was to breathe. I leaned against the rock, exhausted from the effort of resisting the Dark Queen's pull. If she was dark, that made her the queen of the Unseelie Court. The ones who made Vivian. The ones who wanted me dead. Great distraction, Jack. What was not getting into Georgetown compared to facing death and *wanting* to throw myself at her feet? Come to think of it, Jack had been giving me a lot of potentially fatal experiences lately. We'd have to talk about that.

He leaned over, rummaging through his box.

"Who were those poor people?" I whispered, still sick to my stomach from remembering the looks on their faces.

He shrugged without glancing up. "Not people so much, anymore. Unseelie pets don't last long."

I shuddered, wrapping my arms around myself. "You need to take me home. I think those faeries are looking for me, and I'd really rather not be found. Why are we here, anyway?"

Jack straightened with a wide smile that made me feel even worse than the slaves had. In each hand he held a glass bottle of amber liquid.

"You want us to get *drunk*?"

"Don't be stupid. Getting drunk doesn't make the Realms any nicer. Hold these." He handed me the bottles, then grabbed two long strips of damp cloth, stuffing them down into the open bottles so that only a few inches were hanging out.

"What—"

"Do you ever shut up?" Finished with the cloth, he reached into his pocket and pulled out a book of matches.

Oh, bleep no. "Jack! What are you—"

He lit both wicks and grabbed one of the bottles. Grinning maniacally at me, he turned and hurled his bottle. It spun lazily, a trail of light until it disappeared behind the deck of the ship. Maybe it wouldn't work. Maybe—

A massive fireball billowed up, scorching the air and flowering along the boat.

"Evie? You might want to throw that thing."

I looked down in horror at my own burning Molotov cocktail, then flung it as far from myself as I could. It smashed against the side of the boat, most of the flames falling down into the silver water.

Which proceeded to catch fire.

"Wow. Didn't expect that!" Jack nodded appreciatively as the flames spread, eating their way outward along the top of the lake. The boat, now engulfed, creaked and groaned its death cries. "Adding a touch of faerie liquor to the petrol gave it the extra kick, I think."

An unearthly shriek ripped through the air, jarring me to the bones. I did *not* want to meet the owner of that voice.

Jack laughed, taking my trembling hand. "This is the part where we run."

OLD FRIENDS

Jack!" My voice came out unrecognizable, nearly an octave higher. Part of it was terror, but most was a reaction to the thick, acrid smoke, solid as a fist, shoving its way down my throat. The air filled with it as the lake behind us became an inferno.

I could barely see Jack, his hand my only lifeline in this nightmare. "Get ready!" he shouted, and with a dizzying twist the landscape warped. We still stood on the same blasted plain, but far enough away to be out of danger. Tendrils of smoke clung to us like living things, and I tried my best to brush them away.

I watched as the dark clouds undulated sinuously up, blacking out the red night sky. The lake burned evenly, a single body of flame, the Dark Queen's boat barely more than a pile of fire now.

Jack put his hands on his hips, surveying the scene with a satisfied nod. "That turned out much better than I'd hoped."

"Please, let's leave!" If we could still see the chaos, we were far closer than I wanted to be. I could imagine what the Dark Queen's midnight gaze would feel like if she found us. My skin crawled—with fear or anticipation, I couldn't tell. Neither was good.

"What's your hurry? Let's take a moment to bask in the satisfaction of a job well done."

"I didn't want to do that!"

"No?" He cocked his head and raised his eyebrows. "I thought you hated the fey."

"I do, but that doesn't mean I want to run around the Faerie Realms lighting everything on fire!"

"What's the point in hating something if you aren't proactive?" He put his arm around my shoulders, steering me to look at the inferno with him. "You can't tell me that's not satisfying, not after what you saw. Faeries care about very few things, but they're quite fond of their little trinkets. That boat was a particular favorite of hers, not to mention the entire lake. All the centuries she spent crafting this landscape, then *poof*! One excellently thrown firebomb, and you've made her feel anger and pain more deeply than she's probably ever known. And far less than she deserves to know."

Watching the flames, it was as though the lingering smoke wove its way into my chest, dark and seeping, replacing my fear with anger. He was right. They deserved this. They deserved far, far worse than this.

I narrowed my eyes until the brilliant line of fire was all I could see. Come to think of it, it was exactly what this landscape needed. It belonged here.

I turned to Jack. "What else did you have in mind?"

His face burst into a dimpled smile. "I *knew* you weren't useless. A quick stop to gather more supplies and—"

"*You.*"

We both jumped in shock, turning around to find the source of the horrid, rasping voice. Something crouched, feral and twisted. Wild and matted hair half covered sunken features. What had no doubt once been fine clothes were now filthy and torn beyond recognition. But then I found the eyes—her eyes. Ruby red eyes. Ruby red eyes that had once gone with a voice like shattering glass.

Fehl.

The last time I'd seen her had been in Lend's kitchen, when Vivian tried to drain the life from her. She'd gotten away but was apparently much worse for the wear. Gone was the ethereal, disconnected grace of the fey. She was a thing gone wild, her eyes feverish, her movements jerky and darting.

"*You did this to me.*"

I held up my hands, taking a step back. "No, I didn't. I'm sorry, but—" I paused. I wasn't sorry. Fehl had squirmed around her binding IPCA rules to work with Vivian and bring me to what she thought would be my death. What nearly *had* been my death. Besides which, I saved her life that night by stopping Viv from draining her entirely. In retrospect, maybe I shouldn't have. I stood straighter. "I seem to recall you bringing this on yourself."

She let out a laugh, somewhere between a croak and a cough. "Yes, a job well done and well rewarded. But if I finish—if I bring a prize back to my queen—she'll love me again. She'll fix me." Fehl stood up straight, grimacing as though it hurt.

"You broke a faerie?" Jack edged away, not taking his eyes off her. "A little warning would have been nice. I don't want to die now that things have finally gotten fun."

"Relax," I snapped. "We're not going to die. She can't hurt me."

Fehl laughed again, a hint of her old glass coming through. "Little girl, you've no idea what I can do."

"Can you handle her?" Jack asked, and I realized that, for the first time since I met him, he sounded scared. I didn't want to know what he'd faced at the hands of faeries. Faeries like Fehl. I wasn't about to let him get hurt again.

I stretched out my fingers, wondering what a faerie would feel like as I watched Fehl shift back and forth on her feet, twitching like a cat waiting to pounce. It wasn't wrong, it couldn't be wrong, to take some of her soul if it meant protecting myself and helpless people like Jack. It wasn't much different than what IPCA did, anyway. I was like a human Tasey.

Fehl snarled, then jumped forward, covering the distance between us faster than I thought possible. I dodged, but tripped and fell back in my haste to get out of her way. She overshot, sliding along the ground before whipping around as I scrambled backward on my palms, trying to get more space between us.

She bared her teeth at me in a sick grin and stalked slowly forward. Jack was behind Fehl now, frowning as he watched. I wanted to scream at him to run, but he was probably in shock. Why didn't he make a door away from here? I couldn't get up without giving Fehl an opening to attack me. I wracked my mind, desperate for a plan, when it hit me.

"Denfehlath!" I shouted. "Stop!"

Her eyes went wide with fury as every muscle ground to a complete halt. She stood, motionless, frozen before a jump. I might have lost the ability to control Reth when he tricked me into letting him pick a new name, but I still knew Fehl's name. Too bad for her.

I stood, dusting my hands off on my pants. "Don't move." I held back a gloating grin, watching Fehl's tortured face. She was within inches of the vengeance she'd craved for so long, but there was nothing she could do. Jack walked over to me and looked at frozen Fehl as though considering a sculpture in a museum.

"Interesting. IPCA won't give me any faerie names. I'd always wondered about named commands." He turned to me. "Well, what now? Are you going to leave her here?"

I considered it. My fingers twitched at my sides, and I was hyperaware of the extra energy, the ever-present tingling, and the cool, flowing sensation that sometimes rushed through my veins. I could see the glow from Fehl's chest, far brighter in faeries than in vampires. Maybe, to teach her a lesson, just a little . . .

Someone cleared his throat behind us. "Evelyn. I thought I felt you. To what do we owe the pleasure of your company, my love?"

My heart sank to my stomach. Bad timing, thy name is Reth. I turned around to face him, heartbreakingly beautiful, if rather comically out of place in this hellish landscape with his white Victorian suit and golden hair. He looked disdainfully at Fehl, tsked softly, then glanced at the still-raging inferno.

"My, you have been busy today, haven't you?"

Jack nudged me with his elbow. "Don't suppose you know his name, too?"

"No such luck," I muttered, still bitter.

Reth frowned at Jack, the expression doing nothing to sully his perfect, lineless face. "What are you doing here, boy? I believe Dehrn is looking for you. Something about stealing her books of lore."

Jack glared, a petulant set to his lips, but didn't answer.

A shriek, crackling with more energy and destructive power than any fire, reached us from the direction of the lake. "Time to go." Jack grabbed my hand and the landscape twisted away from us, leaving Reth and a frozen Fehl, her eyes screaming the fury that her body couldn't. I felt a stab of anger at losing my chance to—

I needed to stop thinking about it. She couldn't hurt us now, and that was the point. That was the only reason I'd even considered touching her.

We stopped and I sank to the floor of Jack's room, sighing with relief at all the bullets we'd dodged. "I can't believe we got away with that."

"Nor can I," Reth answered, holding a dirty sock at arm's length. "Still, always lovely to have guests."

So much for getting away with it.

DO ASK, DO TELL

Go!" I shouted to Jack, still holding his hand. I didn't want to face Reth, not on his own turf and not after what we'd done. Jack tightened his grip as the room spun around us. I closed my eyes and tried not to let the dizziness get to me.

"Okay." Jack let go and I opened my eyes. We were in an oblong field, surrounded by orange grass that came up to our waists, feather soft and whispering secrets to the deliciously sweet breeze circling us. The field was bordered by pure white trees, bowed over under the weight of more of that blue fruit that I absolutely was not going to get within ten feet of.

"Why couldn't we have come here first?" I asked. Some parts of the Realms I could get used to. Aside from the evil, tempting fruit, of course.

"This is all rather wearisome."

I whipped around to find Reth standing right behind us. Again. I reached for Jack's hand but Reth grabbed my wrist. His hand fit perfectly around the faded scar he'd left there.

"Let me save you the trouble. There is nowhere you can go—in the Faerie Realms, particularly—that I can't find you."

I glared. "What's that supposed to mean?"

"It means that scurrying about like a couple of naughty children serves no purpose. Now, what are you doing here? After all the times I invited you, I'm a bit hurt that you came in with the help."

Jack bristled next to me, glaring at Reth.

"I'll do whatever I want," I snapped.

"My dear, you have a shockingly underdeveloped sense of self-preservation. I would recommend avoiding the Dark Queen's ire, as she already has a rather low opinion of the value of your life. Now." He pulled out a pocket watch that didn't have any hands and frowned at it. "It's been lovely but I really must be off. Try not to destroy the meadow, if it's not too much trouble."

He let go of my wrist and my blood boiled. I'd had enough of him showing up, giving a few cryptic comments, and then disappearing again. I reached out and grabbed his arm. He looked at me, surprise shaping his eyebrows.

"No! Why have you been sending creatures to attack me? And what do you mean, you can find me anywhere? And if you wanted me here so bad, why are you leaving now that I've finally come?"

Reth smiled, his eyes liquid sunshine. "I don't know what you are referring to, as my only goal has ever been to protect you. I would never send something to attack you. However, I think we've established you are nothing if not stubborn and categorically incapable of choosing the things that are good for you." He touched my forehead, then my heart, and I flinched away from his finger. "If only your head were a bit emptier, like your soul. I will welcome you home whenever you *choose* it, but I am expressly forbidden to force you. The Unseelie Court gave Vivian no choice in the matter, and look how well that turned out. Speaking of which, are you going to leave that wretched faerie frozen forever?"

"Fehl deserves— Don't change the subject! You never answered how you know where I am all the time."

He reached over with his free hand and effortlessly pried my fingers from his wrist. Stupid faerie strength. "If you don't mind, my love, your fingers are uncomfortably cold. And to answer your question, how could I not know where you are? It pains me you cannot feel our connection."

I glared. "Bull."

Reth laughed, the orange grass around us swaying in time, dancing to the silver beauty of the sound. "I suppose knowing your true name helps."

He'd teased me with that before, the night I'd freed him by commanding him to take a new name. I didn't buy it. "Yeah, well, hate to break it to you, but *everyone* knows my name's Evelyn, so you're not exactly special. And don't give me this 'real name' crap. If I have one and you knew it, why did it take you so long to find me?" He couldn't deny that. Faeries put a lot of stock in names, and wherever I came from, the faeries hadn't known about me until a couple of years ago at the earliest.

When Reth met me at the Center he didn't even pay attention to me at first. Then one day everything changed, like he'd suddenly noticed me. At the time I'd been flattered (read: madly crushing), but since I learned that the faeries were somehow responsible for my existence, it drove me a bit nuts trying to figure out how a) they hadn't known where I was, and b) he'd figured out who I was.

Reth nodded. "Ah, an excellent story. Perhaps your friend should stay for it?"

I turned to see that Jack had been slowly edging away toward the trees. I shook my head, glaring. "No way, Jack. You brought me here, you're staying with me until I get home."

He sighed, flopping down to sit on the ground so the grass tickled his face. I turned back to Reth. "Go ahead." If he was going to give me answers—really give me answers—it was worth risking a little more time in the Faerie Realms. The hairs on my neck prickled; maybe this was why he'd been so eager to leave. He knew that if I thought I was in control, I'd be more likely to stay.

Oh, I loathe him. But I had to know.

"No doubt you remember when we met." He smiled, and I hated that he knew I remembered every minute we'd ever spent together. Honestly, exes. As if they weren't bad enough in general, mine had to be immortal and a quasi-deity. Good thing I was done with immortals.

Ah, bleep. But Lend didn't count as an immortal.

"When I discovered your unique abilities at IPCA, I told my queen about you and she wondered if here, finally, was the Empty One that was created and then"—he paused, and a brief shadow clouded his radiant face—"lost."

"You didn't create me!" I shouted, surprised at my own vehemence. "You're lying. You probably stole me and changed me, like you stole Jack and who knows how many others! But I got away."

"If you say so."

"Shut up! Tell me the truth or I swear I will burn this whole place down!"

Reth had the nerve to look amused. "It would appear your new friend is a poor influence. Still, I can see this is bothering you. Although I am not allowed to give this information to anyone outside the fey, you are, for the moment at least, *in* Faerie, which could be construed as being within the fey, now, could it not?"

"You lost me at 'although.'"

He nodded, apparently satisfied. "Yes, that works out nicely. Now that you have come to the Faerie Realms of your own free will, which was my queen's stipulation, it opens all sorts of possibilities." He held out a hand. I didn't take it, couldn't take it, and his smile had a strangely soft edge. "Now, now, Evelyn. No need to be frightened."

I clenched my jaw, glaring. I was *not* scared of him. And I wasn't scared to finally get some answers. Oh, who was I kidding. I was terrified. There were so many things I could find out that I didn't want to know. Nothing good would come from what he was about to tell me. But that didn't change anything. I had to know.

I gave him my hand.

He tucked it in the crook of his elbow with a condescending pat. "I do believe I missed this." He turned and we walked through a door that was now in front of us. A panicked yelp sounded and I was nearly knocked over as Jack grabbed me, barely making it before the door closed.

Reth sighed impatiently. "Must he tag along?"

I couldn't believe I'd forgotten to demand it. Five

minutes with Reth and I was already being stupid. "Yes, he must."

Jack took my free hand and the three of us walked together through the darkness. I wanted to ask where we were going, but I didn't want to give Reth the satisfaction of hearing how terrified I was. He'd know the second I opened my mouth.

He opened a door and we stepped out into blinding sunshine. I was disoriented, like when you go to a movie in the afternoon and come out to dark night. How did it become day again? It was late when we left my apartment. Were we on the other side of the world or something?

"Faerie Realms screw with time," Jack muttered, as though reading my mind.

"So where are we?" We had come through a white cinder block wall, facing a massive parking lot. I glanced up and down, wondering what mystical place had such demanding parking needs. And women's restrooms?

Reth, rather than answer, walked along the sidewalk. Jack and I had to scurry to catch up. As we turned the corner, I stopped dead in shock. Of all the places to learn about who I really was—what I really was—this one hadn't crossed my mind as a possibility.

We were at a NASCAR race.

"What on earth are we doing here?" I should have known better than to trust Reth. He'd never been one for jokes, but of course he'd pick now to get a sense of humor.

No doubt he thought this whole thing was hilarious. He turned to me, no trace of laughter in his real eyes, shining beneath his faerie-hiding glamour.

"I think it high time you meet your father."

FAMILY REUNIONS
ALWAYS SUCK

My father?" I stared at Reth, trying to process what he'd said. "I'm going to meet—I have a father? And he's *here*?"

The pack of multicolored logo-plastered cars roared past on the track, separated from us by a massive chain-link fence and a maintenance area. It was too much to process. In spite of Reth and Vivian's claims that I had been "made," I had a father. A father who was going to NASCAR races instead of, say, taking care of me.

Reth surveyed the scene around us, his face a picture of disdain. "Unfortunately, yes. This way, please." He wove his way through the crowds wandering to and from their seats. I nearly got beer spilled on me three times, but everyone moved for him, most (male and female) pausing to stare dazedly at his glamoured glory.

"So," Jack said as we started up an infinite set of concrete steps through the stands, "this is exciting!"

"Can we not talk?" I was finally getting some answers, and I was scared bleepless.

Reth turned to a section of booths that looked far nicer than the aluminum benches everywhere else. He opened the door to the first and gestured for me to go in. Trembling, I walked through. The plushly furnished booth had four armchairs and a side table littered with empty Coke cans.

In the center chair overlooking the race sat a man with shoulder-length hair such a rich brown it looked like polished wood. His back was to us and he leaned forward, intent on the race.

"Do be a good boy and get me something to drink?" Reth asked Jack, shutting the door in his face before he could come in. The man in the chair hadn't turned around yet, and Reth narrowed his eyes in annoyance. "Lin." The man waved us away with one perfect, slender hand.

A faerie hand.

My stomach sank. No. No, not that. Anything but that. It couldn't be—he couldn't be—*I* couldn't be. Reth put his arm around my shoulders, steering me gently down the two steps to the window. When Lin's face came into view there was no denying it. His glamour was fuzzy, as though barely there, and his face had all the faerie features. Far-too-big almond eyes, delicate nose, full lips, ageless skin. But his eyes, an unnaturally emerald green, were ringed with red as though he hadn't slept in days. I'd never seen a faerie besides damaged Fehl look anything but pristine.

"Lin," Reth said again, his golden voice hard.

"Oh, go away. Thirty-three's making a pass."

I looked at Reth, not wanting to watch the strange faerie anymore. He set my teeth on edge, something about him making me instantly wary, tired. There was something there, something that tickled at the back of my mind. Please, don't let it be recognition. Reth looked disgusted as Lin cracked open another can of Coke and chugged it.

"Melinthros," Reth said, his voice ringing powerfully through the box.

The faerie snapped his eyes up, finally looking at us. "Watch it, pretty boy. I've got a nasty headache and if you go throwing around my name, things are liable to get ugly real quick around here."

Since when did faeries call each other "pretty boy"?

Lin turned back to the race. "No!" he shouted, throwing his now empty can against the glass. Then, a wicked smile cutting across his smooth features, he whispered something under his breath and flicked a hand toward the pack of cars zipping by. The car in front flipped onto its side, sliding as bits of it flew off and sparks trailed the ground. The cars behind smashed into it and each other, unable to avoid the wreck. One bright yellow car slammed into another and flipped over the top of it, crushing the roof before spinning off into a wall.

The entire thing took less than ten seconds, and then the track was a mess of smoke and colorful pieces of what used to be cars. An announcer buzzing in the background let off a long string of swearwords, declaring it the worst crash in the course's history.

Lin sat back, a pleased smile on his face. "I love this sport." He grabbed another Coke from the floor and drained it, wiping his mouth before he looked at Reth. "What are you doing here again?"

"I've brought your daughter." Reth's voice was devoid of emotion as it destroyed my life. I couldn't breathe, couldn't process this, couldn't tell whether the room was spinning or I was. Reth's grip on my shoulder tightened, steering me to one of the chairs. I sat heavily, staring at the floor.

I wasn't part faerie.

I couldn't be! It didn't make any sense.

Oh, bleep, when had anything in my life *ever* made sense?

"That's not her." Lin frowned, holding his hand near the ground. "She's about yea high, doesn't talk much, cries a lot. Bound to be around here somewhere." He looked over the top of one of the chairs as though three-year-old me would be there, playing.

Reth's golden eyes darkened. "Yes, that was an accurate description, fourteen years ago when you lost her."

"I didn't lose her." Lin straightened indignantly. "She's—" He paused, scratching his head. Then he looked at me, squinting. "Well, fancy that. You're right. Pale, tragic little thing, isn't she? Still, here she is and she is here. Go take her to the queen or whatever it is she was for. I forget. Ooh, they're clearing the track!"

He stared, transfixed, as what was left of the cars were leveraged off the track while paramedics carried out several people on stretchers.

I looked up at Reth, my lips trembling. I didn't know which was worse—that my father was a faerie, or that he spent the last fourteen years oblivious to the fact that I was missing. Reth's mouth was pursed, his full lips smashed into a single disapproving line.

He picked up a can, holding it with the tips of his fingers as though it were contaminated. IPCA had discovered, at great loss, the only thing from our world that affected faeries was carbonation; it was like hard liquor. Which made my father a faerie alcoholic. Of course. Brilliant. Reth set the can gingerly back down. "This is why I avoided court business. Mixing our fates with humans' never ends well. It's disgraceful. This is what comes of forcing a faerie to live outside our Realms. We've *all* become tainted by the nonsense and decay of this world."

"Reth." I whispered so that my voice wouldn't crack. The tears were already out, but I didn't want to lose it. Not here. Not in front of that thing that was my father. "Please. I don't understand any of this."

Brushing off the seat, he sat in the chair next to me. "I'd hoped he could explain, but once again it falls to me." Reth fixed his depthless eyes on mine and took my hand in his. There were none of the forced flames from before, just reassuring pressure, like he was trying to anchor me. "I suppose the idea for you started about twenty years ago."

He traced a finger tenderly down my cheek. "It was a very bad idea from the start."

WHAT HE SAID

My queen claimed it was our responsibility to accept that we'd created our own prison in the Faerie Realms. The Dark Queen, however, had other ideas. After numerous mistakes, each more disastrous than the last, most of the fey felt making an Empty One, someone who could create and control gates, was impossible. We would be relegated to the Faerie Realms and this sad dirt heap forever. Some asked my queen to help, but she refused, her irrational affection for human life influencing her. I always felt that surely she could at least do better than vampires."

"Vampires?"

He waved a hand dismissively. "Vampires were one of the Dark Queen's early mistakes. She thought if she could kill the humans first and re-create them with her magic, they would become Empty Ones and take in souls. Instead they took life but no soul. Very distasteful, really."

"Wait—you guys *made* vampires?" It was their fault Arianna was cursed like that?

"Please don't interrupt, my love. Our magic became further and further diluted as this world tainted us, which was why we weren't watching for the Dark Queen to succeed. When my queen heard of Vivian, a true Empty One, she knew she had to make one, too, or risk the Dark Queen opening a gate and shutting the rest of us here forever. And so, unbeknownst to any others, she selected a faerie from her court"—he looked derisively over at Lin, engrossed in the race—"and assigned him to create an Empty One."

"Create?" I whispered. I didn't want to know.

"It's not easy for faeries to spend extended amounts of time in this mortal realm. Eventually it wears us down, pulls at the threads connecting us to eternity. We become thin shadows of what we are meant to be." Lin's fuzzy glamour made sense now—even his faerie features seemed strained. "But in order to do what he needed, he was forced to stay here. Finding a willing mortal woman was no challenge, of course."

"My mom?" I had a mom. A human mom.

"No one had thought to try it that way, human

relationships being such silly, messy things. Still, Melinthros had been sufficiently desensitized and was able to make you."

"So I'm—I'm half faerie?" My stomach churned. I was going to be sick. Even the way Reth said it—*make* me.

"Of course not. It doesn't work like that. You cannot become part of eternity with such a definite starting point."

"What are you saying, then?"

"By having a mortal mother and a faerie father, you're not half faerie. You're just not quite mortal. Less than mortal, in a sense. Nothing faerie transfers over."

The cold, empty feeling I'd been running from for so long welled up, threatening to overwhelm me with everything I lacked. I wasn't special. I wasn't paranormal. I wasn't even normal. I was neither. Nothing.

"It's necessary, of course. Human souls, fragile as they are, are incredibly complex, ever-shifting. Impossible to add to or take away from. A real human would never be able to function as a conduit or draw any more energy into herself. You are unique in all the realms in that you can shift energy. As to why you can create gates I've never been clear, although my queen seems to think it revolves around some bizarre human sense of home combined with the extra energy and the souls' pull to leave this world."

He stopped, as though expecting me to say something. What could I possibly say? What could I say to anyone, ever again?

"Of course, there was the matter of Lin losing you, and you have our sincerest apologies for that. As a matter of fact, no one knew you existed at all, save the queen, and she was unaware that Lin had lost you, as she never visits the mortal realm. Imagine her surprise when I described your unique abilities and she realized that you were the Empty One and that Lin was not preparing you for us. Unfortunately I wasn't the only one to recognize you, which led the Unseelie Court to complicate things by sending Vivian after you.

"My queen gave me Melinthros's name and assigned me to determine what, exactly, had happened and how to turn you into what we needed you to be. I had always avoided becoming embroiled in court politics before. Wisely, I might add. It's been exhausting. It was my idea to give you extra soul, but that turned out to be a disaster." He brushed his fingers against my scar.

I shook my head, too much information clogging my thoughts. "I really don't belong anywhere, do I?"

"Nonsense." He stroked my wrist. "I said you were a mistake from the beginning, but you're a very endearing mistake, and with the right amount of adjustments you will fit quite nicely in my Realms. And if you serve the queen's purposes, more the better. You weren't made for this Earth, Evelyn. You do not deserve to be fragile, corruptible, dying. You should be eternal." He leaned in close, a smile equal parts tender and possessive lighting his perfect face. "Eternal with me."

I had to have a place here, a home. I had to have something. "What about my mom?"

Reth's smile dropped and he turned to the other faerie. "Have you found the girl's mother?"

Lin muttered something unintelligible.

"What did he say?"

"He doesn't know where she is."

"No," I whispered.

"I am sorry. Loving the fey isn't healthy for mortals. It becomes an addiction, and if the object of their obsession is removed, they waste away. It's discouraged in my court, unless you bring the mortal to the Realms where they can be satiated living among faeries."

I stood, grief threatening to overwhelm me. I couldn't deal with this. It was too big. Like the draw of the Dark Queen, this feeling would swallow me whole, consume me. I needed to replace it. Jack's words rang in my head—it was always better to be angry than sad.

"You." I stalked over, standing directly in front of the faerie who had created me. He didn't look up. "Melinthros, you will look at me."

His head snapped up, blurry eyes glaring at mine.

"Tell me what happened to my mother."

He spoke as though the words were being forced from him, which they were, thanks to my command. "She took care of the baby until she was no longer necessary."

"Where is she now?"

"I don't know."

"Tell me where she is!" I screamed.

"I can't."

My hands flexed at my sides. He had to tell me. I'd make him tell me.

"Evelyn." Reth's voice was as soft as his touch on my arm. "I tried myself to find her a year ago. I am sorry."

Reth's golden eyes brought me back to reality. A reality in which I was more alone than I had ever been. As bad as it was finding out I was the same thing as Vivian when she went on her killing spree, that was nothing compared to what I felt now. At least then I'd only been forced to admit I wasn't completely normal. I'd assumed that meant *more* than human. Not less.

"Come with me. There is nothing for you here, my lovely Neamh."

The last word reached out to me, raced through my body like electricity. I knew that word. I *was* that word. He really had known my name all along. But I was no faerie, and my name had no claim on my will. No one had claim to me.

"I'm not yours," I hissed.

The door burst open. Jack stood there, breathing heavily, holding a golden goblet in one hand. "Your drink."

"Jack." I walked toward him, reeling, needing to be anywhere else. Needing to be anyone else. "Please take me home."

"You aren't safe from the Dark Queen here, and you will never be whole. Let me take you home," Reth said, his voice slicing through the chill in me. He didn't mean my apartment.

I turned to him. He knew me. He knew what I was, who I was. This was his fault—his and every other faerie's. They destroyed everything they touched. Two could play at that game, though.

"Melinthros," I said, the image of the car wreck fresh in my mind, "you will return to the Faerie Realms and *you will never come back*." His bloodshot eyes bugged out of his head and he clutched at a can of Coke. Shaking, he walked mechanically to the wall and created a door, disappearing out of this world forever. Good riddance. I hoped his withdrawal lasted an eternity. He deserved far, far worse. Maybe someday when I thought of a punishment bad enough, I'd find him again.

I took Jack's hand and stepped out the booth door before pausing. "If I ever see you again, Reth," I said, "I will kill you."

THE TRUTH WILL SET
YOU FREE—OR BREAK
YOUR HEART

I pulled Jack behind me, tripping down the stairs and barely able to see through my tears. I needed to get away from here, now.

"What happened?" he asked, frowning as he tried to open a door in the wall. "Did he hurt you?"

I shook my head, unable and unwilling to talk about it. People passed us on their way to the bathroom, but I didn't care about hiding the door to protect their precious little worldviews. Why should they get to lead happy, innocent, clueless lives? The world was a monstrous place. A monstrous place I had no place in.

Finally light traced a door into the wall. "Home?" he asked.

I squeezed his hand, closing my eyes against the claustrophobic dark of the Paths and not opening them until we walked through to my tiny room.

"Evie!" Lend jumped up from my bed, his face creased with worry. "Where have you been? Arianna called about the letter, said you didn't come home last night, and when I came, I found this"—he held up my iron necklace that I had left lying in the middle of the floor—"and I thought, I was so scared that Reth had—"

He stopped, looking from me to Jack, who was still holding my hand.

"You were with him?" Lend's face shifted and he swore softly. "I thought you were hurt or kidnapped. I've been calling everyone my dad knows, sick with worry. And you've been with him the whole time. Why? What were you doing that was so important you couldn't even call? And why didn't you come to me first when you found out about Georgetown?"

I shook my head, tears streaming down my face. "I couldn't, I—"

"You could tell him but not me? You promised me, you swore you were done hiding things. You lied." He looked so hurt. I hadn't thought my heart could break any more, but seeing his eyes killed me.

"I couldn't face you! Lend, that was our life—that was

everything! And I failed. I didn't get in. I'm not good enough."

He took me by the shoulders, steering me away from Jack. "Evie, there are other options. This sucks, but it's not the end of the world. This doesn't change anything about us. I don't know why you think it would! We've still got the same future."

"No, we don't! We've never had the same future. I've tried my hardest to fix it, but we never will. I'm not—I'm not even human. And you aren't either, so we should quit pretending like this will ever work out."

His face fell. "We've always known we weren't normal. Why does it suddenly matter? So we're paranormal, big deal."

"You don't get it!"

"And he does?" Lend pointed angrily at Jack.

"No! I'm not paranormal, I'm *nothing*! Just another faerie experiment gone horribly wrong. And we don't have a future together because mine is going to dead-end into oblivion and yours is going to go on forever!"

He froze, his expression shocked. "What are you talking about?"

I closed my eyes. I couldn't stand to look into his face, not now, not ever again. I couldn't have him, and it destroyed whatever was left of my heart. I was stupid to ever think we could be together. So stupid. "You're immortal," I whispered. "Your soul is bright and shining and perfect and eternal. You aren't going to die. *Ever.*"

Lend dropped his hands off my shoulders. I wouldn't open my eyes, couldn't see the look on his beautiful face. "How long have you known?"

"Since prom night. When I was filled with the souls, I could see straight through to yours, and—It doesn't matter. I'm sorry that I didn't tell you. I didn't want to lose you." I laughed bitterly, opening my eyes to stare at the floor. "But that was inevitable, wasn't it?"

"Evie, I—What am I supposed to say to this?"

"You'll figure it out. You've got an eternity to."

His voice was angry, desperate. "But we can still—"

"No!" I finally looked up into his water eyes, those eyes I once hoped held my entire future. His heartbreak mirrored mine. But unlike me, he'd get over it. "We can't. I'm not going to be like your dad, left behind, clinging forever to the one perfect love that could never work! I won't be that person. I love you too much to make you try to stay with me when I know you'll want to move on. You'll *have* to move on and become whatever it is you're supposed to be. I'm not going to stay here and wait for it to happen."

I turned to Jack, who opened a door in the wall and held out his hand. I took it, unable to resist a final look at Lend.

He took a step back, not meeting my eyes as he silently shook his head.

"It's for the best," I whispered, wishing, desperately hoping that he would disagree with me, stop me, do anything.

He just stood there.

And so I walked into the darkness with Jack.

SLEEPING BEAUTY

Where to?" Jack asked.

I realized I wasn't crying anymore. There was no point. I was a broken, useless shell of a girl. My entire existence was a mistake. I had no home, no family, no future. All I felt was numb. After all, why mourn the loss of things I never should have had to begin with?

I shook my head, my voice hollow. "It doesn't matter."

"Do you, uh, want to talk about it?"

"You wouldn't understand." No one would ever understand because no one was the same as me.

No, that was wrong. Vivian. She and I were the same.

I was hit with a sudden, aching need to see her. Really see her. I wondered if she knew about us, about what our fathers were. But she would have told me if she did. Now more than ever I could understand her, forgive her for what she'd done. At least I'd been able to grow up with the illusion of normalcy. She'd never had a life free from the faeries.

"Could you find someone? I don't know where she is, but IPCA has her somewhere."

Jack smiled at me in the darkness. "If IPCA has her, I can find her."

He veered to the side and opened a door into a white hallway I knew all too well. We hurried toward Raquel's office. "Wait here." Jack turned the corner out of sight.

I heard him knock. "Jack? What is it?" Raquel asked.

"Evie's missing!"

"What? What do you mean, missing?"

"I went to visit her, but her vampire and that dumb boy she likes were panicking. They don't know where she is."

"Reth." Raquel's voice cut through the air, so menacing even I was a little scared. "Don't worry, Jack. I'll take care of this. I should never have let her out into the world unprotected, but I'll get her back."

The sound of her pumps stomping down the hall was followed by Jack peeping around the corner, grinning. "All clear, then."

"You could have picked something nicer to tell her. I don't want her to worry."

"Oh, relax. Want to snoop in her office with me, or do you want to hide in the hall like a good little girl?"

I glared at him, pushing past. He opened her door and walked in like he owned the place, sitting down at her desk and propping his feet on it as he opened one of the drawers.

"Who are we looking for?"

"Vivian? She'd be . . . I don't know. Somewhere safe, where faeries couldn't get to her? And with medical stuff. And she's a Level Seven paranormal, if that helps." No doubt the IPCA researchers would be thrilled with the information I could give them about myself now. They'd never been able to figure me out before. Lucky them; ignorance was bliss. Or at least less painful.

He hummed cheerily as he flipped through the folders. I fidgeted, sure that at any moment Raquel would come back and I'd be busted. I couldn't face her right now. She'd try to rationalize this, comfort me. There was no way to make this better. There never would be.

"Here we go. The iron wing."

"The iron wing?"

"There's a whole section of Containment where the walls are plated with iron. Makes it impossible to open a faerie door there."

Interesting. That might have been nice to know while I was here. Yet another example of information IPCA hadn't trusted me with. I'd never been one of them, never really been a member. Of anything.

We took a roundabout route to Containment, then went through a supply door I'd never bothered to open. It led to a long, narrow hallway. I thanked whatever luck I had left (at this point it didn't seem like much) that we didn't run into anyone. Jack stopped in front of a plain door, a small, temporary plaque next to it labeled "Seven, Medical." Couldn't they have used her name, at least?

I pushed the door open and there, in a bed in the middle of the perfectly white room, lay the person who was the closest I would ever have to family. I walked slowly up, taking in the myriad of IVs, machines, and monitors she was hooked up to. And instead of the comfort I'd been looking for, I was overwhelmed with guilt.

"What happened to her?" Jack asked, leaning against the wall by the door.

"I did," I whispered. Why hadn't I tried harder to get through to her? I could have stopped her, could have convinced her to stop killing the paranormals. Instead I'd ripped the souls away from her, leaving her with barely enough to hang on.

But if I hadn't taken the souls, Lish still would have been trapped, never set free. I hated this. Why couldn't I ever love someone and not have to worry about all the other ways they made me feel?

I took Vivian's icy hand in my own, careful not to disturb the IV. "Hey, Viv." I tucked a stray strand of blond hair behind her ear, but her eyes stayed closed, the only evidence of life the rhythmic beeping of one of the monitors. Her breathing barely even disturbed the blankets.

"So." I choked back tears, trying to keep my voice even. "Turns out you were right all along. We really don't belong anywhere, do we? I tried to. I tried so hard, but—" The sobs came then, and I leaned my head over onto her shoulder. "I'm sorry," I cried, my words muffled by her still body. "I'm so sorry."

After a few minutes I felt a hand on my back. I stood up, wiping at my face. Great, now I'd gone and gotten her shirt wet, after everything else.

"It's not your fault," Jack said, his voice softer than I'd ever heard it.

"Tell that to her."

"Evie. You didn't do any of this. The faeries did. It's their fault. All of it."

I closed my eyes. He was just trying to make me feel better. I'd done this to her.

But then again, he had a point. If the faeries hadn't raised her the way they did, tried to pit her against me, we wouldn't have had that confrontation. They were the ones who broke her, twisted her until she thought nothing of stealing the life energy of every paranormal she could find.

Bleep, they were the ones who made us in the first place.

It was their fault I was this thing, this cold, empty husk that didn't belong anywhere. It was their fault that Vivian was lying there, that she'd never wake up again. It was even their fault that Arianna was doomed to an eternal life she never wanted. All the people who had been killed or turned by vampires across the centuries. All the kids like Jack who'd gone missing, forced to live among the faeries as pets—or worse. My mother, missing or dead, but gone, never to be mine.

All their fault.

"I hate them," I whispered.

"Of course you do." Jack put his arm around my shoulder. "Come on, we should go before Raquel figures out you're with me."

I nodded and squeezed Vivian's hand one last time.

We walked back out through the hall, passing the open cells I'd ignored before, most of which were empty. I jumped, startled, at a voice.

"*Liebchen.*" Standing behind an electric-field guarded doorway was Uber-vamp. He smiled, one corner of his mouth turned up, his eyes languorously half closed. He didn't stand as straight as before, and even his glamour had a sick, unhealthy pallor to it now. "You look unhappy. Come in to me, let me take you from this world, my little monster."

I stared blankly at him. So this was where Raquel put him to make sure he wouldn't get out again. Jack rolled his eyes and flipped the vampire off, taking my hand in his and pulling me down the hall. I watched the vampire as long as I could, chilled by the look in his eyes, the memory of how it had felt to drain some of him.

His words rang in my ears. *Little monster.* It was true.

Jack found the nearest hallway that wasn't lined with iron and made a door. I didn't look back as we walked through. I was never going to the Center again. I suppressed a shudder at the Paths' darkness and closed my eyes.

"You really hate it here, don't you?" he asked.

"This is how I imagine hell. No fire and brimstone, just black and empty and alone forever."

He laughed. "Hell, huh? Well, hopefully we'll be able to disprove that theory soon. Besides, if it were hell, would I be here with you?"

"I don't know, if hell called for an eternity of annoyance instead of torment, maybe."

"I like you more every day. But neither of us qualifies for hell. We're *victims.*" He smiled, the last word laced with venom. "And if we're occasionally wicked, well, certainly we'd be justified."

I wondered if he was trying to comfort me about Vivian, but he stared into the distance as though anticipating future wickedness. What did he want me to light on fire this time? I didn't think I was up for more destruction.

He opened a door into his Faerie Realms room. I collapsed onto a deep green velvet couch. "Can I please go to sleep and never wake up?"

"I believe your sister has that covered." I glared at him, and he held up his hands. "Sorry. Touchy subject. How about I go get you something to eat?"

I wasn't hungry, but I needed a while to be by myself and disconnect. Jack was so kinetic, always talking, always in motion. He exhausted me even when I didn't feel like this. Still, he felt like my only friend left in the world, and I was grateful to him. We understood each other. "Real food, please. This is the last place I want to be tied to for the rest of my pathetic life."

"Your wish is my command." He disappeared through the wall and I lay back, closing my eyes and willing myself not to think of anything, ever again. If I could only sleep, sleep and not have to think about the future without Lend, the emptiness inside me, that would be enough.

I was nearly out when a pair of hands with razor nails grabbed my shoulders and threw me across the room.

My arm hit the corner of a side table with a sickening crack, and I stayed on the floor, dazed. I could feel blood seeping from the fingernail cuts in my shoulders. What was happening?

"Get up," Fehl's horrible voice rasped at me. "I want to see how badly I can hurt you without killing you." I looked into her feverish eyes as she smiled at me. "How many of your limbs can you live without?"

She wrapped her hand in my hair, pulling me off the ground. I cried out, my arm burning with agony from the movement. I clutched at it, and Fehl's face lit up with cruel delight. She grabbed right where it was broken, and I screamed, lights swimming in my vision. I couldn't handle this much pain; I was going to pass out. I *wanted* to pass out.

"Evie!" Jack shouted. "Don't let her do this! Fight back!"

Fehl's face was right in front of mine, her breath hot and feral. Rage flared past the pain, rage at this faerie and all she had done to me, to Vivian. What her kind had done to the world. I shoved my good hand against her chest. It was time to finish what Viv started.

I opened the floodgates, and Fehl's eyes widened in shock and fear. A thrill went through me, seeing her face. She deserved to look like that.

Her soul connected with mine in a rush of energy and familiarity, my sparks and currents flooding up to meet it, welcoming it, wanting me to draw it in. Her soul was a dark thing, a wild and rushing thing, the wind howling eternally through a black canyon. I could taste its darkness, what it would feel like to own it.

And in that moment I knew I didn't want any part of Fehl inside me.

I shoved her away and she shuddered, crouching on the ground and wrapping her arms around herself.

"What are you doing?" Jack cried.

I trembled, drained from the effort it had taken to close the connection before I took any of Fehl's soul. Exhausted beyond belief, my arm in so much pain I could barely see straight, I shook my head. "I don't want anything to do with her. Denfehlath," I said, and her head snapped to attention.

"Go away and never come near me or Jack again."

She jerked up, her movements stiff and forced like a living marionette, and disappeared through a door in the wall.

I sank to the floor, shivering.

"Why didn't you kill her?" Jack looked at me, incredulous and angry. "After everything she's done?"

"You don't understand. I was going to take her soul. But I don't want any part of her in me, Jack. A faerie soul would be worse than nothing at all."

He looked as though he was about to burst, then let out a deep breath. "Fine, then." Sitting on the floor next to me, he took my good hand in his. "It doesn't matter, anyway. Not after what we're going to do."

"What are we going to do?"

A beatific smile spread across his face, transforming his impish face into an angelic one. "We're going to save the world, Evie. We're going to make sure that faeries don't hurt anyone, ever again."

DIMPLED TERROR

I shook my head at Jack, confused. "What do you mean? How are we going to stop the faeries? I won't drain them. Any of them. Besides which, even if I *wanted* to, I'd never be able to get them all."

"It's simpler than that. Simple, and obvious. They don't belong here; we're going to send them somewhere else."

"Wouldn't they come right back? They can make doors."

"We won't use a door. You're going to make a gate. They can only access the Faerie Realms and Earth with their doors. If you were to open a gate to somewhere else, they wouldn't be able to get back."

How did he know about the gates? I couldn't remember whether or not I'd told him. Maybe Raquel had. Whatever the case, he obviously didn't understand how they worked.

Well, of course he didn't. *I* had no idea how they worked, and I'd made one.

"I can't really do that, I don't think. Besides, isn't that what they wanted? Reth was always talking about me sending them back where they came from. I'm guessing that meant making a gate. I don't especially want to work with any faeries right now, or ever. And I'm not in the mood to make them happy by giving them a shiny new gate to wherever it is they want to go."

"There are other places to send them." Jack's smile was still firmly in place, but his tone was cold, menacing.

I shook my head. He wasn't getting it. "But how would we even get them to go through the gate? And where would I open it to? And how would I open it in the first place? I've only ever done one, and that just sort of happened." The night I'd released all the souls Vivian had taken, the gate in the stars called out to me. The souls of all the paranormals that Viv stole changed me, helped me see things I couldn't before and hadn't since. I doubted I could find that gate— or any others, if there were others—again.

"Relax, Ev. I've got everything figured out. There's only one door into the Faerie Realms from the Paths. Remember?"

I nodded, recalling how it had felt when Jack showed me.

"Very good. That door opens up to any area, but it's still the same door. So if you were to open a gate in that same spot . . ."

"The faeries would go through without meaning to." I stared, finally understanding. It would be like a trapdoor. Trap gate.

"Exactly! No need for confrontation. They'd slip through before they knew what was happening."

"I guess that could work." I frowned. "But even if I could figure out how to do it again, I don't have enough energy to open a gate. I had all those souls from Vivian before."

He raised his eyebrows. "And you're telling me you don't have any extra floating around in you?"

The vampire, the sylph, and the fossegrim: fragments of their souls coursed through me. Shrugging nervously, I shook my head. "Maybe a little, but not on purpose. Well, I mean, I had to. And it's not enough."

"How do you know if you haven't tried?"

"I *guess* I could give it a shot."

"There's a good girl! And if it isn't enough, we can get some more. Too bad about sending Fehl away, though. We could have used her."

"It's not like that." I narrowed my eyes, uncomfortable with how casually he treated stealing souls.

"Come on!" He grabbed my good hand and pulled me through the wall and into the Paths, practically skipping.

I stumbled along, too tired, too overwhelmed to protest. "Here we are." He smiled at the blackness in front of us; I recognized the feeling of the door.

"So I'm gonna send them home?" I was torn. On the one hand, it was what they wanted. But on the other hand, they'd be gone. That couldn't be a bad thing. "How will I know what gate to use? I don't think I can find one."

Jack turned toward me, his eyes feverish. Something in his face reminded me of Fehl, and my stomach turned nervously.

"You're not sending them home. I've read everything there is on gates and portals, and there's a much better destination for them."

"Which is?"

"Hell, of course." I blanched, and he squeezed my hand. "Think about it, Evie. Why should they get what they want, after all they've done? They created vampires. They destroyed Vivian. They ruined your life, and they stole mine. 'Too bad for heaven and too good for hell' no longer applies—if any creatures alive deserve eternal torment, they do. They've earned it. They *made* you, forced you into this life, just so you could open a gate for them. So go ahead—open a gate!"

"I don't know." It was one thing to get rid of them, but to doom all of them to this hell Jack thought I could find?

"Of course you know! You have to know! Do you have any idea what it was like, growing up with them? Desperate for love, for attention, for anything? Adored, then discarded on a whim? The things they did to me . . . the things I was willing to do for them. And still I was nothing—not even a pet. You can't tell me they don't deserve this! You saw the Dark Queen, what she does! Do you think those humans deserve the hell they're living in? And you won't help me fix this?"

The looks on those people's faces flashed in front of my eyes, haunting me, eating at me. They'd been stripped of everything—even their free will—by the faeries. And wasn't that what faeries always did? Took away choices, forced us to play their sick little games?

"And what about Reth?" Jack's voice was softer now, insistent. "After everything he did to you, the way he tried to make you his? Can you really see your scar and not want him gone forever?"

I nodded slowly, looking down at my wrist. Faeries were evil. The nauseating pain in my broken arm was further testament to that. I was done thinking of them as amoral. They might not have the same ideas about life as humans, but they were in the human world. We weren't the ones screwing with their laws, their lives, their rights. And if they were gone, I'd finally be safe. No more worrying about what they had planned, what they were trying to do, how they would attack me next. Jack was right.

Come to think of it, though, I couldn't remember telling Jack about my scar. Or any details about Reth. Or that faeries had made vampires. And I was sure now that I'd never mentioned gates.

"How do you know about all this?" I asked.

"I already told you—I've spent a lot of time studying. IPCA records, faerie lore."

"Wait, you were studying *me*?"

"It's like the Paths. I learned how to use them because it meant freedom. And I learned about you because you meant—mean—the same thing. Freedom from faeries, forever."

His hand on mine was tight, desperate. How long had he been leading me here? He might be right, I didn't know, I couldn't know anymore, but I couldn't do this right now. "I need—I need to think." I was in too much pain to figure this out on the spot.

"No. We need to do this now. Don't let the faeries hurt anyone else. Look for the gate. Feel for it. It'll come to you, I know it will."

A growing sense of the possibilities around me had been nagging since Jack suggested opening a portal. I knew that with a little nudging I could find a gate.

Gates.

Hundreds and thousands, infinite possibilities, and they were all around me. It felt like the Dark Queen's pull, inevitable, heavy, drowning. I could open any of these gates and lose myself forever.

Or lose an entire race forever.

Whereas that night with Vivian only the right gate had called to me, now it seemed that the wrong gates were clamoring, pulling at my senses, begging to be opened. Maybe the gates I found were a reflection of the turmoil in me. Maybe the flux of the Paths, their very nature, supported gates to . . . darkness.

"Think about Arianna," Jack whispered. "Think about Vivian. Think about your *mother*. What that faerie did to her, using her, abandoning her, then forgetting about you. She's lost forever because of them, and you never even knew her."

I closed my eyes. How did Jack know about that? Did it matter? The faeries deserved this; they needed to be stopped. And I'd be helping, protecting so many innocent people. The chaos tugging at my fingertips scared me, though. What if I didn't have the energy to close what I opened? I might not know anything about gates, but I knew I was messing with forces much bigger and stronger than me. I didn't want to leave something like that open.

"I don't know if I can do it."

Jack sighed, annoyed. "Fine, you need more power? How about that crazy vampire? He should do it, right?"

"What, we're going to use him like some sort of living battery?"

"Doesn't he deserve it?"

I rubbed my forehead, trying to think. Sure, the vampire had killed poor, defenseless troll children and tried to kill me, but . . . Well, but what? Why shouldn't I? It wasn't like I hadn't already taken some. And besides, all my life I'd been used—by IPCA, by the faeries. Surely the vampire's life would be better put to use in ridding the world of the faerie menace. He certainly hadn't earned his immortal soul. He'd done nothing with it, no good at all. Like the faeries, he was a monster. What had his words been? "I will kill them all." He was mindlessly bent on destroying other immortal paranormals just for being what they were.

"Oh," I said, softly. Monster indeed, for hating other creatures based on their existence. The clamor of gates unseen swirled around me, buzzing behind my eyes and making my fingers tingle, but instead of alluring, it made me feel sick. How could I consider this? Who was I to decide what fate faeries should have? I couldn't condemn an entire race of creatures to hell for being what they were.

I had a choice, and I wouldn't turn myself into a monster in the name of protecting the innocent. I'd lost so much of myself these last few weeks, chipped away slowly but surely. I'd lost my past, my future, my home, but this last little bit—this sense of right and wrong—*that* was human. Human, and no one could take it away from me.

I thought of Lend and what we talked about so many times, arguing over his dad's methods versus IPCA's. There were no absolutes. You couldn't put things into neat little categories of "good" or "bad." Uber-vamp was bad. Arianna was good. But they were both vampires. Regardless of what some faeries were doing (and I couldn't argue that the Dark Queen didn't deserve hell), that didn't mean they were all irredeemable.

I looked at Jack, his cherub face twisted with eagerness and rage. He was letting his hatred of the faeries destroy him, the same way Vivian had let her bitterness at the world destroy her. I wouldn't give the faeries that victory. Whatever else happened in my life, it was still *my* life, and no one—not Reth, not Jack—was going to force me to become someone I didn't recognize.

"I can't," I said softly, wanting to let Jack down easy. "It's wrong. Faeries are awful, but I'm not their judge. Maybe if I knew how to send them home, but I'm not going to banish them to hell for being what they are."

"What are you saying?" Jack's voice was low, trembling. There was no trace of his disarming smile now.

"I can't do this. Those places—I can feel them, and I can't do it, can't send anything there."

I jumped, startled as Jack burst into a sharp laugh. "You can't? You *can't*? I've been living in hell for the last thirteen years, and you're balking over sending these demons where they belong?" He squeezed my hand so hard it hurt. "I'm afraid that's not acceptable. Not after all the work I put into getting you here."

I'd never thought to be afraid of Jack, silly, cartwheeling Jack, but staring into his eyes, I knew that paranormals weren't the only monsters in the world. "Can we go somewhere and talk about this?"

"No, we can't go somewhere and talk about this." He imitated my voice, sneering. "Do you know how long it took me to figure this out? To steal the faeries' lore books, ingratiate myself at IPCA, convince Raquel to pull you back in? How many missions I had to screw up, how many problems I had to create until she was desperate enough to call you? And do you have any idea, any idea at all, how hard it is to track down a sylph?"

"You were—that was you?" Things started clicking into place—terrifying things. That night at the Center, the faerie hadn't been after me. She had been after Jack for stealing her books. Reth really hadn't been behind any of the attacks.

"Finding the fossegrim was a little easier, but I nearly drowned explaining what I wanted him to do. And still you barely took anything! Then we lucked into finding the vampire. You had more than enough time to drain him in Sweden, but no, you tell him to run away, so I had to drag him unconscious through the Paths on Halloween. Don't even get me started on Fehl. I wait my whole bloody life for a faerie name, then use my only named command to have her hurt you without killing you, and what do you do? Banish her! Heaven and *hell*, Evie, you're worthless!"

I stared at him, shocked. "This whole time. You've been manipulating me, trying to make me—How could you?"

"For all the good it did me!" His face burned with

hatred. "Open the gate. Now."

"I won't!"

He lightened his grip on my hand and I felt a fresh surge of panic. "Jack, I—"

"What was that you told me about your personal hell? Lost in the Paths forever?"

Tears spilled out of my eyes. "Please."

"*Open the gate.*"

"Please take me home. Please."

His dimpled smile, evil in its innocence, snapped back into place. "You don't have a home. But fair is fair. You won't send the faeries to hell, I'll leave you in yours."

"No!" I screamed, trying to grab his hand with both of mine, gasping from the pain in my broken arm. He slipped from my grasp effortlessly and flashed me one final grin before stepping backward into the darkness away from me.

And then I was alone.

HELLO, HELL

I was alone.

I was alone in the Faerie Paths.

Once the connection was broken, you could never find the other person. Ever. Again. And no one would be able to find me in the infinite blank darkness. All the times I'd woken up, panicked and sweating from this nightmare, and now . . .

Oh, please, please let this be a nightmare.

I looked frantically around. Maybe I could find Jack again. Maybe what I'd heard about the Paths was a lie, just another thing Raquel told me so that I wouldn't mess around on transports. "Jack?" I called, my voice ringing through the silence almost scarier than the silence itself. Because once my voice stopped without an echo, snuffed out like a light, the silence felt even heavier, a palpable weight on my shoulders.

I had options. There had to be options. The door! We were right by the door to the Faerie Realms. I put my hand out, shaking and desperate, feeling for it. The only thing I sensed were tendrils of the gates to chaos—hell—those swirling, evil places Jack had wanted me to send the faeries.

What if I tried to open a door and opened a gate, instead?

Oh, bleep, I was in hell and my only options for getting out of it were hells, too.

It would be okay. Someone would help me. Someone had to help me.

"Reth!" I was suddenly desperate for the sight of his golden face. "Lorethan!" I screamed, knowing it wouldn't work, but hoping maybe, somehow, he still kept tabs on his old name.

He would come for me. He told me himself: he always knew where I was. He'd know, and he'd come. I just had to wait.

Hadn't it been long enough?

Surely this was enough time for him to find me.

I counted to one thousand, timing my breaths to the numbers.

Two thousand.

Three thousand.

I was going to die.

Four thousand.

I was going to die, here in the silent dark, by myself.

Five thousand.

And no one would ever know, and no one would care.

Six thousand—where the holy crap are you, Reth? Where are you?

He wasn't coming. My breath came quicker, my heart pulsing too fast in my chest, trying to pound its way out of my body. I took a step, then another, then another and another and another, running, but there was no wind in my hair, no sense of movement other than my feet that kept going and going and going

nowhere.

There was nowhere to go. I was the only thing that existed here. I looked down and was hit with a wave of vertigo. How did I know I was standing on anything? What if I was falling, had been falling this whole time, would fall here in the darkness for all eternity?

I sank down, curling into fetal position. Everything was deadened, numbed. Even my broken arm barely hurt anymore. I couldn't feel anything around me as I wondered what would kill me first. Thirst? Starvation? Finally finding the bottom of this abyss? Or what if I never died at all—what if I just lay here in the dark forever?

My chest was tight, too tight, my heartbeat an actual

pain. Maybe I would die of a heart attack.

I was going to die.

I was going to die, and I'd never see Lend again. He'd never know what happened to me. I'd never get to tell him sorry, or how much I loved him and would always love him, even if I had to leave him. And Raquel, Arianna, David, even Vivian and Carlee—I'd left them all without a word of explanation. I'd been so desperate to find out who I was, find my place in the world, I'd lied to and left behind the people who loved me and were willing to give me a place no matter who or what I was.

Now poor Vivian would be forever alone in her dreams. Maybe before I died I would sleep, and visit her one last time. I'd like that.

I could picture Lend with David and Arianna, worrying. Lend's face—I hated myself for what this would do to him, what I'd already done to him. How could I have been so selfish, lied to him for so long? He deserved the chance to make up his own mind, but I'd taken it away from him by hiding the truth, like so many people had hidden it from me. And, sure, he hadn't chosen me, wouldn't choose me, but it was *his* choice. At least for the time we'd had I'd been happier than I'd ever been the rest of my life.

And I'd had a locker. That was something, too.

I took a deep, shuddering breath, trying to calm my heart rate. If I was going to die, I wanted it to be peaceful, at least. I would lie here and die as I thought of Lend, Raquel, Arianna, and David. Slipping into oblivion filled with my love for them wasn't a bad way to go.

I smiled, remembering the time Arianna cussed out Reth and got thrown into a tree for her efforts. Too bad we'd never find out whether Cheyenne and Landon ended up together. I hoped for Arianna's sake they did. She'd had enough disappointment in her life and death as it was.

David and his ridiculous faith in everyone around him, his undying love for a paranormal that would never, could never, love him back the same way. He wasn't stupid or naive. Loving someone completely like that was far braver than I'd ever given him credit for.

Raquel. Her soft Spanish accent and her infinite arsenal of sighs. I wondered which one she'd use when I never came back. I didn't wonder if she'd be sad. I knew that now, knew I was as much a daughter to her as she was a mother to me. And if we were both screwed up, well, the more I saw of normal life, the more I realized that was typical.

And Lend. My Lend. All I had to do was think of his face. That would be enough to sustain me in the emptiness, had always made me feel like I wasn't empty. I'd never been empty with Lend.

My heart calmed down, the pain replaced by something new: a strange sort of gentle tugging, like I was the needle in a compass. The more I thought about the people I loved—especially Lend—the stronger it got. I wanted him. I wanted to be with him more than anything in the whole world.

I stood, too scared to think about what I was doing,

too scared to hope. I followed the sensation, thinking of Lend. What it felt like to hold his hand. Watching him draw. Those precious times when he got to be nothing but himself around me. The way he laughed. The look he got in his eyes when he was about to say something he knew was clever. The way he looked at me while I talked, like I was all he had ever wanted in the entire world.

I closed my eyes, walking forward with my good hand up, smiling as I followed this feeling. I held on to my image of Lend, surrounded by Arianna, Raquel, and David. That image felt like a place, felt like what I'd always imagined home would feel like. The dead air in front of me stirred, solidified, and I tripped and tumbled out of the darkness and straight into Lend.

My Lend.

And then he was holding me, and I was crying, and Raquel and David and Arianna were there, too. Lend stroked my hair, repeating the same thing over and over.

"It's okay, you're home. You're home."

And for the first time in my life, I knew it was true.

MEET ME IN THE MIDDLE

Honestly, you little brat," Arianna said, carefully putting the finishing touches on my splint, "if I'd known you were going to be so high maintenance, I wouldn't have agreed to be your roommate."

I smiled, my teeth gritted against the pain. "I love you, too, Ar."

"And you're an idiot, by the way. If you had let me talk to you, I would have explained that I took the liberty of putting together applications for you to American University and George Washington University, both of which are a quick train trip away from Georgetown."

"You—what?"

"And if those don't work out, I'm more than willing to use my vampire tricks on an admissions officer. Just because I can't have a life doesn't mean I'm going to let you be so stupid about yours. You can thank me later."

I stared, shocked. I didn't know what to say. I'd been so set on Georgetown, I'd never been willing to think of other options. I was beyond touched that Arianna had been watching out for me like that.

Of course, being close to Lend might not matter anymore.

"Are you sure you don't want to go to the hospital right now?" Raquel's eyes were still tight with worry. She'd come immediately to David's house when Jack told her I was gone. They sat now, shoulder to shoulder.

"It can wait until tomorrow."

Raquel heaved a *why must you be so stubborn* sigh, then shook her head. "I can't believe it about Jack. We'll be on the lookout for him; if we catch him, the iron cells will hold him. The little demon can't make doors there. Speaking of which, I'm still not sure how you got out of the Paths alone."

"I don't know. Reth and Jack both said you had to have a sense of the place you wanted to go, have a connection to it. For Reth it was names; for Jack it was seeing it before. For me it was—" I blushed, looking over at Lend, who sat next to me, but not touching-me-next-to-me. "Well, it was you. All of you. Once I focused on memories of you, I sort of felt my way here."

Arianna looked confused. Admittedly they had a lot to take in, between the whole Jack-is-a-psychopath-who-wanted-me-to-destroy-a-species thing, and also the turns-out-I'm-less-human-than-we-thought thing. Lend stayed silent the whole time, which made me increasingly nervous. Was he going to be awkward around me now? I still loved him, I always would, and I'd do whatever he wanted with our relationship, but this whole not-touching-not-talking thing was gonna have to end.

Okay, so maybe I wasn't quite ready to let him go.

Okay, I'd probably never be ready to let him go.

Arianna frowned. "But when you were stuck in the Paths, why didn't you call that one faerie, your father? Didn't Reth tell you his name?"

My jaw dropped. "Bleep. Wow. It didn't even cross my mind." I couldn't believe how stupid I was, ready to rot and die on the paths when I knew a faerie name other than homicidal Fehl's. But that meant something, too. When it came down to it, I didn't even think of my "father" or where I came from. I thought of the people I had, the people who meant something to me.

So that whole faerie parentage thing? Screw it. Knowing where I came from didn't change who I was. My stupid father could rot in the Faerie Realms for the rest of eternity. He was nothing to me.

And I most definitely was *not* nothing.

Too bad I couldn't have figured that out before destroying my relationship with the love of my life. I had messed everything up, so fixated on trying to create my ideal of a life and so paranoid about losing Lend and being hurt that I sabotaged myself. I looked over at Lend, wishing he'd do something, say something.

As if in answer, he stood and held out his hand. "Can we go for a walk?"

"Sure!" I let him help me up, unsure whether or not I could keep holding his hand. But he didn't let go as he led me outside and down the path toward the pond. He stopped abruptly halfway there.

"I can't—" His face twisted somewhere between anger and sadness. "I can't believe you didn't tell me. Why?"

I couldn't stand to look at his face, so I studied the blanket of dead leaves on the ground. "You're the most important person in my life, the best thing that's ever happened to me. And I kind of hate that, how much I love you. Because I've been left a lot in my life, and loving you meant that it'd happen again. The thought of watching you drift away, become someone like your mom who couldn't love me anymore—it's easier to get it over with sooner. It won't kill me now, I don't think, but it might later. And I'm sorry, I should have told you, but I thought if you didn't know we could make it work somehow. You always made me feel warm, forget the emptiness. It was selfish, and it wasn't fair of me. Everyone deserves to know what they are."

"Evie—you—GAH!" Lend shouted, and I looked up at him, surprised. He had both hands clenched into fists and was staring up at the sky. After a few seconds he looked back at me, all the anger gone from his face. "I'm not an immortal."

"But I saw—"

"I know what you saw, and I'm sure you were right, but *being* immortal doesn't make me *an* immortal. Don't treat me like I'm my mom. She's always been that way—she can't be any other way. She doesn't grow, she doesn't change. Are you saying that I'm the same?"

"Of course not!"

"Then don't act like I have no choice! I've never wanted that life, that world. And I know I'll have to decide what to do someday, but bleep, Evie, I'm eighteen! I don't have to face forever for a long time yet."

"But you will, eventually."

He rolled his eyes. "You act like I'm gonna pack my bags and jump in the nearest river next week. Which would be a terrible idea because I have a huge paper due. That isn't my world. This is. And I'm going to live out my life the way I want to. Which is by getting a degree, and making leaps and strides in cryptozoology, and having kids, and being ridiculously conventional aside from helping take care of paranormal creatures and being able to shape-shift. And I am going to do all that, every minute of it, with the girl that

I love, who is going to promise to *always* be truthful with me about *everything* from now on so that I can actually be there for her."

I blinked back tears. This was exactly what I wanted to hear, what I hadn't dared hope I would hear. But he didn't know. How could he be sure? "What if you change your mind? I don't even know how long I'm going to live."

He stepped forward to close the distance between us as he rested his forehead against mine. "The only life I want is one with you. I don't understand this gap you see between us, but can't you meet me somewhere in the middle?"

"The middle of what?"

"I don't know, the middle of tomorrow and forever, the middle of life and death, the middle of normal and paranormal. Where we've always been."

I bit my lip, nodding against his forehead. "There's a place for us there, right?"

"Always." He put his lips to mine, sealing our own little spot in the world. Together.

ACKNOWLEDGMENTS

Turns out writing the second book in a series isn't as easy as you'd think. Or maybe you thought it would be really hard, in which case clearly you are smarter than I am. So, as usual, I have many people to thank for getting this book out there. Perhaps I should start interspersing these paragraphs with kissing scenes to reward you for reading them.

First and foremost, my adorable genius of a husband. Thank you for all the Saturdays you took the kids to the beach while I sat locked in the library. (Wait. Maybe *you* should be thanking *me* for that.) Thank you for your unfailing belief in me. Thank you for no longer suggesting I kill

Evie in every scene; I kind of like her alive. Most especially, thank you for making me laugh every single day of my life. I love you, Hot Stuff.

(Sorry, no kissing scenes between Noah and me. Much as I enjoy kissing him, that would just be awkward.)

Elena and Jonah, you are endless sources of delight and joy. Watching you grow is the greatest privilege of my life, and there is no title I am prouder of than "Mom."

Mom and Dad, you are the best parents anyone could ask for. Kit and Jim, thanks for having the best son ever and letting me marry him. Erin, Todd, Lindsey, Keegan, Lauren, Devin, Matt, Tim, Carrie, Seth, Shayne, Eliza, Christina, Josh, Emma, Beverly, Thomas, Colton, Dee, and Mary: I'm really glad to be related to all of you. And really glad I don't have to get gifts for everyone at Christmas, because boy there are a lot of you.

Natalie Whipple, thank you for being there. Thank you for reading my stuff as I write it and overlooking the first draft issues to help me finish so I can clean up the mess. I couldn't write without you. Stephanie Perkins, none of my drafts are ever done until they have passed muster with you. Your brilliant advice always makes my writing even more *mine* than it was before. I'm so grateful to count both of you among my dearest friends.

(Okay, I'm not going to kiss Natalie or Steph, either. Even though I love both of them.)

Cristina Gilbert, my awesome marketing director, and

Kim Bouchard, the publicist for *Paranormalcy*; Christina Colangelo, Kristina Radke, and Caroline Sun, the marketing and publicity team behind *Supernaturally*, thank you all for your enthusiastic and greatly appreciated efforts on Evie's behalf. Torborg Davern and Alison Donalty, your covers are freaking works of art. Thank you for dressing Evie's books in a way she would flip out over. If she were real. Which she is not, but I do enough flipping out for ten imaginary characters. Tyler Infinger, thank you for assisting and otherwise being awesome. Any day I get a package with your name on it is a good day.

(Guys, I just don't know who should kiss who. Imaginary characters? Real people? I want to thank Snow Patrol, Paramore, and Ingrid Michaelson, but I don't think they should kiss each other. However, if anyone tried to kiss Lend, Evie would Tase them, and then the acknowledgments would get way too violent.)

Erica Sussman, brilliant editor extraordinaire, you are nothing but a joy to work with. I am so glad that I get to create these books with you. Thank you for the editorial letters that fix what needs fixing but are generous with the smiley faces. Even your handwriting makes me happy.

Michelle Wolfson, I'm not usually one to believe in fate but you and I were meant to be. Thank you for being my tiny spitfire agent of awesome. I'm so lucky to have you on my side as an agent and friend. You are unbelievably wonderful.

(The other question is, are you looking for a full-on kiss? Or maybe a friendly peck? I don't think tongue is appropriate for an acknowledgments section. I'm totally over-thinking this. Curses.)

And finally, to my readers. You. Thank you for reading *Paranormalcy*, telling your friends about it, writing me notes, and everything else you did that buoyed me up and helped it to be such a success. I hope you loved *Supernaturally* just as much; I can't wait to show you where Evie's story ends in the next book.

(I know—I love you all so much, how about *I* kiss *you*? Then again, that would take a very long time, depending on how many of you read this. And it could lead to some awkwardness, since I would be going in for the cheek, but what if you turned your head the wrong way, and we bonked noses, or maybe your significant other misinterpreted the cheek-kiss as something more than friendship, and then we'd have to say, "No, no, it's just to make the acknowledgments more interesting!" but it would be this whole mess and really we're probably better off if I just give dramatic air kisses to everyone.)

So. "Kiersten lifted her hand to her lips, grinning impishly (as there are few better ways to grin, in her opinion) as she blew exaggerated kisses to everyone reading the acknowledgments section to show them how much she appreciated them for joining her imaginary worlds."